CAST IN ANGELFIRE

THE MAGE CRAFT SERIES

SM REINE

CAST IN ANGELFIRE

The Mage Craft Series
Book One

SM REINE

In paradisum deducant te Angeli...
Æternam habeas requiem.

ONE

Billings, Montana—September 2030

There was a bounty on the life of a girl named Marion. The dollar figure was high enough that the real question wasn't whether she would die—it was how quickly, and who would land the reward.

The bounty was passed around on darknet forums where killers sought their next paychecks. The darknet had become more advanced as unseelie sidhe developed technology so complex that it seemed to be magical, and the content was immune to the eye of law enforcement, since the servers were hidden in the Winter Court. Only people invited to the darknet could access it. Invitations were not cheap, and they could never be purchased with money.

The original posting of the bounty said that the target answered to "Marion," and that she had multiple last names. This Marion had been born in 2011—four years before Genesis rebooted the world, spewing vampires, faeries, and a thousand other preternatural breeds across the face of the Earth.

It also said that she needed to die before the first of November. That meant that there was less than a month to form a plan, track her down, and murder her.

The bounty's poster included a blurry photograph of the target taken from a distance. Only her wavy brunette hair was distinct, but she stood near a bus shelter, which allowed Geoff Samuelson to approximate her height at five feet, ten inches—perhaps a bit taller.

The information wasn't much, but it was enough for Geoff to get that bounty.

And he didn't plan to share.

"She's only nineteen," said Vasicek. "A baby."

"Nineteen's old enough to screw, and it's old enough to die for your country," Geoff said.

Vasicek slipped a magazine into his sniper rifle. "I'm not saying it's a problem. I'm stating fact. My little sister is older than she is."

"She musta done something to piss people off," Geoff said. Nobody got million-dollar bounties put on their head unless they really deserved it. That was the thought that had been comforting Geoff while crossing the North American Union on Amtrak, rushing toward the target's last known location in Montana. If someone was willing to pay that much money to knock off Marion

Multiple-Last-Names, then she probably deserved it.

The thought of what Geoff would do with all that money was its own kind of comfort, too.

Vasicek had a dreamy look that said he was contemplating something similar. Even the serpents coiled over his ears looked like they were fantasizing about the bounty. "What do you think you'll do with your half?"

"I'm out of this business," Geoff said. "Out of the business, out of the country, retiring for life."

"The money's good, but not *that* good."

It would be once Geoff murdered Vasicek, ensuring that he didn't have to split the bounty in half. "What are you planning to do with your cut?"

"I'm franchising. Got lots of connections who are, you know, like *me*." Vasicek probably meant demons in general, not specifically megaira. His specific breed made good assassins, though. They fed on aggression the way vampires fed on blood. "Us types do good with this killing stuff. I'll buy 'em, pay 'em a salary, collect lots more bounties. Get some fat stacks going."

"Like the Mary Kay of murder?"

"The Wal-Mart of murder. We'll be huge. We'll *dominate*." The snakes creating Vasicek's hair laughed along with him in a chorus of cruel hissing.

It was a nice fantasy all right. Before Genesis, Vasicek might have been able to do such a thing. Demons had been almost as numerous as humans back in those days, and there had been no sidhe or shifters to compete with. Now there weren't many demons for Vasicek to hire. They'd all been shoved into the Nether Worlds, then the key to the door tossed away.

Geoff didn't bother pointing out how impractical the plan was. Vasicek should enjoy the fantasy while it lasted. In a few hours, he'd be bleeding sulfurous blood onto the pavement, his soul dragged to the Nether Worlds to be with his brethren. No Wal-Mart of murder for him. Not on this plane.

"It's a nice idea." Geoff got to his feet as the train halted. He shouldered his backpack, which was a lot smaller than Vasicek's gun-laden duffel bag. Geoff didn't need weapons to kill. "Dream big, bro."

"Dream and keep on dreaming," Vasicek agreed.

The train station wasn't far from the target, so Geoff braced himself for competition—the legions of assassins, primarily sidhe, who would be closing in on the same million-dollar skull that he was. It felt anticlimactic to step off the train to no fanfare, no blood, no gunfire.

He hoped they weren't too late to kill Marion.

Their destination waited on the other side of the street. Original Sin. The name was picked out in bold neon sparkling with magic.

It was one of many clubs under the same name —a franchise not unlike Wal-Mart. This was the kind of franchise that mundane humans couldn't see, though. Mundane humans passed on the sidewalk without ever glancing at it. Their eyes skipped from the tattoo parlor to the lingerie shop on the other side, like that space between didn't exist.

Even Geoff had a hard time focusing on any of the Original Sins he'd visited. Like the darknet, Original Sin was intended only for the kind of souls who could locate it, and the owners didn't make that an easy chore.

"What time did the email say?" Geoff asked.

Vasicek said, "Midnight."

The train had been delayed at its last station; the time was already after eleven thirty. Geoff and Vasicek wouldn't have much time to set up.

The bouncer at the door for Original Sin had the strange glittering flesh that was a hallmark of sidhe—also known as faeries, though the sidhe had made it clear that wasn't their preferred term. And most people were smart enough to call sidhe whatever the hell they wanted.

Sidhe were a whole other deterrent to visiting Original Sin. The sheer power of their magic warped the world, consuming all light and emanating it from their glittering flesh. It was hard to think straight around the unseelie sidhe, harder still to focus on them, and near impossible to murder one of them.

If Geoff and Vasicek pissed off the bouncer, they'd die before they could track down the bounty.

This particular sidhe seemed too bored to fight. Vasicek paid their cover fees, and the sidhe didn't even glance in their bags before stepping aside.

Eleven thirty should have been too early for any club to be so busy. Under ordinary circumstances, the creatures of the night didn't get partying until the witching hour struck, but Original Sin wasn't an ordinary circumstance. The regulars simply never left. It was as packed with bodies that evening as it would have been in brilliant, burning midday.

Every version of Original Sin was essentially the same, with minute differences. Geoff scanned the room to orient himself to the changes in this location.

The bar was at the back as it usually was, glowing like a beacon in the midst of inky shadow. Liquor bottles seemed to hold inner lights all their own, as if pixies had been trapped at their bottoms.

The dance floor was on a level below ground. Geoff skimmed the faces of the dancers as he walked along the mezzanine, picking out all the preternaturals he could. Shifters were easy to spot, golden-eyed as they were. Vampires were the pallid and frail. There were only a couple of sidhe besides the doorman. Having too many sidhe around was bad for business.

This particular version of Original Sin had columns of fire in each corner, a shade of white-blue that suggested magic. Geoff passed by one. It looked deadly, but it wasn't hot. He still wouldn't risk bumping into it. Original Sin was exactly the kind of place where they would decorate with something fatal at a touch.

"Up there," Vasicek said, jerking his chin toward the south wall. Scaffolding supporting the lights that strobed over the dancers, lighting their preternatural flesh like prisms.

Geoff climbed the scaffold. Vasicek was right behind him. Much like the doorman, none of the regulars seemed interested in the fact that two men were scaling the rigging for the lights; of all the strange things that demons did in Original Sin, crawling up the walls was the most ordinary.

The scaffold gave them an excellent vantage point overlooking the rest of the club. Geoff could see into the curtained booths on the far side of the bar. He could even see the hallway behind the DJ.

When the target came in, he would know.

Geoff turned on his cell phone to read Marion's emails again. An anonymous person had contacted Marion to ask for help, and despite the message's brevity, Marion had readily agreed to meet that person at Original Sin at midnight. The target must have known the individual she was due to meet.

He checked the time again. *Almost midnight.* Geoff rolled the moonstone charm in his fingers as Vasicek set up. "Do you feel that?" Vasicek asked, scratching at the back of his neck. His nails were sharp enough to leave red streaks on his greasy skin.

Tilting his nose up, Geoff took a sniff. The club was filled with a nauseating cocktail of lethe, pot smoke, liquor, sweat, and piss. One smell was so strange that it rang alarm bells in his head, even though it was faint—the smell of burning oak.

His eyes swept the crowd, and he spotted the target near the door.

Marion shone among all the other preternaturals. She wasn't the most beautiful of them, but there was something compelling about her willowy figure, high cheekbones, and cold blue eyes. She didn't look like she was only nineteen. She didn't exactly look older, either.

Ageless was the word for it.

Unease crawled over Geoff. *What is she?*

The options slithered through his consciousness—cherubim, gibborim, or messenger, maybe. He wouldn't have expected any of them. Ethereal types seldom left their territory in the Levant, and they would never deign to socialize with mere gaeans.

He felt less guilty about Marion's impending death.

Marion glided toward the bar and slipped into a booth. A waiter brought her a drink in a martini glass, which she accepted with a smile. It must have been her regular drink. She wasn't old enough to have a regular drink.

She sat out in the open, oblivious to how many creatures would be circling for her blood. Trusting enough to meet an unnamed contact in public, trusting enough to sit with her back to a room filled with strangers.

Vasicek extended the stand on his sniper rifle,

propped it against the rails of the scaffold, and aimed it down. The light coming through the sight shone on his eye. Black swirled over the iris like pools of ink. "I have her in my sights."

"Remember the plan," Geoff said. "Wait until I'm down."

"I'm waiting, I'm waiting." Vasicek's finger looked awful twitchy. "Hurry up."

Geoff swung off of the scaffolding, landed behind the dance floor, and slipped out the back door to the alley. The moonstone charm was burning a hole in his pocket—almost literally. He needed to use the magic before it expired.

He stripped his clothing off and stuffed it behind a trashcan. The moonstone scorched his palms. He bounced it between them, waiting for the signal that it was time to change.

Muffled gunshots popped from within Original Sin.

People screamed.

That was Vasicek's signal.

Doors burst open, and Original Sin's patrons flooded onto the sidewalk. Geoff watched them from his hidden position at the back of the alley.

Some people clutched bloody wounds on their arms, shoulders, necks. Vasicek hadn't deliberately been aiming to kill. He had been trying to create mayhem, and it had worked.

"Come on," Geoff muttered, pressing his thumb against the stone.

Gaean magic settled over him.

It didn't hurt to shapeshift into his wolf form

when he allowed the Alpha to control him, as most shapeshifters did. But using a charm between moons to force the change—that was different.

He shapeshifted a piece at a time. Fast and brutal.

His knees broke. Switched positions. He collapsed onto his hands as the fingernails fell out. Silver claws thrust from the skin, oozing blood around the edges.

He threw his head back and roared through his breaking jaw, which extended into a muzzle.

Nobody heard him. They were too busy running from Vasicek's attack inside. There were more gunshots, more screaming, the wail of a fire alarm.

After his spine extended into a tail, vertebrae replicating, grinding, twisting, the fever of fur extruding from his skin was nothing. It barely even itched. Within a minute, he had swollen to quadruple his former size, perhaps more, and Geoff could no longer hide behind the trashcan.

A pair of women burst through the rear door.

One of them Geoff didn't recognize. She was a petite nobody with hair the color of straw. Most likely the anonymous person who had emailed Marion asking for help.

The other one was tall, with lots of curly brown hair, and bright-blue eyes.

Even Geoff's wolf brain recognized the target, and it remembered how much she was worth.

A million dollars.

He could retire permanently.

Geoff lunged.

Werewolves were faster than any other gaean breed, so he flashed across the alley in a heartbeat, and he was on top of her the heartbeat after that. He slammed her into the wall hard enough to knock her out. Maybe even hard enough to kill her, if her skull hit in just the right way. He'd struck her with half a ton of werewolf at a hundred miles an hour, after all.

He reared back to rip her face off.

His claws halted inches from Marion's cheek.

It felt as though a fist had closed around his body, holding him suspended in the air. He thrashed, howling. But no matter how he snapped, there was nothing to bite. Nothing physical held him.

Marion slid out from underneath him, hands outstretched, pupils white with magic. Her hair swirled around her neck, lifted in a wind that didn't touch him. "Bad dog," she said, and she flicked her fingers. "Down, boy."

Geoff hurtled into the far wall hundreds of feet down the alley.

He'd been tossed around by Alpha shapeshifters before. He'd been shot more than once. He'd even been crushed by a car before.

None of that hurt as much as Marion tossing him with a single, magical gesture.

"Stay down," she said. Her voice rattled within his skull. The very sound of it hurt.

Geoff scrambled to his feet while his head was still spinning.

Marion was holding hands with her straw-haired friend, ignoring Geoff as though he presented no threat whatsoever. "Are you okay?"

"I think so," the girl said.

"Get back into Original Sin." She pushed the other woman through the back door.

Geoff launched himself at Marion again, faked a left, and then swung right. All with lightning speed. The fastest that he had ever moved.

She stepped out of his way effortlessly.

He skidded past her, paws scrabbling uselessly on pavement.

Marion saw his lightning speed and raised him by summoning real lightning. She pointed one hand toward the sky and the other toward Geoff. "I told you to *stay down*."

Electricity danced down her upright arm and clustered on her fingertips. It arced from her fingernails.

Geoff dodged—barely. The lightning struck the wall behind him. It lanced up the bricks, sizzled against the roof.

He leaped toward Marion from the rear.

She swung around, annoyance twisting the graceful lines of her face.

"No," she said, side-stepping him again.

The neon lights outside of Original Sin popped in a shower of sparks. Every single street light within range blacked out.

The night was absolute.

Unable to see, Geoff slammed into the trashcan. It exploded around him in a shower of stinking garbage. He shook it off, but old beer and vomit weighed his fur down.

His worst fears were true. There was only one type of creature that disabled all electricity simply by existing.

Angels.

The bounty on this kid should be a lot higher.

Light glowed at the end of the alley. Marion's magic was gathering again, illuminating her the way that lanterns were illuminated by inner flame. Her eyes spilled ethereal blue down her cheekbones. She advanced on Geoff. "Who sent you?"

The back door banged open, bouncing off the wall. Geoff glimpsed Vasicek emerging from over Marion's shoulder.

The megaira raised his gun. He fired as Marion turned to look at him.

Geoff didn't get time to feel hopeful that Vasicek would finish the job. Marion plucked the bullet out of the air an inch in front of her nose. "Silver," she said, rolling it between her fingers. "Whoever hired you must not know me well at all."

She hurled the bullet at Geoff before he could react. It embedded in his foreleg as though shot from a gun.

There was no pain quite like silver burn. Geoff's howls shook the bricks of the alley. His vision blurred, his head rang, his blood turned to acid.

Vasicek gave a strangled yowl.

And then he was silent.

Geoff couldn't see what had happened to the demon. He could see nothing, think of nothing, *feel* nothing but the bullet. Marion seemed to have aimed it so that the point would flatten against the bone deep within his flesh. The moon was scorching him from the inside out.

Vasicek was probably dead.

Not enough money in the world for this.

Marion crouched and ran her hand through the ruff of hair at Geoff's neck. He whined and snapped at her fingers. She pushed his muzzle to the pavement, as casually as though that were something she'd done to werewolves before. "I want you to shift back and tell me who sent you."

If he could have, he would have. Anything to make her back away. Anything to stop the pain.

The charm wouldn't wear off for another hour, and there was no way to tell her that.

She stood suddenly, distracted by another person appearing in the alley. Marion stood and turned to face them. The smell of her shock came off of her in waves so powerful that they pierced Geoff's suffering.

"*Mon dieu,*" Marion said softly. Her hands balled into fists. Her voice strengthened. "*Qu'est-ce que toi, tu fais ici?*"

There was no responding voice. There was only blinding darkness, immense and total.

When the street lights flickered back on, Vasicek was dead, Geoff was still bleeding, and Marion Many-Last-Names was gone without a trace.

TWO

Ransom Falls, California—October 2030

It had been a long night in the emergency department of Mercy Hospital, but that was no surprise; the days surrounding new moons were always achingly busy. Shapeshifters who rejected the control of the Alpha went wild on the new and full moons. Even if they didn't manage to hurt other people, they often hurt themselves.

Wild shapeshifters meant broken bones. They meant scratches.

Worst of all, they often meant bites.

There were procedures to prevent those kinds of incidents, but locking shifters in the safe houses hadn't helped much as of late. They were always smashing their way out and biting people anyway.

That was what happened when you failed to pair the public's safety net with a budget to match.

Without adequate government funding, the burden of cleaning up preternatural messes fell upon the hospitals.

Dr. Lucas Flynn wasn't paid enough to deal with that kind of crap, but he hadn't gotten into it for the money.

He stopped in the doorway of the waiting room, cursorily studying the patients triage had lobbed his way. Luke's reputation for being able to identify the origin of preternatural wounds meant he got first shot at every possible preternatural injury that happened within a hundred miles of Ransom Falls.

Most of the injuries on that particular night were ordinary. Dog bites were easy to pick out by the narrow bite radius and slow-healing defensive wounds, so he dismissed them in an instant.

There had also been a bar fight, judging by the men nursing black eyes in the corner. Hardly preternatural.

The women with the broken bones in the nearest chairs had been attacked by a shifter—or at least a gaean with super-strength. However, they hadn't been bitten. Bones would heal without Luke's intervention.

The two remaining patients jumped out at him.

"Which ones do you want to see?" Nurse Ballard asked, hurrying to greet him with an armful of paperwork. She shoved her thick-framed glasses up her nose with the back of her wrist.

"Those two," Luke said, pointing. "Charts?"

Nurse Ballard handed them to him and nearly dropped the rest of the papers in the process. "I think this first one's a chisav mauling. We've had sightings."

"Right before a new moon? Unlikely."

Luke examined the chart anyway, double-checking the photos of the irrigated wound before it had been bandaged. That was definitely the bite radius of a human mouth, not a chisav or dog. She'd been attacked, and it had been a shifter in his human form who had done the biting.

"Get a dose of Retrolycathol in her before dawn. Call the OPA for a priest in case I'm wrong." He was never wrong. "We'll need a priest for the patient in the blue jacket anyway."

Nurse Ballard frowned at the second patient. "Him? That's definitely a werewolf bite."

"Demonic influence," Luke said.

"How can you tell the difference?"

He always could. The why of it didn't matter, and explanations would delay getting necessary drugs administered and priests summoned. "You'll want him in isolation until the priest arrives. Thanks, Charity."

She took the Retrolycathol prescription to the pharmacy.

Luke would need a closer look at the patient before she got the Retrolycathol. There was no point subjecting her to months of unpleasant side effects unless it was truly necessary.

She was lucky to be eligible for Retrolycathol in the first place, though. Not all patients were that fortunate.

Luke stepped into an inpatient room to check on one such patient.

Mrs. Eiderman was a relic of another era: the kind of woman who would have been young and beautiful in the eighties, with hair teased tall, a love of shoulder pads, and a terrible smoking habit. Those had been the days when people understood that smoking was a deadly habit, but were too rebellious to stop. Women of the eighties had been high-powered business magnates, and they had been immortal.

She had been right not to fear lung cancer. It wasn't lung cancer taking Mrs. Eiderman down, but lycanthropy.

How a shifter had managed to evade capture by the OPA on a full moon was one mystery. Why it would have sneaked into Sunny Vistas Retirement Home was another. Those mysteries weren't Luke's problem. What mattered was this: Mrs. Eiderman, a delicate woman of seventy-something years, had been bitten. She was too frail to survive multiple doses of Retrolycathol. And she was dying.

Three moons had passed since Mrs. Eiderman had been assaulted by a shifter, and all three moons had happened in Luke's hospital. He hadn't thought she'd survive the first of them. Now the fourth approached and she was still there, shrunken and frail, in a hospital bed.

There was no hint of weakness in the smile she gave Luke as he entered her room. "Good morning,

Dr. Flynn."

He glanced at his chart, looking for reports of mental failure. "Morning?"

She laughed. "Just seeing if you're on your toes. I know it's evening."

"I'm supposed to be the one testing you, Mrs. Eiderman." He sat on the chair at her bedside. Three moons he'd sat with her. Three sunrises. She was still smiling despite the golden eyes and unhealed bite wound on her forearm. "How have you been feeling?"

"Like I could lift cars above my head."

She didn't look it. If she'd been twenty years younger—even five or ten years—she might have been able to lift a semi truck, assuming she survived all six moons of transformation. Mrs. Eiderman was guaranteed not to last that long, though.

"Can you rate your current pain for me between one and ten?" Luke asked.

"Zero," she said.

The last nurse to visit her had drawn a frowning face and number eight on the white board. Eight of ten. That was how bad her pain had been during an earlier visit. The painkillers were working. No wonder she was smiling so much.

Luke rested a hand atop hers, rubbing his thumb along her knuckles. "I don't like having to bring this up, but you need to know...the moon is coming again. It's tomorrow night."

She sighed. "Will you be here for me?"

"Do you want me to be?" The patient had refused his company during her last transformations. Her dignity was too great to be seen when her bones were breaking and skin was splitting.

"I think so." Mrs. Eiderman could barely open her eyes, but she was still giving a sleepy smile. The wrinkles on either side of her mouth had been carved deep by an entire lifetime of smiling. "This will be the last one, after all."

"There's no way to know that," Luke said.

"Promise me you'll be here?"

He wasn't supposed to be on shift for that moon. "I wouldn't dream of missing it."

"It's a date." Her sleepy smile had turned lascivious. Mrs. Eiderman had made no secret of admiring Luke's body. The fact that she didn't mention it out loud this time spoke volumes about her condition.

Her last moon *was* coming.

"Damn," he sighed, pulling the curtains around her bed to allow her to rest.

He was stepping out of the room when another nurse jogged to his side, eyes wild, stethoscope slipping from his shoulders. "Luke! Thank God you're here!"

"What's up, Ollie?" Luke asked with far less urgency.

Nurse Oliver Machado was a bit dramatic, to put it nicely. If Oliver had his way, Luke would have personally attended every single patient to come through the emergency department, including the ones with stubbed toes and mosquito bites.

Oliver stopped a foot away, leaning his hands on his knees as he tried to catch his breath. "The woman. In the forest. White eyes."

"Slow down and start from the beginning." Luke might as well have prefaced every conversation with Oliver like that. "Aren't you supposed to be camping this week? Scrubs are an odd choice for camping."

"Well, I *had* to come in once I found her. She was wandering around the forest."

"Who was?" Luke washed his hands in the sink, scrubbing his fingernails thoroughly.

"The *woman*," Oliver said, frustrated. "You need to see her."

"It's almost the new moon, Ollie. I'm on preternatural rotation. We've already got two patients who need my attention and it's not midnight, so I'd wager I'll be too busy to see any random forest nymphs tonight." He was joking, but if the woman were a nymph, then she wouldn't have been the first one to wander into his emergency room.

"You have to see this one. She's asking for you, Doctor."

Luke's eyebrows lifted. "For me? Specifically, by name?"

The expression on Oliver's face was opaque, but the urgency in his eyes said that he knew.

He *knew*.

Worse than that, the patient knew, too.

This was someone that Luke needed to see.

"All right," he said. "Take me to her."

The other patients would have to wait.

When Marion woke up, she only knew those two things: That her name was Marion, and that she was awake.

That was all.

She catalogued a few other facts in the moments that followed. Her body was female. She had large breasts, wide hips, and a flat stomach, all hidden underneath a starched white sheet that made her think of hospitals.

Hospitals—Marion knew what a hospital was.

Marion sat up and the sheet puddled around her waist. She was wearing blue pajama pants. Ribs jutted from beneath her breasts. She looked as though she hadn't eaten in quite some time, although she didn't feel hungry.

The crook of her elbow itched. Someone had taped an IV needle to her arm. She tried to pick the tape off with her fingernail.

The door opened.

A man entered, and the sight of him made her forget about the IV. He was an attractive man in his prime years, with a square jaw, narrow shoulders, and brown skin. His black hair was cut short to the scalp.

He spoke in a language she didn't understand.

His mouth moved with harsh syllables. An American voice, somewhere from the western side of the country, and it was infuriating that Marion could identify where he came from but didn't know the words themselves.

This man wore plain blue medical scrubs—something else that Marion recognized. He had a badge clipped to his chest. The name was blurry at a distance. Marion needed to wear glasses, she realized.

When he moved near enough to sit beside her bed, the badge came into focus.

Lucas Flynn. He appeared to be a doctor.

"I'm not sick," she said immediately. She was speaking in French, which must have been her native tongue.

He stared at her as though she were a ghost haunting his hospital. His hand rubbed his jaw. He must have been on shift for hours because a beard shadowed his chin.

"I'm not sick and I don't need a doctor," Marion said, speaking slowly in the hopes he would be able to pick up a word or two. "I need to find Seth Wilder." The name was rattling in her head, bouncing around, clearer than anything else she knew. Clearer than her gender, clearer than her own name, clearer than the overwhelming confusion.

Marion *needed* Seth Wilder.

The doctor's eyes narrowed. He clasped his hands in his lap, then unclasped them, then sat back in the chair. The request displeased him.

He said something.

"I don't understand you," Marion said, thrusting her arm toward him. "Please remove this. I don't need it and it's uncomfortable."

The doctor lifted one finger, telling her wait a moment non-verbally.

He put gloves on before removing the IV. It stung a little, but Marion felt much better without it.

"Thank you," she said.

And he replied with something that she suspected meant "you're welcome," which was such basic English that surely she should have known it. She could only understand the context, though.

Dr. Flynn took the gloves off again, tossed them into the trash, and extracted a cell phone from his pocket. He continued to speak in that frustrating American accent as his thumbs moved over the screen.

After a moment, his phone spoke in an automated, robotic voice. "Do you know any English?" The doctor's phone was speaking her language. Dr. Flynn smiled at her expression and turned the phone so that she could see the screen. He'd opened some kind of translation app.

"No, I only speak French," Marion said.

He seemed to understand that. He typed again, and the phone said, "My name is Dr. Lucas Flynn. Do you know where you are?"

She held her hand out to take the phone. He dropped it in her palm. "I don't know anything," she typed, and the phone read it aloud in jilting English. "I can't remember anything before waking up in this hospital room."

They exchanged the phone again. "You're in Ransom Falls, California, which is in the western North American Union. You were found walking in the forest outside of city limits, alone and confused."

Marion didn't remember that part either. It explained why she felt sore, though.

"A nurse found you," Dr. Flynn went on, still using the phone. "The nurse said that you've been asking for a man named Seth Wilder."

"Yes," Marion typed. "I need him." She felt as sure of that as she was of her name, and as unsure as she was of everything else.

"What's your name?" he asked.

"Marion."

"Do you have a last name?"

"I'm sure I must, but I don't know it," she said.

That was a fact that seemed to bother the doctor as well. "How old are you?"

"I don't know."

"Where do you live? How did you end up in the forest outside of Ransom Falls?"

"I don't know. I've already told you everything I can remember," Marion typed. "If the only things I remember are my name and Seth Wilder's, he must be important to me somehow. I believe he will be able to help me remember everything."

When she passed the phone back to him, their fingers brushed.

The instant that they touched, Marion felt as though a door had opened in her mind.

She jerked away from him.

The violence of her reaction surprised both of them. "I'm sorry," Dr. Flynn said aloud, and he quickly typed the apology in his phone to be translated into French as well. "*Je suis désolé.*"

"It's okay," she said in English, and her accent was similar to the doctor's: harsh, American, West Coast in origin, as natural as though she'd been speaking it her entire life. "You didn't hurt me."

"Well, damn," Dr. Flynn said. She understood the second thing he'd said as well as she had the first. He leaned back in his chair as though trying to put a few more inches between them. Who could blame him?

Marion looked down at her chest. Nothing had changed physically, but her hand was clenched into a fist, and her knuckles ached as though she had just rapped her hand hard against the door in her mind, asking someone to open it.

And someone had.

Coming in contact with Dr. Flynn had helped her remember...something.

"Can you help me remember everything else?" Marion asked, and it surprised her how easily it came out.

His mouth opened. It closed.

"I can order some tests," Dr. Flynn said.

He moved to leave the room, and sudden fear struck her. What if she only spoke English when she was in this doctor's presence? What if someone else came in to draw her blood, and the doors in her mind shut again, blocking out the words she had learned—maybe even her name?

She whipped the sheets aside and leaped from bed. "Wait, Doctor."

He stopped in the doorway. His knuckles were ashen because he gripped the tablet with her chart on it so hard. "Yes?"

"Can you run the tests yourself?" Marion asked. His brow furrowed, and she added, "Please."

After a pause, he said, "Okay. I can do that for you."

Luke got Marion a hospital gown, clean socks, and a hairbrush, then sent her into the bathroom to change. "You'll wait for me?" she asked, lingering in the doorway with a hand on the knob.

He'd been planning to check on the other patients, but he said, "Yes."

She left the door open a tiny crack when she went inside. He could hear her rustling around in there—the slide of cloth against skin, bare feet padding on linoleum, a comb through hair. Luke was painfully aware of every little movement she made.

Marion shouldn't have been there.

Oliver rapped lightly on the doorframe before stepping into the room. "Are you okay, doc?" he asked without preamble.

Luke gave himself a moment to compose his thoughts by filling a cup with water at the sink. "How did you know to get me for her?"

"I've always known," Oliver said. He cleared his throat. "You always see the preternatural patients anyway."

"How did you know that she's preternatural?"

"You had to have seen her eyes. Didn't you?"

Luke drank the water just as slowly as he'd filled it. It would have been impossible not to notice Marion's eyes. They were such a pale color that they barely qualified as blue.

"I'm going to be busy with this patient for a while," Luke said. "I want you to validate the werewolf bite on the patient Charity pulled aside for me. Make sure it was, in fact, a shifter. Can you do that?" Luke didn't wait for Oliver to agree before saying, "And then we need to talk about... everything. I need to know what you know about me. Don't leave the hospital."

"I won't. I'm looking forward to talking." Oliver didn't immediately leave. He was watching the door to the bathroom, as though contemplating whether Marion should be left alone in there.

Luke was wondering the same thing, though he wasn't sure if Oliver's motivations were the same.

Oliver knew who Luke was. If not for Marion, the doctor would have run from the hospital and never looked back. He was still tempted to do it.

But first things first.

"Go," Luke said.

Oliver finally stepped outside. He shot one last look at Luke before shutting the door behind him.

THREE

Dr. Flynn showed Marion where the shower was and waited in the hospital room while she cleaned the dirt off her body. She appreciated having him nearby, even when he was in a separate room. She was acutely aware of his physical presence and the deep murmur of his voice on the other side of the wall, and it was irrationally comforting.

His presence made her feel safe enough to strip down in the chilly bathroom—a thin-walled room with a drafty window over the toilet. Patterns of moonlight frothed on the tiles, shadows foaming as howling wind bent the trees outside. It felt as though there were enemies lurking in wait for Marion.

She wasn't alone, though. She could get dressed without fear.

At least, she didn't feel fear until she inspected

her naked body. Her legs were mottled with bruises from the knees down, she had several scrapes along her hips and shoulders, and she felt like her back was injured, although she couldn't see anything in the mirror.

Whatever had happened to Marion—however she had lost her memory—it had not been gentle.

Speaking of the mirror, Marion was pleasantly surprised to find that she was not just female, but a beautiful female with striking features. She had a strong bone structure. Chestnut hair made her blue eyes look unnaturally bright—the white-blue of a Husky's eyes, which did not match her otherwise dark coloring. She suspected she was no more Caucasian than Dr. Flynn was, though her memories seemed to have left a gap that would have explained her geographic origin. Somewhere that spoke French, apparently.

"I'm a model," she said, testing the words to see how they felt. They didn't resonate with her.

What would a French-speaking amnesiac model be doing stumbling around Ransom Falls?

Marion dried off and combed her fingers through her tangled curls, never once breaking eye contact with her reflection. Some part of her feared that she might somehow vanish if she stepped away from that mirror.

Her neck was lean, her shoulders bony, her large breasts perky. Definitely young. Very little muscle definition, though not in poor physical condition. No old scars.

She stroked her hands down her cheeks, neck,

and chest. Her skin was dark-olive in color. Not a wrinkle or blemish in sight. "I'm a student. I'm an artist. I'm an actress."

None of that stuck out to her.

Marion pulled her hair over her shoulder. Her fingers moved swiftly, twisting it into a thick brown braid that got all of those curls out of her face, revealing her high cheekbones, wide eyes, and pointed chin. Marion liked the look of it. She wanted to let the others in the hospital see her face. She wanted to know if anyone recognized her. And if they happened to admire her in the process, that wouldn't be such a terrible thing, either.

Whoever she was, and whatever role she held in society, she was a little bit arrogant. "No harm in that," she murmured to herself.

Marion wrapped herself up in a hospital gown, as it was much cleaner than the pajamas she had been found in.

She hesitated when she turned away from the mirror. The door into the hospital room was waiting, and the sight of it made something strange ring within her skull.

Marion lifted a hand to knock.

Why did she want to knock? It didn't have a lock, presumably in case she fell trying to use the bathroom and needed a nurse's assistance.

She pushed it open.

Dr. Flynn waited on the other side. His expression was guarded. "This way, please."

She studied him as they walked down the hall. It was hard to tear her eyes away from a man as attractive as Dr. Flynn. The doctor was probably too old for her, she acknowledged internally. He must have been through eight years of medical school, and her reflection made Marion suspect she would have been lucky to have completed eight days of university. But still attractive. Easily the sexiest man she'd ever seen.

To be fair, her memory didn't extend very far back, but if the world had many men sexier than Dr. Luke Flynn, people surely couldn't get very much accomplished. Such men would be terribly distracting.

"Do I know you?" Marion asked.

"If you've been in Ransom Falls for long, you might have seen me around. It's a small town," Dr. Flynn said without looking at her.

"Do you know me?"

A flicker of a smile crossed his mouth. "I do now." He was being evasive. Marion wasn't quite optimistic enough to call it flirtatious.

Dr. Flynn led her to another room, this one with blue walls and an arched white doorway. When she passed through, her skin broke out in prickles. She rubbed her upper arms. "What was that?"

He tapped his tablet, making a note. "Sit in the chair, please."

Marion did.

Another man, whose nametag identified him as Nurse Machado, approached her with a wheeled tray. He had a needle, an elastic strap, a couple of empty vials.

Her spine stiffened. "You'll not take my blood. Only Dr. Flynn may touch me."

At a look from the doctor, Nurse Machado stepped back. Dr. Flynn took the tray.

"Explain what you're doing before you begin," Marion said.

"All right. This needle here is for drawing blood. I'll take three vials. That's not enough for you to feel any side effects from blood loss, although it will pinch when I insert the needle. I'm going to run some standard labs and see if we can narrow down a reason for your memory loss. The lab will take a few hours to get through everything."

"Not if you take the samples to test yourself," Marion said. "You'll be able to work quite quickly, I'm sure." The men exchanged looks. She lifted her chin to shoot a look at them down the bridge of her nose, arching an eyebrow. "Will that be a problem?"

"The lab here is great," Dr. Flynn said. "I can attest to that. I trust them."

"Regardless, I'd like you alone to handle my case."

Nurse Machado flung his hands into the air. "Why pay our lab techs thirteen dollars an hour when a doctor with a quarter million-dollar salary can do it? I'm out of here. You know where to find me, Luke."

The door had barely swung shut behind him when another nurse entered, this one female. Marion knew instantly that this woman was attracted to Dr. Flynn, though she couldn't have put her finger on why that was. Marion simply *knew* it.

This nurse's nametag said Ballard. She was a diminutive woman, though it was more to do with posture than stature, as though her confidence had been drained by a vampire. She hid her face behind glasses with thick black frames. "I've called the priest. He should be here in an hour. We're almost out of Retrolycathol and—"

"Not now," Dr. Flynn interrupted.

"But Doctor—"

"Not *now*, Charity." It came out a little sharper the second time.

Being snapped at by Dr. Flynn must have been an unusual incident. Nurse Ballard looked as shocked as though he'd dropped an anvil on her head.

She slunk away, hugging the paperwork to her chest.

Marion wanted to tell Dr. Flynn that it was okay. That he could attend to other patients, particularly ones in such a state that they needed the attention of a priest.

But it wasn't okay.

Until she walked out the doors of that hospital, Marion had no intention of letting the doctor out of her sight.

Dr. Flynn had different plans.

He returned Marion to a private room and instructed her to sit. "You'll be safe here," he said. They had just finished running several tests, one of which had involved a very large, alarmingly noisy MRI machine. "I'll make sure nobody comes in while I'm gone."

She didn't sit. "I want to come with you."

"You can't. The lab is a secure area."

"You'll be escorting me."

"No," he said sharply. "You'll be staying right here. You'll be safe. There are other people in this hospital who need my help while your labs are performed."

Her cheeks warmed. She sat on the bed. Marion was rewarded by another of those warm smiles from the doctor.

"I'll check in on you soon," he said.

And he was gone.

Marion counted to ten, using the clock on the wall to measure the seconds.

Then she tested the door.

The handle turned easily under her hand. It wasn't locked. She was almost offended by that. Wasn't the doctor concerned for her safety? Did he want to permit any hospital employee to wander in at will?

Luckily, doors that allowed people in would also allow them to come out.

Marion stepped into the hall.

The hospital was pleasantly quiet, sterile, and tan-walled. It was also very small. Marion suspected that she had seen everything there was to see when walking from her room to the MRI machine, including a nurses station that was currently unoccupied. Nurses Machado and Ballard were nowhere in sight.

She stepped behind the desk, pressing a button on the workstation keyboard. The screen flicked to life. It was locked with a password. *Disappointing.*

No papers had been left out on the tables, no drawers left open. Marion didn't try very hard to break into them. She wasn't even sure what she was looking for.

Footsteps echoed down the hall. She stepped through the door behind the nurses station to hide, and she found herself in a break room. There was a table, a microwave, a mini-fridge.

A pair of thick-framed glasses sat unattended beside that microwave.

"Hello there," Marion murmured, picking them up. She cleaned them off with a paper towel, blew a fleck of dust off of the glass, and then slid them onto her nose.

The room came into focus. Now she could see the far wall clearly, though the lenses were a mite strong, making the world look fish-eyed. It wasn't too distracting. They would work.

Nurse Ballard didn't really need those more than Marion did. Marion removed them, folded the arms, tucked them inside her hospital gown.

"Do you need something?"

She turned to see a very suspicious Nurse Machado in the doorway. He didn't look angry, so she believed that he hadn't seen her taking the glasses.

"I was alone in my room and became afraid," Marion said, most likely too confident to sound properly frightened. "I was looking for company."

Nurse Machado stepped into the room. He was very imposing, large enough that he would have been able to pin down struggling patients if necessary. "Where did you hear the name Seth Wilder?"

"It's not your concern." She flicked her fingers. "Out of my way. I'll return to my room now."

Nurse Machado advanced on her. "I thought you wanted company."

He was a very large man.

"You'll get away from me, or I will scream," she said.

"For whom?" he asked. "You sent Dr. Flynn to the lab. It's in the basement. And Nurse Ballard's down in the waiting room."

Another step forward.

Marion braced herself, refusing to move back in response. She squared her shoulders. Lifted her chin. "What do you want from me?"

Now he was so close that she could smell his aftershave—and underneath that, the coppery scent of blood.

A threatening aura haloed him, his mood sour on her tongue and making her hair stand on end. Marion could feel it crawling over her skin the way that she had felt that Nurse Ballard was attracted to Lucas Flynn. It felt like if she squinted hard enough, she might be able to see through his skull to the specific phrasing of his unfriendly thoughts.

"You don't remember, do you?" Nurse Machado asked. "Where I found you?"

The lights in the break room flickered. She glanced up at the ceiling and held her breath, praying they wouldn't go dark. They didn't. "I don't remember anything before waking up in my room here."

"So you expect me to believe that you don't remember the circle."

She blinked with surprise. It was the only outward show of emotion she permitted herself. "Circle?"

"You're a good liar, but I still know you're lying," Nurse Machado said. "Watch yourself. And know that I'm watching you too."

"Are you done? Now get out of my way."

After a moment's hesitation, he did as she ordered.

She kept a hand on the glasses within her hospital gown so that they wouldn't slide as she strode down the hallway.

The nurse didn't follow.

When she shut the door to her hospital room, Marion's knees gave out. She sat on the edge of the bed. Marion was shaking all over—shaking with fear, she realized, which she hadn't felt when she'd been making demands in the break room. She'd reacted on instinct. And her instinct, apparently, was to be imperious and demanding.

Marion took the glasses out of her hospital

gown. What was she thinking, stealing some nurse's glasses? And then ordering a man around when she was trapped alone with him.

Who had Marion been that these were the behaviors that came naturally?

She set the glasses on the counter where Nurse Ballard would be able to find them later. Then she wedged a chair against the door, crawled into bed, and pulled the covers over her head.

Marion didn't feel any safer alone with herself than she did with Nurse Machado.

It took less than an hour for the doctor to return. The longest, most miserable hour in Marion's short memory.

"The results have come in." Dr. Flynn sat on the stool by the counter and rolled it to Marion's side. He held the lab sheet so that she could see it, even though the medical codes didn't make any sense to her. "The good news is that you're perfectly healthy. I see nothing in your blood work that should impact your memory."

Hot worms of anxiety writhed through her heart. "What about the MRI?"

"You need to see something else to understand that." He flipped to the second page. "The doorway into the lab has magical stones set into it. Each one reacts to a different preternatural breed. When you walk through, it records your presence, registers which stones react, and a witch analyzes the results." He pointed at one box. "You aren't a demon."

"Is that good news as well?" Marion asked.

"Very good news." His forefinger slid to the next box. "You aren't a werewolf, shapeshifter, sidhe, or other common gaean breed."

"Gaean?"

"Okay, damn. There are three major factions: gaean, infernal, and ethereal. Infernal creatures come from the Nether Worlds—they're usually called demons. Gaeans are all the preternatural creatures natural to Earth and the Middle Worlds."

Marion tipped her head to the side, surveying him thoughtfully. "What does the test register for you, Dr. Flynn?"

"None of the stones react to mundane humans." He lifted the page to show her the other side. "The stone that detects witches reacted to you faintly. So did the stone that detects angels."

A word surfaced in Marion's memory. "I'm a mage."

"Based on your blood tests, you're most likely a Gray mage," Dr. Flynn said. "Gray is a word we use for anyone who has two factions in their ancestry —in this case, human and angel. Either your angel parent was a mage, or your human parent was a witch. Whatever the mix, it resulted in you: a half-angel who can cast magic."

She turned her hands over to look at her palms, expecting flames to explode out of them. That seemed like the sort of thing that a half-angel, half-witch mage would be able to do. Nothing happened. Marion clenched her fists. "What else did you learn?"

"That brings me to the MRI results." He opened the folder to a photo. It looked like shattered glass: white lines shooting out on a black background, with the indistinct shape of a skull blurred in the background. "I couldn't scan you because of your unique physiology. If there's something like a tumor, we have no way of knowing. Angels don't get medical care from human hospitals and half-angel Gray are too rare to study."

Her heart sank. "I see."

"I can't help you, Marion. I'm sorry."

Perhaps that was why she believed she needed to see Seth Wilder. He must have been some kind of expert in angels—her breed, much to Marion's surprise. She didn't feel like an angel, half or whole or any proportion thereof.

In the meantime, she was left with no memory, no clues, and no plan.

Her throat burned. "What am I going to do?"

Dr. Flynn patted her knee. "I wish I could help you."

"Thank you, Lucas," she said, and then it struck her that she had slipped, addressing him informally. "I'm sorry. Can I call you Lucas?"

He opened his mouth, as though to argue with her—to ask her to call him a different name. But then he stopped. Considered it.

"Call me Luke," he said.

Outside of Marion's hospital room, at the nurse's station, Oliver Machado sat beside Charity Ballard. She should have been working her way through heaps of paperwork. In theory, the hospital's records were electronic. In reality, their budget couldn't accommodate enough equipment or assistants to catch up with the laws about digital record keeping. Charity felt like she was constantly drowning in paperwork.

She was taking a break from fighting the hurricane of bureaucracy. Instead, she was watching a live stream of the news on her computer monitor. Charity didn't bother turning it off when Oliver joined her. If he reported her for procrastination, she could report him for a hundred more dangerous infractions.

"Anything interesting on the news?" Ollie asked, rolling his chair over.

"More summit crap," Charity said. "I'm so tired of hearing about it." The news had been talking about the upcoming summit around the clock ever since it had been announced earlier in the year. The werewolf Alpha, Rylie Gresham, had made a rare public appearance to invite every faction to join her at the United Nations to hash out preternatural issues. At this point, Charity would have preferred to have teeth pulled than hear more about vampires, werewolves, angels, and demons.

"Why are you watching if you're sick of it?"

Because pulling teeth still wasn't as awful as staring down her stack of paperwork. "It's important to be well informed."

"It's not going to have jack to do with us mundanes," Ollie said.

Charity coughed into her fist. "Mundanes. Yeah." Still, she didn't close the video stream. A reporter was interviewing an angel about the issues the ethereal delegation hoped to tackle. That angel had the same shocking eyes as their newest patient, Marion. It was deeply unsettling.

"Can't believe we invited those things into the NAU," Ollie said.

She was inclined to agree. More angels in the region could only lead to badness.

Charity sighed and closed the news stream. "You look like you aren't busy right now. Can you help me catch up on these forms?"

"I came here to help you, but not with paperwork." He lifted his cell phone so that she could see the screen. "This was in the white pages today."

Charity squinted. She hadn't been able to find her glasses, so she couldn't see what he was trying to show her. "Is that a photograph of the patient you found camping? Marion?"

"With a number for a tip line," Oliver said. "Someone's searching for her."

She took the phone from him and scrolled down to read the text. There wasn't much information to go along with the blurry image of

Marion; just a request that people report sightings.

"I wonder if she's part of the ethereal delegation that arrived for the summit," Charity said. "Although it's strange she'd have ended up in this neck of the woods."

"Strange and scary, isn't it? We don't need angels around here." Oliver stood without taking his phone back. "I'm heading down to the lab to pick up a copy of her results. I'll be back in a few minutes."

Charity swiveled in her chair to watch him go.

Someone was looking for Marion. That was likely a good sign—wasn't it? They would be happy to know that the missing person had been found. There might even be a reward.

And then they would take the angel-girl out of Ransom Falls before she could cause any real harm.

She rolled a few inches to the left, peering through the cracked door into the patient's hospital room. Luke was sitting a few inches from Marion, his hand resting on her knee. They looked to be having a rather intense conversation.

Charity dialed the number in the ad, and someone picked up on the second ring.

"Hello?" asked a voice.

"Is this the tip line?"

"If you have something to report, then yes, it's the tip line." There was a hint of humor to the voice, and Charity shivered at the sound of it. His voice brought to mind her childhood before Genesis, listening to the radio in the car with her father. That professional, silken voice that DJs used to have.

"I saw your advertisement. She's here at Mercy Hospital in Ransom Falls, California."

"Thank you." Now that musical voice sounded deeply relieved.

There was rustling on the other end of the line, as though the man were about to hang up. Charity spoke quickly before he could. "Is she dangerous?"

"Very."

"Should I call the police? Or the OPA? Wait, are *you* the OPA?"

"No," he said. "But you might want to evacuate before we get there."

Charity didn't get a chance to ask whom she was speaking to or when "they" would arrive.

He hung up.

FOUR

The next afternoon, Luke found Marion negotiating for her discharge at the nurses station. There was no way to tell that the patient had been speaking in French only hours earlier, completely incapable of understanding the language she now used with the confidence of a native.

"I'm sorry," Charity was saying. "I can't discharge you without speaking to Dr. Flynn." Her eyes lifted over Marion's head, expression brightening at the sight of Luke. "Here he is now. You can talk to him yourself."

Marion rounded on him. She had eschewed the hospital gown for scrubs, which must have been donated by one of the female residents. One of the main purposes of scrubs was modesty: they were formless linen, tight enough to keep from creating a hazard, but not so tight as to be construed as offensive. On Marion, the scrubs looked like a fashion statement. Her thick brown hair, twisted into a sloppy bun, dangled along the lean lines of her throat. Luke could make out the lacework pattern of veins crossing under her jaw.

"They won't let me leave. Why?" Marion asked.

"Typically, in a case like yours, we would contact social workers to help take care of you," Luke said carefully.

"A case like mine? A half-angel?" She said that too loudly.

The nurses weren't paying attention, but Luke guided her a few feet away and lowered his voice. "Someone who obviously needs help."

"Was your plan to hold me here until I could be turned over to a homeless shelter?" She brandished her medical records at him, which she must have bullied out of Charity. "You've left spots blank on my records. You don't even have my breed written down here. I would go into the mundane human system!"

She had no clue how much of a favor Luke was doing for her with that. The preternatural benefits system would have chewed a kid like her up and spat her out broken, and that was assuming that she wasn't snapped up by a higher governmental power. The girl was a mage, after all.

"Look at me!" Marion touched her jaw, her neck, showed her hands to him. "How old do you think I am? Sixteen? Seventeen?"

"I'd guess more like eighteen or nineteen."

"My parents will be worried about me.

Furthermore, there's likely a school missing me." She shook her finger in his face. "You would have me sent into the system, abandoned, made someone else's problem!"

"You're making a lot of assumptions." And all of them were wrong.

A wounded look flashed through her eyes. "I thought I could trust you, Luke."

"You can trust me when I say I'm trying to do you a favor."

"Don't contact any social workers. You certainly don't need to do me any favors."

"Okay." Luke caught Charity's eye and circled his finger in the air. "Put together the discharge paperwork." The sooner that Marion was out of Luke's hospital, the sooner he could return to his normal life.

Marion was braced for battle, and didn't appear to know what to do without getting one. She deflated. "Yes. Excellent. Do that."

Oliver wheeled the patient who had been bitten by a werewolf the previous night down the hallway. At the sight of him, Marion's anger vanished. She stepped behind Luke and gripped his sleeve.

"What's wrong?" he asked. Did she recognize the patient who had been bitten? Or did she recognize Oliver?

Marion didn't respond until the nurse and the patient rounded the corner. "What's the best way for me to get out of town? Is there a subway?"

"In Ransom Falls?" They didn't even have a

coffee shop, unless you counted the diner, which served sludge that could only very generously be described as coffee. "All we have is the bus that passes through here on the way to Sacramento from Eugene. There are probably schedules in the waiting room, but—"

"Sacramento." She nodded sharply. "I'll start there."

Charity approached with the paperwork. "Dr. Flynn—"

"Thank you," Marion said, taking the papers from her. She signed the highlighted lines, then tossed them onto the counter. "I'll be leaving now."

"Wait." Luke extracted his wallet and gave her cash. He didn't check how much. "Buses aren't free."

"Thank you." Marion managed a small, grateful smile. Then she was gliding down the hallway, tall, elegant, and inhumanly graceful. A creature unlike any that Luke had ever expected to see in Ransom Falls.

That was why he had moved there, after all. To get away from people like her.

"Do you think we should let her go?" Charity asked, wringing her hands. "It's raining out there, and—and she has no idea what's going on."

Luke ignored his instincts shouting the same thing. "We can't hold her against her will unless she poses a risk."

"How do you know she doesn't?"

He didn't respond to that. He just went to his office.

Luke locked the door behind him. He couldn't lock out his worries, though.

The issue was that he already knew that Marion was not going to find a school missing her attendance, or Seth Wilder at her home. She might, however, find people who were looking for her. Some of them might be friendly. Most of them wouldn't be.

Luke didn't want any of those people hearing Marion ask after Seth Wilder.

Over the years, the man who called himself Lucas Flynn had grown accustomed to refusing to give help if it might make his identity vulnerable. He did his best using the tools that a doctor typically had, sacrificing time, energy, and money to treat patients. He ignored the other resources he might have been able to access, even if those other resources could have saved lives.

He was Luke Flynn, a mundane human doctor working at a small rural hospital in NorCal. The problems of a Gray mage like Marion Garin should not have been his issue.

Yet when he gazed out the window to see a slender teenage girl waiting at a rainy bus stop, he felt a powerful sense of responsibility that he couldn't shrug off.

She needed help from Seth Wilder.

"No." He closed the blinds on the window and turned to face his office. "No way."

A medical degree for Lucas Flynn hung on the wall. His computer displayed paperwork for several shifter-bitten patients who needed his help.

He had a cup of pens, a leather desk blotter, an executive chair. No guns, no knives. No signs of Seth Wilder at all.

He leaned back in his chair, pushing the blinds open with a finger.

Marion had good timing. A bus pulled up to the stop after a few seconds, leaving her little time to get drenched by the downpour. As he watched, Marion climbed inside, used the money he had given her for a ticket, and sat down. The bus pulled away from the curb.

She had officially left to find Seth.

"Damn," Luke said.

He started to let the blinds fall closed. An instant before they obscured the sliver of street, the bus swerved. Brakes squealed.

Luke shoved the blinds aside as the bus tipped onto the two right-hand wheels. It teetered, then rolled and smashed onto its side. It skidded into a tree on the side of the road. The bus was crushed.

"Damn," Luke said again, less calmly than the first time.

He yanked open a desk drawer, grabbed a handgun from its depths, and ran for the hallway.

The instant his foot crossed the threshold, all the power in the hospital went out. The lights died and there was no generator hum to follow. He skidded to a stop in the hallway.

People he didn't recognize were heading toward Marion's former room. They warped the walls around them. Their skin glistened with pure magic.

Sidhe. Faeries.

And probably assassins.

The nearest of them was a leather-clad young man with broad shoulders and black hair that glistened faintly blue. He carried a bastard sword as long as he was tall. Luke could imagine Marion cleaved in half by that sword all too easily.

He raced toward them. "Hey!"

They ignored his shouting. As soon as they realized that Marion's room was empty, reality distorted around them with a hard twist, a swirl, and an audible *pop*.

The assassins vanished.

Marion felt the assassins coming before they shoved her bus off the road. Unfortunately, she wasn't sure *what* she was feeling at first—that tickle in the back of her mind, the buzz at her crown, her itching knuckles. It was as meaningless to her as Luke's English had initially been.

She understood once the windshield shattered and the killers leaped in. They were squat creatures with curly brown fur covering their human-like bodies.

They were urisk, and they wielded knives.

Marion was startled to recognize the creatures. She was even more startled when her mind was flooded with trivia about them. Urisk were tough creatures from a common caste of sidhe known primarily for their craftsmanship, although their nimble fingers were just as good at destruction. More of them had ended up in mercenary work than craftwork since Genesis.

How she knew this, she didn't know, and she didn't have time to dwell on it.

She leaped to her feet and flung a hand toward them on instinct—why, she wasn't sure, because nothing happened.

An urisk slashed the bus driver's throat. His body flopped onto the steering column. The bus veered on the slick road, tipping onto two wheels, and Marion tumbled back to her seat.

Glass exploded. Seats snapped from their moorings and a tree branch punched through the floor. Metal groaned as the bus collapsed at its center like a soda can in a crusher. The collapse separated her from the trio of urisk assassins.

She couldn't remember if there had been any passengers at the front of the bus. If there were, then they stood no chance of surviving. The urisk would dispatch them as rapidly as they had the bus driver.

The people who sat near the back with her still stood a chance.

Marion took quick inventory: an older man, and a woman with a child. The child was bleeding from a cut on his forehead, but conscious. No fighters. Nobody who could help her.

She scrambled toward the crumpled center of the bus. There was a hatch in what used to be the roof. It had a bright-red handle visible even among the destruction. "Follow me!" she shouted to the other passengers. Her command was echoed by pounding at the front half of the bus.

"What the hell is going on?" asked the older man, helping the woman lift her child.

Marion didn't have an answer for him. She gritted her teeth and slammed both heels into the door on the roof. It popped open.

She slithered onto the pavement, then reached into the bus again.

"Give me your hands!" she shouted.

The child did as she ordered, and Marion hauled him out onto wet pavement. Then she dragged his mother out. And then the man with the flannel shirt.

By the time they had all escaped, one of the urisk had ripped through the collapsed section of the bus. It launched itself through the shattered seats to attack Marion.

Its cruel fingers seized upon her ankle and yanked hard.

Marion was jerked toward the bus.

"No!"

She stomped at the urisk wildly. It was more luck than planning that drove the toe of her lost-and-found sneakers into its noseless face. Sidhe blood cascaded down its lips in glimmering shades of copper.

Fingers curled around Marion's sleeve and yanked her a safe distance from the bus. It was the mother. "Are you okay?" the woman asked, hair wild around her face.

Marion scooped the boy off the ground, shoved him into his mom's arms, pushed both of them toward the shoulder of the road. "Run!"

A urisk plowed into Marion from behind. They tumbled to the pavement together, Marion on the bottom, assassin on top.

She twisted to look at it, and the fractional motion meant that the urisk's knife slammed into the street instead of her skull. The blade embedded two inches into the ground.

Marion gripped the hilt of the knife atop the urisk's hand and bit its wrist, getting a mouthful of wiry hair. Coppery blood gushed into her mouth. The urisk released the knife. Marion wrenched the blade from the ground and stood.

"Get away from me!" She swiped the knife at the urisk.

It leaped out of range. There was no fear in its beady eyes—only wariness. The creature didn't seem convinced Marion presented much of a threat.

Unfortunately, her assassin was right. When Marion swung again, it slammed its elbow into the crook of her arm, bending the joint until it nearly broke.

Her fingers released the knife.

The other two urisk emerged from the wreckage. Both held similar knives. One of them was dripping in human blood from the unfortunate bus driver.

Marion turned to bolt, but a fourth urisk was behind her.

Individually, none of them would have looked too frightening, as their slender builds made them resemble human children.

Collectively, clad in leather armor with thirst for violence glittering in their eyes, they were the stuff of nightmares.

They closed in on her.

Marion threw herself to the ground and rolled between the feet of two of them. She crawled past them as quickly as she could.

One of them knocked her over. This time she landed on her back. Another of the assassins pinned her arms to either side of her head, ensuring that she wouldn't be able to twitch away from the killing blow.

There was nothing she could do but watch a knife descend toward her face.

A gunshot whip-cracked through the drizzly evening.

The urisk's hand sprayed blood. The knife fell from its grip.

Another gunshot, and another.

Skull fragmented. Wiry hair exploded. The assassin fell off of Marion.

The doctor, Luke Flynn, stood behind it. His gun was still leveled at the assassin he'd killed. He was distant enough that Marion's nearsighted vision cast him in a slight blur. It looked, in a way, like he was glowing.

He shifted his aim a couple inches and fired again.

The urisk pinning Marion down let go.

Luke kicked its body off of her. Then he hauled her to her feet, wrapped an arm around her shoulders, and swiveled to fire at the third and fourth urisk. The gunshots reverberated through her entire body. Her eardrums ached.

The surviving urisk scrambled toward them with shocking speed. Luke smashed his heel into its face. The urisk's skull collapsed and it fell to the ground with a shiver of dying magic.

Rain immediately began washing all the sidhe blood away.

Only then did Luke release Marion in order to reload his gun, exchanging one magazine for another. He chambered a round, flicked on the safety, holstered it again. Smooth motions, practiced motions. Something he'd clearly done thousands of times.

Then he gripped her shoulders in both hands. "Are you okay, Marion?"

She searched for words and found none.

Was she okay? Was such a thing possible?

Dr. Lucas Flynn's eyes were endless, such a dark shade of brown that they might have been black.

"Yes," she said slowly, "I think I am."

Marion and Luke didn't wait on the road long enough for emergency personnel to arrive. At the first whine of sirens, the doctor pulled her toward the trees and leaped down the embankment.

He watched over the side of the road as police cars swarmed the crash scene.

Marion remained seated near his feet and started to tremble. She kept mentally reliving the events that had just happened: the windshield shattering, the bus driver's slit throat, the collision.

And then Luke, calm among the violence.

He extracted gloves from the pocket of his jacket, wiggling his fingers into them one hand at a time. "Who were those urisk?" Luke asked, sitting beside her. "Why did they want you dead?"

She spread her hands in a helpless gesture. "You know as much as I do. Why are we hiding from emergency responders?"

"I know all the local firefighters, cops, and EMTs," Luke said. "I don't want to tell them what happened. I don't want them to know..." He trailed off.

"How good you are with a gun?"

He glanced over the embankment one more time. "The people who came to the hospital for you were sidhe, but not urisk. I think there are two separate factions among the faeries searching for you."

From his tone, she assumed that was a bad thing. "Oh."

"We need to figure out how they found you," Luke said. "I need to know if my patients at the hospital are still vulnerable."

"I told you, I don't know anything." A thought struck her as soon as she spoke. That wasn't entirely true. "Except...when I was at the hospital, one of the nurses was acting strangely. He seemed to be trying to threaten me."

"Oliver Machado?"

"How did you know?"

"Only two nurses were in my department last night, and only one a man. But..." He heaved a sigh, raking a hand over his hair. "Ollie was already acting strange."

"How so?"

"He's the one who found you in the forest," Luke said shortly, as if that was all the explanation she needed.

Frankly, he could have refused to tell her anything at all, and Marion wouldn't have attempted to do anything but thank him. There was nothing Luke could do to offend her at that moment. She'd been inches from having a knife embedded in her brain until he'd descended.

Luke gripped Marion's hand and pulled her further from the road. The leather of his glove was as warm as his skin might have been.

"Where are we going, Doctor?" she asked.

"Oliver's house. We need answers, and I've got a strong suspicion that he has them."

FIVE

Oliver Machado lived on a lonely road in the shadow of the mountains. His home wasn't quite dilapidated, but it was far from loved; his flowerbeds grew only weeds and his fence hadn't been stained in years.

His car wasn't in the driveway.

"He must still be at work," Marion said.

"He's not supposed to be on shift." Luke pounded his fist against the front door.

Marion hung back on the front path, which was as crumbling and weedy as the flowerbeds. It was quiet so far from town, not that Ransom Falls was much of a town to be "out of" in the first place. All she heard was water trickling through tangled branches, the sighing of leaves, and the occasional snap of a twig. Nature sounds.

Would she be able to hear more urisk coming,

or would they sound like the rest of nature?

Luke beat the door again. "Come on," he muttered, trying the doorknob. "I know you're home."

"I don't think he is. There aren't any lights."

The doctor slipped off of the steps, cupped his hands around his eyes, and peered through the crack in the curtains. His jacket gapped under the arms. Marion glimpsed the straps of his holster.

She remembered how secure she had felt when he'd pulled her away from the urisk. He'd shot so quickly, so calmly. Hanging back on the path kept her a safe distance from Oliver Machado's front door, but she didn't feel safe at that distance from Luke.

Marion picked her way toward him through the grass. "I really don't think he's home."

He ignored her and stepped around the side of the house. She stuck close, eyes on the empty road behind them. Luke found another window behind an unkempt cluster of ivy. He wiggled his fingers into the bottom and opened it. Marion stayed on the ground, watching his kicking feet vanish into the shadowy room.

"Wait here," he whispered over his shoulder.

Marion clutched the windowsill, which high enough that she could barely peer over it. "You want me to wait alone?" The dark forest was the natural home of some sidhe. She would know if a car was coming, but another urisk could attack without warning.

Luke wasn't immune to the urgency in her

tone. He thrust a gloved hand through the window, offering to help her climb up.

She grabbed him.

Oliver Machado smoked so much weed that tar layered the carpet and stained the walls. Otherwise, his home's interior was as unremarkable as its exterior. He had a lot of cheap furniture and as much clutter as one would expect in the home of a bachelor who worked shifts.

Luke headed past the kitchen, past the bathroom.

"Where are we going?" Marion asked.

He put a finger to his lips, indicating that she should be silent.

Then he opened the bedroom door.

At first, Marion only saw a bed that seemed to double as a laundry pile, along with many curling movie posters serving as cheap wallpaper.

Then she saw some of that laundry shift.

"Don't run, Ollie," Luke said. "I don't want to chase you."

The nurse emerged from the closet by the bed. "I won't run. Not from you, Doctor." Oliver glared at Marion over Luke's shoulder.

Her crown itched, as though an electrical current were running over her scalp. Something wasn't right. "Luke..."

"Step out where I can see you," Luke said.

Oliver moved forward inch by inch. "Careful, Luke. You don't want her at your back. Keep both eyes on that thing at all times."

"I'm not a *thing*," Marion said indignantly.

"If you don't trust her, why'd you bring her to the hospital?" Luke asked.

"Because I wanted you to reveal yourself. We all do. And we're tired of waiting for you." The nurse's eyes were filled with a ghastly light. "If anything's going to bring you out, it would be that *thing*." He emphasized the offensive word, and Marion's skin prickled.

It wasn't just insult that made her feel that way. That strange sensation she had felt since entering Oliver's house continued to grow until it gripped the back of Marion's neck. She rubbed her fingers over her skin, but the sensation didn't subside.

That feeling was coming from Oliver.

"Magic," she said suddenly. "That's magic."

The nurse lifted a hand. He was clutching a fistful of paper.

Luke shoved Marion aside with a shout.

Oliver's pages erupted and a column of fire punched through the air. She hit the ground. The flames splashed onto the wall over her head, instantly fizzling out.

All that magic nearly cracked Marion's skull. She clutched her temples and cried out—at least, she thought she cried, but she couldn't hear herself anymore.

But she did hear the gunshot.

The roar of more magic.

And then Luke swearing profusely.

She looked up through his legs at the place that Oliver Machado had been standing. All that remained was a smoldering circle on the carpet and an entire book's worth of half-burned pages.

"Teleportation," Luke muttered, running his fingers along the circle Ollie had scorched into his carpet.

"What did you say?" Marion was sitting in the corner of the bedroom, knees hugged to her chest. She looked so pale that Luke thought she might pass out.

"Oliver Machado just teleported himself out of here. I can't tell where. I'm one of those people who can't do anything with magic." If Marion had been her usual self, she would have been able to track the nurse's magic easily—but then again, she wouldn't have needed to. A half-angel mage would have out-witched him any day. Oliver would never have disappeared.

"Most people can do magic?" Marion asked.

"Yeah, but even so, few witches could do this kind of magic. It's really powerful stuff, way more powerful than Oliver should have been able to cast." Luke wondered if Ollie had designed the spell himself or if he had powerful friends.

He kicked the ash around, scuffing the lines so that another witch wouldn't be able to reuse Ollie's spell.

"He said that he wanted you to reveal yourself," Marion said. "What did he mean by that?"

"No idea." Luke helped her off of the ground,

careful not to make skin contact.

Oliver had left his laptop on his desk. Luke opened the lid to find that he was still logged in to the darknet. He had a specific forum post open: a post with Marion's name at the top, followed by a low-resolution photo that looked like it must have been taken via telephoto lens.

Marion gaped at the page with such confusion that Luke couldn't help but feel bad for her.

"Is that some kind of...advertisement?" She reached for the keyboard.

He pulled the laptop out of her reach. "A bounty. Yeah."

"On me?"

"Seems to be the case," he said, swiveling the computer so that she wouldn't be able to see it. He scrolled down. There wasn't a lot of information on that page—not enough that anyone should have been able to locate her in Ransom Falls. Marion must have been tracked in some other fashion.

Until Luke could determine how she was being tracked, he couldn't be certain that more assassins wouldn't show up at any moment.

He pushed a button to send the bounty to Oliver's printer, then shut the lid.

"Can I see?" Marion asked.

The bounty had been followed by comments discussing how easy it would be to kill a teenage girl. The forum participants had also said what they'd like to do before and after her death. "I've printed the bounty off in case we need it later."

The bounty, and only one comment with information more useful than horrible.

She reached the printer before he did. The damp ink was still glistening when she lifted it from the tray to stare at the words.

"What day is it?" she asked faintly.

"October," Luke said. "The twenty-eighth."

"They want me dead before November. There are...what, thirty days in October?"

"Thirty-one."

"Oh," she said. "A whole extra day. Then that isn't so bad."

He took the paper out of her hands. "Someone commented with your home address. We know where you live, and that means we know where your family should be. Vancouver Island isn't a long drive. Less than a day."

"The killers will be looking for me there," Marion said.

"And you'll have family to protect you," Luke said with conviction—more conviction than he felt.

"I'll go home," Marion said. "Yes. That's a good idea."

"Sure," he said.

Marion would return to a powerful family, who were surely accustomed to people attempting to assassinate a girl like Marion.

Then she would be out of Luke's life as quickly as Oliver Machado teleporting from his bedroom.

Luke lived in the only apartment complex in Ransom Falls. It had twelve units: six on the bottom floor and six on top. Half of them were usually empty. He had the corner unit upstairs.

That was where he took Marion.

"What are we doing here?" she asked, hanging in the doorway when he opened the apartment. "Is this something to do with the nurse?"

"This is where I live," Luke said.

"Ooh. It's your *home*." Marion looked around with renewed interest, as though seeing everything for the first time.

Luke could imagine what she was seeing. The living room was sparse, though not so sparse as to attract attention by random people who might see inside, like Tony the pizza delivery guy. Luke had decorated by going to a Home Outlet two towns over and buying a matching set of decor. None of it was to his taste, but he didn't hate it, either. Wicker this, linen that, an abstract painting with an inspirational quote.

"Make yourself comfortable," he said. "I can cook something if you're hungry and your standards are low."

"I'm not hungry yet. I seem to have lost my appetite." Marion peered into his bathroom. He leaned around her to pull the shower curtain closed, but not before she saw the camping stove that he'd set up inside the safety of non-flammable porcelain. "Are you brewing potions in there?" she asked, wiggling her fingers as though she itched to check. "Or making methamphetamine, perhaps?"

There was no point in lying. She wouldn't understand the implications of the truth without her memories. "I was casting bullets."

"Your own bullets? Why?"

"Ammunition purchases are monitored." And nobody sold silver bullets anymore. Not legally.

"A doctor with a secret gun hobby," she said.

"It's only for self-defense," Luke said. "I'm a libertarian. I don't think the government needs to know what kind of guns I have and how much ammunition I keep."

He went into his bedroom and left the door open so that he could keep an eye on Marion. There were a few personal effects in his bedroom. Nothing sentimental, but important items, like his diplomas, certifications, letters of reference.

She tugged on the fringed end of a blanket he'd folded on the arm of the couch. "Do you have a laptop I could use?"

"Sure. Behind the TV."

Marion fished it out and spread her hands over the keyboard, as though unsure what to type.

"There's no password," Luke said, reentering the living room with his bag slung over his shoulder.

"I see that."

"What's the problem?"

"It feels like there are websites I want to visit. I don't know which ones." She noticed him carrying luggage. "Why have you packed?"

"I just killed a bunch of assassins within eyesight of my hospital. It seems like it's time to find a new job."

"I'm sorry," Marion said.

He shrugged. He'd known it would happen sooner or later. Luke's life in Ransom Falls had been too pleasant and rewarding to last very long.

Marion started typing. He looked over her shoulder to see that she was searching for the name "Seth Wilder." The top results were for a book—an autobiography written by the Alpha of the North American shifter pack, Rylie Gresham.

"Seth Wilder is a historical figure," Marion said. "How interesting. Do you own this book?"

"Nope," Luke said. He'd chucked his hardback copy of Rylie's autobiography in the trash years earlier.

"I don't suppose there are any bookstores in Ransom Falls. I'll have to check when I get to the next city."

"And which city will that be?" Luke asked.

"Whichever one the next bus goes to, I suppose."

Marion couldn't be considering trying to get on a bus again after what had happened the last time. She was clearly a public safety risk.

But how else was she supposed to get around?

Luke sighed. "Look...it's late. You should get some sleep. I'll take you to Vancouver Island after sunrise."

Her eyes brightened. "Really?"

"Really. God only knows what'd happen if I let you hitchhike. I just have to check in at the hospital before I can go anywhere."

Marion's face fell. "I see." She scanned his apartment and her eyes fell on the car keys dangling on the hook over by his front door. Luke didn't need to be psychic to tell that she was thinking about hijacking his car.

Then she picked up the printed version of the bounty. It was strange seeing striking eyes like hers —the eyes of an angel—filled with helpless fear.

Luke sat next to her on the couch and searched the air for words. "Marion..." Nothing comforting sprang to mind.

The problem was her lack of memory. The Marion Garin that Luke was aware of—the mage, the political figure, daughter of powerful people— wouldn't have been daunted by the idea of people out to kill her.

Marion had been silent for long minutes, and Luke thought that she was worrying until he glanced at her again. Her eyes were getting heavy. The assassination attempt was catching up with her.

"Stretch out, use the blanket, take a nap," he said.

That woke Marion up. "What are you going to do?"

He grabbed his keys. "Like I said, visit the hospital. I'll be back as soon as I can. Keep the lights off, be quiet, and you should be safe. All right? Don't go outside."

Marion settled back on the couch, pulling the blanket over her legs. "You don't need to remind me."

"I'll be fast," he said.

Her head was already resting on her arm, eyes sliding closed.

He waited for a moment to see if she was going to go anywhere. It didn't seem likely. Her heart was already slowing with fatigue—he could see the way that her pulse decelerated in the faintest flush of skin on her throat.

Luke made himself look away from her veins, clutching his keys hard enough that they bit into his hand, and he left.

Marion waited until Luke left. She counted to ten. And then she followed him.

Lucas Flynn was a man of mystery folded within mystery. It wasn't natural for someone to be as helpful as he was, particularly when his mysteries involved such skill with a sidearm, deployed on behalf of a total stranger like Marion.

It would have been nice if she weren't suspicious, but that simply wasn't the case.

He took his pickup. She couldn't keep up with him on foot, but she didn't need to. She found his vehicle parked behind the hospital down the road, halfway hidden by the trees. He had gone to work and was trying to be subtle about it.

Marion walked along the open windows of the hospital, peering inside. Most patients were asleep. A few rooms were empty. Others she couldn't investigate at all because their windows were shuttered and locked. The instant that Marion saw the glint of gray metal, she knew that those shutters were lined with silver.

Many urban hospitals had safe rooms for shifters, but it was strange to see such a safe room in a rural area. Stranger still to see one shuttered window hanging open on the night of a new moon.

Marion crouched below the window and peeked over the sill, shrouded in the shadows of the trees.

The safe room was small, but without glasses, her vision was still too blurry to read the whiteboard on the far wall. It was impossible to tell the patient's name. A shrunken old woman rested in the bed. She was sleeping, but twitching occasionally.

Luke sat in the chair beside her bed, gazing at her face with an inscrutable expression.

When the patient moaned in her sleep, he smoothed his hand over her papery skin. "Mrs. Eiderman." Her brow crimped, and he said her name again, louder the second time. "Mrs. Eiderman, it's Dr. Flynn."

The patient's eyes opened with effort. "You came."

"I'd never miss a date," he said, giving her a slanted smile.

Marion was watching something much too private—the answer to one mystery she never should have stumbled upon. Yet she couldn't tear herself away from the window. Her eyes were fixed to the place where Luke gently rubbed Mrs. Eiderman's arm.

"It hurts," Mrs. Eiderman said.

"I'll turn up your drip." But once he inspected the IV pole, he hesitated. "If I kick this up, you'll have a hard time remaining conscious."

"I don't care anymore. This is it, Dr. Flynn."

The doctor pushed the button to increase the dosage. "Call me Luke."

"Luke," she said with a sigh.

Marion couldn't stay back anymore. She climbed over the windowsill.

The patient's eyes focused on her. "Oh, beautiful."

"Marion," Luke said, rising from the chair.

"I'm sorry," Marion said. "I'm sorry." But she didn't leave. She slipped around the bed to join Luke. "Hello, Mrs. Eiderman. My name is Marion. I'm—I'm a patient at this hospital, too. A patient of Dr. Flynn's." The introduction felt inadequate, but that was the only thing she knew about herself.

"Beautiful," Mrs. Eiderman said again.

Luke sank into the chair again. Rested his elbows on the bed's rail, put his hand over the patient's. "The new moon is rising."

A shiver rolled through Mrs. Eiderman's body. Her face twisted. "I know." Shivers turned to seizure, her eyes rolled back, and her skin roiled.

Even without her memory, Marion recognized the symptoms of lycanthropy.

She could tell by Luke's expression that it wasn't normal, and that Mrs. Eiderman wasn't going to survive.

This was why Luke had delayed their escape from Ransom Falls. This was the one thing he needed to do that was more urgent than trying to escape assassins.

He needed to be with one of his patients for her final night.

While Luke watched Mrs. Eiderman's tremors, Marion watched him. What kind of man killed with such grace yet treasured life so immensely? How could a doctor be so deadly, but so merciful?

Mrs. Eiderman's breathing grew labored. Her lips were turning blue. Fur thrust from her arms, then fell out, spilling atop the sheets. Too weak to change, too sick to stay human. She shook so hard that something inside of her body broke. Marion could hear the muffled pops.

There was no turning up the drip. Nothing could take away her pain now.

For a third time, Marion said, "I'm sorry." She rested her chin on Luke's shoulder, and her cheek brushed against his.

She hadn't meant to touch him, but intent didn't matter. Only action.

Her mind opened.

Mrs. Eiderman was the most brilliant star in the sky, so bright that she dimmed the world around her. Her soul gleamed pristine even when she was dying. And there was no doubt about it: the old woman was drawing the last breaths she would ever take. Her heart simply didn't have the ability to beat much longer. The fact that she'd waited long enough for Luke to witness it was a miracle.

Thought and memory and spirit tangled over the surface of her mind in silver fibers. They spoke of a long and beautiful life. Of a woman who had known love in marriage and motherhood. Of someone who had forged a satisfying career. Of a survivor who had lived through Genesis and lived to see grandchildren, with a great-grandchild to come.

All of that was sunsetting below the horizon of her life. The pain reduced the glory of her final moments.

Marion also saw how to take the hurt away.

She reached toward Mrs. Eiderman to fix it.

Luke caught her wrist. "Don't, Marion."

She only realized that she was starting to cry because his face was blurry despite being inches away. "Please trust me."

He released her.

Marion linked her fingers with Mrs. Eiderman's.

Runes appeared in Marion's mind. She read them as easily as she read the English language, and as easily as she had spoken French when she'd woken up. Some of those runes were to relieve pain. Some were for grace. Some were for emotional peace. All of them tangled together were intended to take a person beyond the harsh cruelties of reality. It would elevate her to something very much like Heaven.

"Come with me," Marion whispered. "Come with me, Elena." That was Mrs. Eiderman's name. It was spelled out among the runes, stamped upon the crystalline perfection of her soul.

Magic braided with a lifetime of moments.

Marion couldn't take the pain away, but she could lift Mrs. Eiderman above it. And she did. She took her consciousness somewhere lycanthropy and old age couldn't reach.

The patient stopped shaking. She sagged into the bed.

"You're okay," Marion said, eyes burning, throat thick. "I'm with you." She was with Elena Eiderman—not just in her last minutes, but in every minute that had come before.

"Beautiful," Mrs. Eiderman breathed.

When she exhaled, she didn't inhale again.

There was no pain in the end.

SIX

No animals sang in the depths of night. The forest was hushed. Cool wind breathed the scent of rain over Luke where he sat beside Marion on the tailgate of his pickup.

Black coffee stolen from a hospital break room warmed his hands. Marion held hot chocolate made from years-old powder and water. She didn't complain about it, but that might have been because she wasn't drinking, just as she wasn't moving or speaking.

"That was impressive," Luke said.

Marion's eyes lifted to his, as though she'd been startled by the sound of his voice. "Hmm?"

"Your spell. I thought you didn't remember any magic."

"I don't," she said.

"That's not what it looked like." For a few

minutes, when Marion had been holding Mrs. Eiderman's hand, her eyes had shone with inhuman light and her flesh had glimmered.

Her thumb traced around the rim of the mug. "I didn't remember any magic," Marion amended. "Not until I touched you."

Luke wasn't comfortable with that: not the way that she had suddenly spoken English when their fingers had touched, or how the brush of her cheek against his had given her magic.

But he was grateful for it.

Marion hadn't remembered magic at a time when she needed to save herself from urisk. It had only come to her in a moment of mercy, when she had been trying to deliver a woman to the other side.

"What I did for Elena must have been an angel thing, wasn't it?" Marion asked.

He laughed softly. "No. That wasn't just some angel thing."

"Isn't that what they do? Help people when they..." She bit the inside of her cheek and ducked her head. "Angels help people when they need it."

"Angels aren't like that." He hesitated, questioning how much he should tell her. She was clearly sensitive. If he delivered the truth about the role angels had played in the world lately, she would internalize it, turn that on herself. But after what she'd done, he owed her whatever truth he could afford. "If they ease anyone's death, it's because they're doing the killing."

Marion clutched her cup tightly enough that

the foam bent. "Angels are the bad guys?"

"That wouldn't be the most nuanced analysis of world affairs, but it's not wrong, either." He rested his hand on her knee. "It doesn't matter. We know one thing now. Whoever you were before you lost your memories, you were selfless. You're kind."

Spots of pink appeared on her cheeks. "I know something about you now too, Dr. Flynn." She drained the foam cup of stale hot chocolate, then hopped off of the tailgate. "How far away did you say Vancouver Island is?"

"Twelve hours if we don't stop."

They climbed in. His pickup had an extended cab—the most spacious model that had been on the market three years earlier. There was enough room for another person to fit between Luke and Marion, perhaps two if their passengers had been small enough. It felt like too much distance, sitting behind the wheel and watching Marion slip into the seat on the far side.

Demons, angels, and sidhe flitted through his mind. All the things that might be able to rip half of a pickup off the road, killing Marion in an instant.

Who would hold her hand while she died?

Fatigue took Marion before they got out of Ransom Falls. When she woke up, they were still driving.

"Welcome to Oregon." Luke must have stopped driving at some point because he had gotten her a fresh cup of hot chocolate, which he offered her as soon as she sat up.

Marion yawned and stretched. "Thank you." She inhaled the chocolaty scent, which was far richer than the drink she'd gotten from the hospital.

Chocolate was exactly the mood boost she needed. Her sad, confusing dreams had been tinted with silvery light, the glimmer of souls, and the end of a life. Walking someone through the final moments of her life was a sacred thing. Marion doubted she'd ever forget Elena Eiderman.

The old woman hadn't been the sole focus of her dreams, though. Marion had dreamed of magic—not magic that healed, but magic that destroyed, bending the world to her will. She had dreamed of lightning. Shattering bodies. A sky that wept crimson rain.

She had dreamed of war.

Luckily, chocolate healed all imagined hurts. She emptied her cup all too quickly.

Before long, Luke stopped for gasoline at a farm town. Marion emerged from the pickup yawning and rubbing her eyes.

Oregon looked like a completely different world to Marion. The subtle differences shook her the most: the spacing between lanes on the road, the stoplights hanging from cables, the density of the trees. She had never seen anything like it in the brief expanse of her memories. The air tasted different in Oregon, too. It was wetter.

How many changes could she be expected to adapt to within a span of mere days?

"I'm going to stretch my legs," Marion said. She needed to get her heart beating and blood flowing to clear her head.

Luke handed cash to her. "Could you get me another drink?"

"More coffee?"

"Whatever they have with lots of caffeine," he said. "And get whatever you want, too."

She managed a smile. "Dangerous offer, Dr. Flynn. Perhaps I'll buy myself the lobster."

"If you can find lobster in central Oregon, you'll have earned it."

The gas station was at the end of a rustic strip mall decorated with beams like tree trunk halves. Marion bought two coffees from a clerk who stared openly at her dark hair and shocking eyes. She couldn't imagine many half-angels visited his gas station.

She paused by his door before leaving. There was a worn, wind-blasted sign posted beside it. "We Report Preternaturals," it said. It was so battered that Marion thought it might be older than she was.

Report preternaturals? To whom? She would have to ask Luke.

He was leaning against his pickup as an attendant pumped his gas. She hesitated to approach. The attendant looked ordinary enough

—as human as anyone else she'd seen—but after her earlier encounters, she was feeling paranoid about strangers.

Marion wandered down the strip mall instead of rejoining Luke. There weren't any places that might sell lobster, but there was an antique shop and, better still, a used bookstore. That was where she entered. It had a paper notice much like the one at the gas station. "We Report Preternaturals."

The bell jingled when she pushed the door open. Shelves covered every wall, and every inch of those shelves was packed with books.

"Oh my," she whispered, breath catching in her throat.

"Can I help you?" A woman sat at the counter with a pile of paperbacks as tall as she was.

Marion must have looked stupid gawking at the bookstore. She floundered for words. "I want Rylie Gresham's autobiography. Tell me where to find it."

"Nonfiction, memoirs," the clerk said. Suspicion flashed across her face.

Marion ducked into the shelves before the woman could speak to her again.

Wandering the aisles taught Marion something new about herself: she loved books. All of them. Skimming their spines made her heart beat faster the way she imagined the touch of a lover might.

Any one of those books could tell her a thousand things about the world she'd woken up in. If Marion had been given infinite time, she could have stayed in that store until she had pored over every page, every word, and gotten to know every character within.

One hardback in particular caught her eye. She'd located Rylie Gresham's autobiography.

Marion set the coffee cups at the end of a shelf before pulling the book out. The dust jacket had soft corners and the pages were yellowed. The Alpha's face took up the entire back cover. She was a beautiful woman, as golden-haired and -skinned as Luke was brown. Rylie Gresham might as well have been assembled from pure sunshine.

She flipped it open and searched for Seth Wilder's name. He was all over the early chapters. Rylie introduced Seth Wilder as the brother of the pack's Alpha male—a human man who helped run the pack in its early days. Seth Wilder was described as compassionate, kind, and intelligent.

She didn't immediately see any clues as to how such a man might be able to help Marion get her memory back, but it did say that he'd lived at the shapeshifter sanctuary at some point. A map in the appendix showed that the sanctuary was in a range called the Appalachian Mountains.

Marion needed to buy the book. Luke would understand if she used his money for that.

She flipped to the first page as she wandered to the cashier, drinking in the foreword, which had been written by the current Secretary of the Office of Preternatural Affairs. Fritz Friederling's writing style was clipped, unsentimental. He didn't mention Seth Wilder. He did, however, say that Rylie Gresham was the single most important preternatural to have ever been born.

"I don't serve your type."

Marion's gaze snapped up to the woman at the cash register. "Pardon me?"

"We don't deal with your kind of 'people' in these parts," the bookseller said. She jerked a thumb toward the paper sign that said "We Report Preternaturals." The confusing words took on menacing connotations in light of the clerk's tone.

Marion's cheeks went hot. "I would like to buy this book." It came out in French because she was so flustered. It took effort for her to remember how to say it in English. "Please, I'd like to buy this book."

"I don't want your money." The bookseller was flushed, too. Her mental signals were blazingly obvious, even easier to read than Nurse Charity Ballard's attraction to Luke had been. She was offended that a preternatural had wandered into her rural town and dared to patronize the bookstore.

Marion hugged the book to her chest. "Can I just—"

"Get out of here!" The woman reached over the counter to wrench the autobiography from her grasp. Marion didn't let go of it. She wanted that map.

Rationally, she was aware that there would be other copies of the book at other bookstores. She didn't need *this* one. But this appalling red-faced woman was struggling for the autobiography, and Marion's only instinct was to clutch it closer.

Then suddenly, the woman let go. She sat back on her stool, staring beyond Marion.

Luke had appeared behind Marion, glowering with fury. The "We Report Preternaturals" sign was crumpled in his fist. He set it on the counter. Then he set a twenty-dollar bill beside it.

"Come on, Marion," he said, wrapping his arm around her shoulders and guiding her out the door.

The cashier was left spluttering behind them.

The jingling of the bell over the door was much too cheerful for Marion's mood. Her tremors had nothing to do with the cool forest air.

"Get in the pickup," Luke said.

She stopped to stare at the bookstore again. "What was that in there? What did that sign mean?"

"It means people are terrible, that's all. I told you to get in the pickup."

She hesitated by the tailgate. "But..."

"Come on. Let's go."

Marion scrambled into the passenger seat. Luke gunned it out of the parking lot as she buckled. "Are there laws against preternaturals buying from bookstores?"

"No. And there are no mandatory registration laws for preternaturals anymore, either. That woman belongs in a goddamn museum." Luke peeled around a corner, and that tiny town in the middle of Oregon nothingness vanished between the trees. His eyes flicked to hers. "Are you okay?"

"Yes, but...confused."

"You didn't do anything wrong," he said forcefully. "Read the autobiography. It'll explain most everything."

Marion opened it and she read.

Unfortunately, the autobiography did explain most everything. It explained how most people hadn't known that demons and angels existed before Genesis. They had been considered mythology and little more.

Until a demon publicly assassinated a state senator.

Then the ugly truth had become public: humans weren't alone in the world, and the things that went bump in the night sometimes weren't friendly.

Legislators had missed that "sometimes" part. They had responded to the assassination with hostile legislation involving registration, travel restrictions, and even taking children away from preternatural families. There hadn't been time for preternaturals to fight back before Genesis birthed a thousand new breeds including urisk, vampires, and sirens.

Much of the damaging legislation had vanished with the rebirth of the world, as gaeans now matched mundanes in number. As Marion had seen at the bookstore, fear lingered where laws did not.

She looked up to find that they were still driving through forest, which hadn't changed since she'd started reading. "The autobiography doesn't talk much about Genesis itself. What *is* Genesis?"

Luke's eyes flicked her way. He had one hand on the wheel and the opposite arm resting on the pickup's door, tapping out a rhythm like a heartbeat with his fingertips. "It was the end of the world. Gods got to fighting. The old ones were killed by the new ones and everything got remade. Most people believe that the new gods died during Genesis because they haven't been seen publicly."

She closed the book slowly.

War between gods? That was a lot to take in.

"Where were you when Genesis happened?" Marion asked.

"I was dead." At her expression, he laughed. "Everyone died in Genesis. There was a thing called the Genesis void—this blackness that devoured the entire world. If you died because the Genesis void took you, then you were reborn. If you died because of something else, like getting run over by a truck in the chaos, you stayed dead."

"No wonder people cling to hate and fear. It sounds incredibly traumatic."

"It was," Luke said.

He was focusing on the road, so she had carte blanche to stare at his sculpted profile. A sly smile crawled over her lips. "How did your girlfriend handle Genesis?"

"No girlfriend. I've been single for years."

"I can't imagine someone like you being alone

for long," she said, wrapping a lock of hair around her forefinger.

"I wasn't always single, no. I had a fiancée once." There was such grief in his voice that Marion immediately felt guilty for probing. She should have realized that "everyone" dying in Genesis might have included people who mattered to Luke.

"Gods, I'm sorry," she said.

"It's not like that. My ex is alive." He focused on the road so hard that it was like his gaze could burn a hole through the asphalt to the core of the Earth. "We didn't work out, though."

Marion hesitated before venturing, "Because of something she did?"

"Someone. My brother."

That was almost worse than his ex-fiancée dying.

It was obvious he still loved her, this woman who had left him for his brother. When he spoke of her, there was so much emotion rippling over his brain that Marion couldn't help but pick it up. Until that moment, she hadn't felt much from Luke's thoughts at all.

And as Luke said, he'd been single for years. His ex might have moved on, but he hadn't.

"Why haven't you found someone to love again?" Marion asked.

"Personal choice. I made an oath to myself to find a way to be happy while alone." His tone was as empty as his brain was wracked with chaotic emotion. "I wouldn't survive all that crap again."

"You shouldn't be afraid to love again. Heartbreak hurts, but it can't kill."

Annoyance touched Luke's memories of heartache. "How do *you* know? Are you getting memories of being a love expert?"

He had a point, but Marion wasn't going to let that deter her. "Do you wish you'd never treated Elena Eiderman, even though your final shared moments were sad?"

"I'd never regret knowing Mrs. Eiderman."

"Of course not. We love, and we lose." Marion crossed her hands over her chest. "We carry those who have gone within our hearts for the rest of our days. I'm certain of this."

"Are you, now?" His tone was still strangely flat.

"I am," she said firmly. "You'll love again, Dr. Lucas Flynn, and it will be all the sweeter when you do because you'll understand what it's like to have lost it. Love and loss are two halves of a whole, a critical part of the human experience. Genesis happens to us all on a personal level a thousand times over. I don't need memory to know that."

Luke didn't respond. Marion felt like she'd overstepped an important boundary, but it was too late to take it back.

Oh well.

She plucked Rylie Gresham's autobiography off of the dashboard. She'd dog-eared the last page where she had seen Seth Wilder's name, making it easy to return to that position. "She didn't deserve you anyway," Marion added. "You're much too good for a woman who'd leave you for your brother."

He made a weird sound. It took a moment to realize he was choking back a chuckle.

"Well it's true," she said defensively.

"Read your book, Marion."

"I could read it aloud, if you like," she said. "This road is very long. You must be bored."

"Thanks but no thanks. I'm not interested in politics."

He punched the button for the radio with a knuckle. Sports reporting came on. She tried to immerse herself in the book—not just in Seth Wilder's story, but in Rylie Gresham's, and the history of the frightening world she'd woken up in.

But she never quite dropped her attention from Luke Flynn at her side.

Even though he didn't look her way again, she thought that she had his attention, too.

Luke and Marion stopped for the night in Port Angeles, a town on the coast so close to Vancouver Island that its shore was a dim line on the horizon.

"There aren't any ferries until morning," Luke said as he slid into the driver's seat. He had stepped out to speak to the people working for the ferry line, and despite what had looked like an attempt to bribe them, he'd returned disappointed. "We'll have to be here at first light if we want to get across."

"What if we go back down the Olympic Peninsula and leave from another city with a ferry?" Marion asked.

"We'll still have to wait until morning." He shifted the pickup into gear. "We're just lucky that Canada's not a thing anymore."

"Canada?"

"Before Genesis, there was no North American Union. There were multiple countries on this continent, and we'd have both needed a passport to get to Vancouver Island."

"Lucky indeed. I don't have a passport." Chances weren't terrible that she *did* have a passport, but she had no clue where it was. Much like the rest of her life. And her memories. So the existence of a passport was neither here nor there.

"Neither do I. It wouldn't have been the first time I jumped a border without the paperwork, but any time I don't have to skirt the law is a good day."

"Canada." She mused the name. "Why'd it go away with Genesis?"

"It went away after, actually. A few years after everyone came back, the border's restrictions started to dissolve. There were too many preternaturals crossing to stop them. North America had already started working in tandem to provide a benefits system for preternaturals, so instead of cracking down on border controls, they removed them."

"Interesting solution."

"Smart solution," Luke said. "That's something Rylie Gresham did, actually. She probably doesn't talk about it in your copy of the book. That edition was published ages ago."

Luke parked around the corner of a nearby hotel as the sun dipped behind the trees. He checked in while Marion read a pamphlet for the ferry over and over again, wishing that she could change the operating hours by force of will.

She was so close to home—so close to *answers*. Family was waiting for her, along with her home.

All she needed was a boat that would take her across the bay.

Ferries weren't the only things that could cross water. Marion toyed with the idea of chartering a boat, or even stealing one. She didn't know how to drive a boat, but she also hadn't known how to speak English at first. Stubbornness could clearly take her all sorts of interesting places.

Through the hotel's window, she could see Luke getting a room in the lobby.

If she went to her home on Vancouver Island, her time with the doctor would be over.

She folded the pamphlet in half, creased the seam with her fingernails, and tucked it neatly into the folder where Luke kept his insurance. Moments later, the doctor emerged from the hotel holding a key card. His smile of greeting was heart stopping.

No, Marion was not interested in hastening her separation from Luke Flynn.

The hotel room was repulsively musty, though

she liked its tall windows overlooking the ocean. There was only a single queen bed, and inspecting the couch didn't reveal a pullout. "I'll sleep on the floor," Luke said, catching her worried frown. "You can catch some rest if you want."

The bed held no appeal for her. For the first time since waking in the hospital, her stomach was grumbling. "How do you feel about going to dinner?" Marion asked, picking up a menu by the phone.

Luke glanced at the ocean through the windows, then whipped the curtains shut. "We can order in if you're hungry."

"I don't think a town this size has much by way of takeout aside from pizza. I don't like pizza."

He smirked. "When's the last time you had pizza?"

"I don't need to remember disliking pizza to know it's foul." Marion rubbed her hands on her jeans, imagining the grease and tomato sauce she would get on her fingers. Disgusting.

"It's not safe for us to go to a restaurant," he said.

But they had gotten all the way to Port Angeles without being attacked again, leaving behind Nurse Oliver Machado, the urisk, and the attempts on Marion's life. She was nearly home. And in a few hours, she would part ways with Luke— possibly forever.

Marion was not going to sleep.

"I don't want to sit in this room all evening. We'll go somewhere they would never expect to find us," she declared.

"They'd never expect to find us eating pizza and watching *Mythbusters* in a Best Western," Luke said.

She looped her arm through his and pulled him back toward the door. "Come, Dr. Flynn. We're somewhere new and I want to explore."

"That's not a good idea." A note of warning had entered his voice, but it wasn't without that soft edge of patience he always had while speaking to Marion. He wasn't telling her no. Just "probably not." As far as Marion was concerned, anything that wasn't a firm refusal was as good as cheerful consent.

"If someone attacks, I'm sure you'll save my life again," Marion said with a smile she hoped he'd find charming.

Charmed or not, he didn't argue. It was as good a start as any.

SEVEN

Marion picked a bar in downtown Port Angeles using the map, claiming that any place with "Barnacle" in the name was bound to be disgusting and therefore not a bar where assassins would look for her. She dragged Luke down the hill with all the enthusiasm of a local, though she clearly had no idea where she was going. They kept getting lost.

Luke didn't mind. He liked seeing Marion in such a good mood. The crisp ocean air brought color to her cheeks and the wind frothed her hair around her face like sea foam. Her laugh carried for blocks.

But he couldn't share in her cheerful mood. He'd felt an uneasy, itching sense of wrongness ever since entering Port Angeles, and he kept having to resist the urge to look behind them.

There was *something* there—something nearby. He suspected that even if he looked, he wouldn't see anything.

Whatever Luke felt wasn't human.

He made sure that Marion was on his left side in order to keep his right hand free to draw a gun.

On one of their random diversions down a side street—which Luke was becoming increasingly suspicious were not random at all—Marion's eyes suddenly brightened. "Ooh, wait!"

She ducked into a clothing shop before Luke could stop her. The sign was in French. They were selling wares expensive enough that they didn't dare put them on mannequins in the windows.

Luke couldn't resist the urge to scan the street for attackers any longer. Nobody was looking in their direction. There were certainly no sidhe nearby. Hell, there weren't even any shifters, and those had become a dime a dozen in the world outside Ransom Falls.

Port Angeles was a boring, mundane place. Nobody wanted to kill Marion there.

He followed her inside.

Marion was whipping clothes off the rack and measuring them visually against her body. A fashionable, rail-thin clerk waited nearby, eager to help her spend money.

Luke leaned an elbow against the changing stall. "Is this the time for shopping? You can't even pay for it."

"I must have money," Marion said.

"Not on you, you don't."

"Well...on *you*." She all but batted her eyelashes at him as she snagged a few more hangers off of the rack. She whirled to face the clerk. "I want to try these on. Will you help me?"

Both women vanished into the changing room.

While Marion tried on clothing, Luke watched the windows to the street. There was still nothing to see outside and his sense of being watched had faded. If assassins were stalking them, they found the idea of lurking while Marion tried on designer clothes just as boring as Luke did.

After a few minutes of giggling behind the curtain, Marion emerged from the changing room. "*Et voila!*"

He had to admit that Marion looked a thousand times more comfortable wearing designer clothes than she had wearing scrubs. This was who she was: a woman who probably seldom wore the same clothes twice, much less hand-me-downs from a hospital lost and found.

"You look great. Now change back. The fun's over," Luke said.

"The fun is only beginning. I'm sure I'll be able to repay you once we get to my house. I imagine my parents must be rich if I have such tastes." She mounded her curls atop her head, twisting to look at the back of her shirt in the mirror. "What do you think?" She dropped her hair and spun in place.

He had been trying not to look at her too much, but it was impossible to ignore her statuesque beauty. Marion looked every inch the half-angel, from the narrow pinch of her waist to the noble curve of her jaw.

"The clothes are fine," he said, dropping his attention to his shoes before she could see what he was thinking.

He caught her impish smirk out of the corner of his eye. "In that case, I'll take this outfit." Marion waved down the clerk, who was organizing hangers in the changing room. "Can I wear this out of here? Oh! And bring me those boots in a size nine narrow if you have them."

"Wait," Luke said. "Price?"

It looked as though the idea hadn't occurred to her. She plucked a tag from the hem of the shirt and showed it to him.

The number shocked a laugh out of him.

"No," he said.

Even mild confusion was lovely on her doe-like features. "No?"

"I'm not buying anything from this store. If you want something clean, we can find a thrift store."

Horror filled her eyes. "A *thrift* store? Clothes that other people have owned before?" She looked as though she might faint.

"You're wearing scrubs from the hospital."

"My alternative was nudity." Marion clutched the hangers to her chest. "Now I have another alternative."

"You don't, in fact, because I'm not buying designer clothes for you." He checked the price tag again, and it was just as high as he'd thought. Too many digits for a single article of clothing. "Not happening. No way."

"You're a doctor. Aren't doctors paid well?"

"Whatever I make is none of your business because it's not your money. I've already done you a hell of a favor by driving you here, Marion. I'm not asking you to pay me back or thank me. But I also don't owe you anything."

Her throat worked as she swallowed hard. The way that her eyes shimmered almost made Luke want to take it back—almost.

Marion carefully set the clothes on a shelf and stepped back with visible effort. "I got excited and wasn't thinking."

"Don't worry about it," he said gruffly. "You've had a bad week."

She ducked back into the changing room. It took much less time for her to put the scrubs back on than it had to take them off. She emerged looking deflated. Marion turned to the clerk, but couldn't quite meet her eyes. "I'm sorry," she said before heading out of the shop.

The woman was scared and alone without memory, and Luke had made her cry.

"Damn it," he muttered under his breath.

Luke gave Marion a moment to compose herself before joining her on the street corner. When he approached, she lifted her head to reveal that her cheeks were already dry. "Still hungry?" he asked.

"I don't need to eat. I won't starve." She

pinched at her belly under the baggy shirt.

"Come on," he said, hooking an arm around her waist. She was a little too tall to comfortably wrap an arm around her shoulders. "Let's go to that disgusting bar you picked. I'm buying."

"Okay," she said in a tiny voice.

Luke probably shouldn't have touched her like that. Not when he was an inch from brushing her skin and causing a strange magical reaction. But pinning Marion to his side meant it would be easier to remove her from danger once they were attacked, and Luke was sure they were going to be attacked.

They were still being followed. He could feel it.

It was weird that they hadn't been approached yet. Surely the assassins wouldn't be deterred by the public location. The bus attack had made it clear that neither witnesses nor collateral damage were an issue for the people who wanted to kill Marion.

"There it is," Marion said.

Her prediction that the Salty Barnacle would be "disgusting" turned out to be correct. Its boarded windows were crusted with salt blown in from the ocean. The only signs of life were the neon sign and the fact its front door was propped open by a barrel. Marion stopped in front of the door, nose wrinkling.

"Pizza's sounding good now, huh?" Luke asked.

She gathered herself. "No. Let's try this place first." She moved boldly into the bar. Luke followed, skimming the room for signs of danger.

Unless blue-collar workers hunched over bowls of chowder were dangerous, Marion had picked well.

Her nose seemed to have taken on a permanent crinkle. "It's so...sticky."

"We can go somewhere else." *Like back to the relative safety of the hotel room.*

"No, I like this," she declared.

He knew for a fact that wasn't true. Angels were fastidious. Marion in a sticky restaurant was like Luke watching someone perform surgery without washing their hands first.

He wasn't going to argue with her, though. The smell of chowder left him hungry. Human bodies liked to eat a lot.

They took stools at the bar. "What can I get you?" asked the bartender.

"I would like a drink," Marion said with the boldness of a queen making a decree. "Something very strong."

The bartender lifted his eyebrows. "Would you?"

"Yes." She did that thing where she fluffed her hair and batted her eyelashes. It was a tactic that young women had used to get drinks without showing ID for many generations. It worked, as always. The world had changed, Genesis had killed everyone, and Marion's memory had been wiped, but it still took only a smile from the pretty girl to get liquor.

A quick sniff of Marion's drink told Luke it was a Long Island Iced Tea. Strong indeed. He pushed it over to Marion.

"Beer for me," he said. "Chowder too."

The bartender blasted cheap beer into a mug and headed into the kitchen to get them food.

Marion was so tense from trying to avoid touching the bar itself, the stool, and even the floor that Luke thought she might self-destruct. When the bartender returned with bowls of chowder, soup was dripping down the sides from his lazy ladling. Her eyes got a little wider.

"Let me know when you want to go back to the hotel," Luke said, and he dug in with gusto.

She took a long sip of her drink, as though she needed to fortify herself before she could eat. It wasn't enough. She took a napkin and gingerly wiped the outside of the bowl clean. Then she folded the napkin and set it aside.

"Delicious," she announced after her first taste of chowder.

Luke couldn't help but laugh.

"I don't appreciate being laughed at," Marion said.

"I'm not laughing *at* you, exactly. You gotta admit this is a little funny."

She admitted nothing, giving him an imperious look that was only slightly ruined by her attempt to stop smiling. "Tell me more about this thing we were discussing on the drive, this Genesis."

"I don't know what else to tell you," he said. "The world ended. Everyone died. That's basically all there is to it."

"Don't insult me by oversimplifying it. An

event of that magnitude must have been the result of numerous complicated factors."

"Sure," Luke said. "Factors that are beyond the reckoning of mortal minds."

"And everyone died because gods got into a slapfight."

"Everyone died, but most people came back, many of them changed. For instance, all of the sidhe—faeries—who exist now used to be straight up human before Genesis. But even though everyone started out as one species, they fragmented into two major types of sidhe: the ones with dark power, the unseelie, and the ones with light power, who are called seelie. And then there are hundreds of breeds of each type beyond that."

"Have all my attackers been the evil unseelie?" Marion asked, blowing on another spoonful of chowder.

"I said dark, not evil. Like nighttime versus daytime."

Marion set her spoon down without eating. "The fact that I'm a preternatural…"

"You're wondering if you were changed by Genesis."

"I must have been young if I had." Marion studied Luke with her cheek pressed to her shoulder. "You must have been young during Genesis too. Do you remember it well?"

He didn't remember it at all. He'd been dead for a year before it happened. "Nope."

"I'm sure that's for the best."

"Yeah, probably," he said. "Most folks aren't

over it. There are a lot of support groups thanks to the werewolf Alpha." He focused on scraping chowder out of the bottom of his bowl. "Rylie set up social programs for people reborn as gaean species. One of those programs is publicly funded therapy."

"This Alpha sounds very caring," Marion said.

Luke took a long drink of his beer in lieu of an awkward pause. He swallowed it down, cleared his throat. "Anyway, that's what's been going on for the last fifteen years. All these people came back as shifters, vampires, whatever. It's hard. But we're working it out."

"How lucky that there are doctors like you who help people," Marion said.

His beer had mysteriously vanished. Her Long Island Iced Tea was running low, too. Luke flagged down the bartender and ordered two more drinks. "I'm just doing my part."

"Don't sell yourself short, Dr. Flynn," Marion said. He appreciated the way she said his name, sort of like she was teasing him. Being called Lucas Flynn had never quite sat right with him. There was cognitive dissonance even when his nurses said that. But when Marion used his name, it was sort of...cute.

"This is yours." He gave her the second drink.

She took it with an appreciative smile. "Tell me how you got interested in doing preternatural medicine."

"Not much of a story there," Luke said. "I saw how many people needed help after Genesis, so I jumped in where I could."

"You are quite the hero," Marion said.

He was transfixed by the paleness of her eyes, the way that she stared at him.

Luke could almost ignore the fact that she looked like a woman he had known once upon a time, in a very different life. A woman whose features couldn't cross his mind without being followed by a swell of hatred in his chest.

He took another drink, and another. He didn't even feel buzzed. "So what'd you get out of the autobiography? Anything I didn't tell you?"

"I've learned that Seth Wilder was a human man who helped run Rylie Gresham's werewolf pack. He built their sanctuary, too. Not because he was rich—he came from rather humble beginnings, in fact. He simply invested his whole soul into the project."

"Huh," Luke said. "The whole sanctuary? And the pack? That's what the book says?"

"Indeed. He sounds interesting. I can't wait to meet him."

He hummed noncommittally into his beer. "Anything about where we can find him?"

"Unfortunately the Alpha parted ways with Seth Wilder around Genesis, and his current whereabouts weren't mentioned. I skipped ahead in the book, you see. I enjoy spoilers." Her cheeks dimpled when she smiled. "Regardless, I thought I might go to the sanctuary to see if someone can refer me to him. That will happen after I visit home, of course."

"Of course," he echoed faintly.

Luke was spared of trying to think of something else to say by the TV behind the bartender. Someone had flipped the channel from sports to the news. A reporter named January Lazar sat behind a desk, staring intently into the camera as she spoke.

"With only days until the first summit at the United Nations, significant members of all preternatural factions are closing in on New York City," January said. "A security risk? War waiting to happen? Or something more insidious? We turn to senior correspondent Amber Gregory on site at the United Nations for more information. Amber?"

"Don't watch that," Luke said. "January Lazar's trash."

But Marion's eyes were fixed on the TV. They were cutting to footage of people arriving at the UN building. The ethereal delegation arrived by wing at a zeppelin dock, and their entrance was filmed from a wavering camera that suggested distant helicopters.

Even at that distance, the images of the arriving angels were blurry, but the footage was good enough to see the imposing figures they cut. They were each tall and statuesque, with wingspans that easily tripled their height. Most of them were also carrying swords that burned with fire.

Fear flitted through Marion's pale eyes. "*Those* are angels?"

"They're with the ethereal delegation, so yeah," Luke said, scooping clam chunks out of the bottom of his bowl. "The news station is most likely using warded cameras to film them."

"What makes you say that?"

He kept forgetting how little she knew. "Angels are near impossible to photograph. Whenever their energy flares up, they knock out everything electrical for blocks. In order to film them, an angel has to restrain their power and cameras have gotta be warded by witches."

"You know a lot about angels," she said.

He knew a lot about a great many things. "Folks have talked a lot about the non-human factions since Genesis. People are especially interested in angels since they're so reclusive. They're mysterious."

"I'm mysterious?"

"Angels in general," Luke said.

Marion was clearly internalizing this information. She was turning it inward and examining herself through the lens of the other angels. The way that the newscasters talked about them with fear and respect. How intimidating the ethereal faction looked. The amount of power they held.

And the swords.

He had a hard time imagining Marion with a sword. Entitled as she might have been, she struck him as being roughly as threatening as a three-legged kitten. She seemed to come to the same conclusion, since she shook her head and returned her attention to her second Long Island. "This summit the angels are attending. What is it for?"

"I'm not paying all that much attention. I only worry about preternatural medicine, not preternatural politics."

"That's happening on the East Coast, yes? And we are west."

"That's right. Most angels live in the Ethereal Levant, though. That's not even on this continent."

"In that case, I doubt I have anything to do with the likes of them." She drained her second drink.

While she was still drowning her worries in liquor, the door to the bar creaked open. A man entered.

Luke's eyes and brain registered two completely different sets of stimuli from the newcomer's arrival. His eyes registered a narrow-shouldered human with skin the color of peaches and cream, like he'd never been in the sun before. There was a boy band look to him—untouched, polished, and vain.

That was what Luke could *see*.

His brain told him something else entirely. Mostly that reality was distorted by the powerful glamour magic draped over this stranger. Luke felt like someone was pushing on the backs of his eyeballs from within his skull.

This man had been following them since Ransom Falls.

"Check please," Luke said. The bartender, annoyed, slapped their receipt on the bar and shuffled off.

Marion looked disappointed. "I'm still hungry.

I've barely eaten."

"Sorry," he said. Boy Band sauntered toward a booth and sat down. "I don't want to alarm you, but we were followed here." She twisted to look, and he grabbed her wrist. "Don't."

Marion's eyes went blank. He had touched her bare skin again.

Luke drew his hand back, but it was too late.

"Oh," Marion breathed, lifting her hand. White light crackled around her fingertips.

Luke felt things opening inside of him when he touched her. He'd felt it at the hospital when they'd been exchanging translations using his phone. He had felt it when she'd carried Mrs. Eiderman to the other side.

And he felt it now.

At this point, Dr. Lucas Flynn knew what destiny felt like. He knew when it was rubbing against him with feline eagerness.

He drained his mug and pushed it away. "Damn." When he settled back on the stool, he let his jacket swing open, giving him easy access to the gun.

Nobody was looking their way. It seemed impossible that nobody could have sensed such a massive shift in the world—in the damn *universe*—but nobody was looking.

He threw a paper napkin over Marion's glowing fingers before dragging her toward the exit. "Don't let anyone see," he said. "Mages aren't common and witches don't cast magic like that."

"Sorry." She stuffed the offending hand into

her pocket.

The two of them stepped outside to find an empty street under a drizzly gray sky.

And there he was.

The young, handsome assassin stood six feet in front of them, holding a sword as long as he was tall.

"I found you, Marion," he said. "*Finally.*"

EIGHT

Marion barely had time to register the presence of the assassin before Luke shoved her behind him and drew his gun. The doctor fired three shots: two toward center mass, and one toward the head.

The sidhe killer moved even faster than Luke. He blurred the street around him as he erupted into starlight, becoming a form larger than human, larger than should have been able to fit within the confines of a single town.

He enfolded Marion in glittering magic that burned into her skin, simultaneously cold and hot. Her mind couldn't seem to decide how to process the sensory information.

She could tell that her feet were lifted from the sidewalk, though.

The assassin was trying to carry her away.

"Luke!" she cried, flinging her hands in his

direction. She didn't know if he heard. Marion's voice fell flat within the rippling magic.

She thought that she could hear a distant orchestra, like cellos playing sour notes.

And under that, more gunshots.

The shining gold fog evaporated.

Luke caught Marion by the hem of the shirt and yanked her toward him. He fired his gun into the fog as it darted down the street. The further the light got from them, the more it returned to human shape. But even as it dwindled, its magical reach extended over Port Angeles, blanketing the town in shimmering distortions like a heat mirage.

Marion had no idea what she had just experienced. She could only cling to Luke's shirt and gape in the direction of her attacker. "What...?"

"Move," Luke said tightly, shoving her into the alley.

Even with the sidhe magic lifted from her mind and body, she felt brain-blind, like her every nerve had shut down. Marion was running on sheer instinct.

She skidded around the end of the alley and Luke pushed her again, nudging her downhill. Marion let momentum carry her past an antique store, a restaurant, a fence.

They leaped onto a rocky beach. Luke pulled her under a pier and looked over the top, gun uplifted, ready to fire. "Damn," he muttered before dropping back beside her.

"Do you see it?" Marion asked.

He nodded. "Up the hill."

Marion's sense of direction was scattered, but she knew that "up the hill" was meant to indicate their hotel—and worse, Luke's truck. Their only potential mode of escape.

Her eyes tracked across the rocky beach, wetted by crashing waves that were black in the dimming light. Marion couldn't make out much detail beyond twenty feet. Without glasses, her vision was too blurry. She could tell that there was a boat tethered a few hundred feet away, though.

Perhaps the truck wasn't their only mode of escape after all.

"We're not waiting for the morning ferry," she said decisively.

Marion didn't even get a chance to stand up before Luke yanked her back again. "Are you crazy? We can't steal a boat!"

"Better stealing than dying!"

"No way," he said. "It would attract too much attention."

"I've already caught the attention of the assassins. I'm not afraid of being seen." She threw her shoulders back and lifted her chin in defiance. "Better still, if it brings law enforcement upon us, then they can protect me!"

"I can't believe we're discussing this. Hasn't anyone in your entire life told you no before?"

She almost argued with him, wanting to remind him that she had no clue—but then she stopped. "You have. Several times."

He faltered. "I have." Marion grinned. She

imagined that a smile on her striking features must have been very disarming, particularly when she bit her bottom lip as she did at that moment. He sighed. "All right." Luke straightened enough to look up the street. "The glow from the assassin's light has faded."

"That's good?"

"Not exactly. Means I can't see where he is."

And Marion assumed that meant that the assassin could look like anyone, too. That degree of magic must have been able to cloak virtually anything. "We'll be safest on the island, far from here," Marion said.

"It's not that far," Luke grumbled. But he followed her down the beach anyway.

Marion's feet were light on the rocks, though her shoes had no traction. She slipped repeatedly. It made her slow. Luke was more agile, but patient; he waited with her even as he kept his eyes on the city above.

The roiling waters stank of seaweed. Waves crashed over the rocks, leaving thick ropes of kelp and froth in their wake. The kelp was filthy, murky, slimy—nothing Marion could bear to touch.

They clambered onto another pier, closer to the harbor. White boats bobbed in the night. Big boats, little boats.

"I wonder if I know how to drive one of those." Marion squinted at the nearest boat and cast her mind for memories, fishing around for anything aquatic, preferably sailing-related. She came up with nothing. Not even a hint of familiarity, like she'd felt upon finding a shop selling designer clothes.

They didn't have any alternatives. Marion might not have been able to see the light from her would-be assassin anymore, but she sensed a certain weight in the air that suggested nearby magic. *Strong* magic.

They climbed over a fence to get into the harbor. Luke selected a small boat with the word "Sparrowhawk" on the hull and helped her climb inside. "Do you hear anything?"

She strained her ears. Marion didn't think he meant the crashing waves. "What do *you* hear?"

"Singing," he said. "That means you're driving the boat." He released the ropes tethering the boat to the harbor, and they bobbed a few inches to the left.

"I don't know how," Marion said.

"Neither do I." Luke checked the magazine on his gun, then positioned himself near the motor. "It'll be safer if you're behind the wheel. Trust me."

Marion shrugged. Why not? She was a smart girl. An angel. Surely she could drive a boat. "The only problem is that it looks like it needs keys," she said. He held up a key ring. "Oh. Where'd you find that?"

"Around," he said. "Don't worry about it."

She didn't worry about it. At that point, she would have trusted Luke if he'd told her to launch herself over the side of the boat into the murky waters.

Marion turned the engine on, throttled

forward.

They bumped the boat in front of them.

Okay, less of a bump and more of a strike. Not a gentle one. Her chest slammed into the controls and she winced. "Sorry, Doctor!"

Luke didn't respond. He was glaring at the ocean like he heard something strange.

She steered more carefully, pushing out onto the water. Once she got away from the pier, she increased the speed to put distance between themselves and the shore—and, more importantly, the sidhe assassin.

Marion found the controls simple. She soon got into the rhythm of steering through the waves, weaving between the other boats toward the mouth of the small harbor.

"Not that way," Luke said suddenly.

"It's the only way we can go," Marion said, accelerating. "What's wrong?"

He didn't get an opportunity to answer before they broke into open water.

A plume of salty water gushed in front of their boat, as tall as the hotel they hadn't slept in and as wide as a car. It arced in midair, twisted, and smashed toward Marion like a fist.

She didn't even get a chance to cry out.

Water clogged her nose, ears, mouth. She was cold. Soaked. Suffocating. Her lungs spasmed within her chest, but found no oxygen.

It splashed to the bottom of the boat with such force that they tipped sideways.

Marion clung to the wheel. Her feet slid from

underneath her.

Then the boat righted itself, coming down from the crest of the wave to bob in calm ocean once more.

Where there had been a pillar of water, there was now a woman with opalescent flesh. The starlight behind her twisted into spirals. She was suspended in midair by broad wings of ocean film, green and dripping, her gaunt face hardened into cold resolve. She held blades of coral.

It wasn't the glittering sidhe who'd attacked them on the shore, but Marion wasn't sure if she should take that as a good thing or bad thing. Either way, they hadn't escaped danger.

"Get down!" Luke shouted. Marion threw herself under the wheel.

He rose up, shot his gun twice. Even though he was drenched from the spray of ocean, the gun still fired. But it didn't seem to matter that the gun functioned. The bullets passed harmlessly through the sidhe, carving tunnels into her chest that sealed instantly.

She landed on the front hull of the boat with a thud, bare feet denting the metal.

The assassin leaped over the windshield and landed on the deck between the doctor and Marion.

"Luke!" Marion shouted.

The sidhe's coral blades came down on the wheel. Coral should have been fragile enough to shatter on impact against the manmade material, but they sliced right through it.

Marion dodged the attack so narrowly that she felt coral scratch her arm.

Luke plowed into the sidhe and threw her over the side of the boat. He took the wheel, throttling forward again at maximum speed. They tore into the bay as the water surged behind them.

The sidhe assassin was following with a tidal wave.

"Take control again," Luke said as the engine sputtered dangerously.

Marion's hands slipped on the broken wheel. "What do we do if we can't shoot that thing?"

"Drive," he said. "Keep driving."

They were still so far from Vancouver Island that it appeared as little more than a line of inkier black against the black sky on the horizon. At least an hour away, Marion would have wagered.

The water moved much faster behind them.

In fact, the rear of her stolen boat was already lifting from the force of the wave. It was driving them forward faster, faster. They were hurtling out of control.

It was like the assassin was trying to push them toward something.

Pale figures appeared in the water ahead. Marion glimpsed slender faces with predatory features, sharp eyes, thin lips. The women were comfortable within the water even though there was no craft nearby. Doubtlessly they weren't human.

Their mouths were open and moving. It looked like they were speaking—or singing, as Luke had mentioned earlier.

Marion couldn't hear anything.

"Sirens," Luke said.

The word helped no memories surface, but Marion assembled the definition rapidly. Sirens must have been one of the preternatural creatures that had emerged after Genesis. They dwelled in the water and sang enchanting music that Marion couldn't hear, but Luke could.

He covered his ears, shut his eyes. A groan tore through his chest, and a line of blood dripped from his nostril.

The music Marion couldn't hear was hurting him.

Trapped between naiad and sirens, with a gun Marion wasn't sure could hurt anything, she only knew one thing: this time, she needed to save her own life.

"Give me your hand!" she shouted to Luke, loud enough that she hoped that he'd hear her over the sirens. He didn't react. Blood poured down his upper lip.

The female bodies were slicing through the water, pale forms among the dark waves.

Marion lunged toward him, seized his hand.

Doors opened. Magic unfolded.

The world went white.

Marion remembered a garden. She had been as

tiny as the trees had been large. They towered over her with trunks as wide as small cities—trunks so huge that they couldn't have been natural to Earth.

She'd liked how the dense trees stretched for seeming eternity, the dim blue light that radiated from everywhere and nowhere, and the hint of green in the leaves miles above her head. Marion had even liked how she never saw the sky, not once, because the canopy was too dense.

More than anything else, she'd liked the company she kept there.

"It's really easy to go wherever you want," the boy had told her. He'd been older than Marion, tall and skinny, on the brink of adolescence. "I can show you how to do it."

He'd walked up to a tree then and knocked on its trunk. A door had appeared. It had been a terribly ordinary door, white and four-paneled, like any door that Marion had seen in her homes on Earth. Except that this one was set into the tree.

"How did you do that?" Marion had asked.

"Try it yourself," he suggested.

So she had. Marion had been pleased, but not surprised, when knocking on another tree produced a door just as readily.

"Wonderful," she'd said. She had been speaking in French. That was the only language she'd spoken as a little girl. Her older playmate, the tall boy, had spoken only English. They'd had no trouble communicating anyway. The things they said transcended words.

"You can do that any time you want, anywhere

you want. They're always listening."

Marion had asked, "How do you know?"

And he'd said, "Because I'm one of them."

She hadn't understood what he meant at the time. But later—later, it had all made sense. Marion didn't remember any of it now. She was grasping at distant truths, flailing for scraps of memories and almost reaching them...but not quite.

Marion remembered the garden. The doors. The boy with the curly hair.

Everything else remained just out of reach.

Luke's mind cleared and his eyes opened on a starry sky. Everything hurt. That was a novel sensation. He couldn't remember the last time that he had been in so much pain, and for a moment, the humanity of it all excited him.

Pain. *Pain.*

Then he remembered that pain meant something must have hurt him.

"Marion?" Luke was immersed in a good three inches of chilling water flooding the *Sparrowhawk.* It sloshed when he stood.

"I'm here." Marion picked herself up from underneath the console. Her normally voluminous hair clung to her cheeks, giving her the shrunken, angry look of a cat tossed into a bathtub.

She was alive, though. And so was he.

Luke looked around for the sirens and the naiad. They were nowhere in sight. In fact, he saw nothing at all: no other boats, no land, no lights. They were floating in the midst of a quiet ocean.

"What happened?" The last thing he remembered was Marion pulling his hand away from his ear, and then such immense pain that he'd instantly passed out.

"I cast magic." Marion showed her fingers to him. They sparked with white electricity, which fizzled out within seconds. "I think..." She drew in a breath and let it out slowly. "I think I might have killed them all. I remembered something while I cast magic, too. A garden."

"Like, with vegetables?"

"With doors," she said softly.

"I'm not following you."

"I don't get it, either." Marion wrapped her arms around herself, hugging her body against the cold. Her chin trembled. "I'm sure I killed them."

"They were trying to kill you," he said.

"I know. I *know.*" Two tears painted parallel tracks down her cheeks.

"Marion," he sighed. He enfolded her in his arms. Marion was very tall for a woman, so she easily rested her chin on his shoulder. Her hands clutched the back of his shirt, and he gripped her in return. She smelled like a bonfire—fine furniture shattered into pieces and burned on a beach.

Marion was a mage powerful enough to rip sirens and naiads apart when she was angry, but she was trembling.

"You're okay," he said. It wasn't a question, but an order. "You're okay, Marion."

"What kind of person must I be to have so many people out to kill me? Nobody invests so much into killing the nice people."

"They do when the nice people are dangerous," Luke said.

"I don't want to be dangerous."

"You'll get your memories back soon, and I bet we'll find that you haven't done anything to deserve this." Luke wasn't certain if he believed those words himself, but they made her trembling subside, so it was worth saying. Anything to make her stop shaking like that.

"Thank you," she said, lifting her head from his shoulder. She lifted a finger to brush it over his bottom lip, but didn't quite touch. "Where'd you get that?"

She meant his scar. He had several, but the one on his face was most obvious. "A fight."

"What could have possibly hurt someone like Dr. Lucas Flynn thoroughly enough to leave an imprint?"

"Long story. Doesn't matter."

"It matters to me," she said.

He touched her sleeved elbow and used it to guide her hand away. He still didn't release her once the offending fingers were safely at her side. From only inches away, he could see into the depths of Marion's white eyes, glowing in the night. Alien as those angel eyes looked, there was more humanity in them than he'd seen on most mundanes.

Even without any skin-to-skin contact between the two of them, Lucas gazed at Marion and felt... things. Things that he didn't trust.

Light arced through the sky in an eye-scorching shade of gold. Luke had barely an instant to register it before that light slammed into the deck of the boat. Water sprayed where it connected.

The light resolved into a human form.

Luke pushed Marion behind him, shielding her with his body. "Stay behind me!" He drew his gun.

"Wait!" the new man shouted. "Don't shoot me again! I'm not trying to hurt either of you, damn it!"

It was the sidhe who looked like a member of a boy band. He wasn't carrying that massive sword anymore. Lucas didn't fire.

All three of them froze, watching, waiting to see who would twitch first.

"Who are you?" Marion finally asked, clutching the back of Luke's jacket.

The assassin laughed disbelievingly. "Marion, it's *me*."

"She asked you a question," Luke said with a hard edge to his voice. His gun didn't waver. "You need to answer."

"My name is Konig—ErlKonig," he said. "Marion...I'm your boyfriend."

NINE

Luke didn't fire, but he also didn't lower the gun. Marion curled her fingers over his shoulder. She studied Konig from safety, half-hidden behind Luke.

ErlKonig. A powerful sidhe who could appear and disappear like fog rolling in off the ocean, who had tracked them across Port Angeles and into the bay.

Her boyfriend.

If this man was her boyfriend, then he must have been someone she knew well. *Very* well. But his features didn't trigger any memories, and she found it hard to believe she could have forgotten a face like Konig's. He had a long nose, big violet eyes, and black hair that glistened blue when light hit it. He looked like a male model who had been sprayed with glitter.

The differentiation between seelie and unseelie sidhe made a lot of sense when Marion looked at him. Luke had said that they were like day versus night. Konig was every inch the nighttime taking human shape. He was also the same breed as many of her would-be assassins.

"Prove you're my boyfriend," she said.

Konig laughed disbelievingly. "But Marion—"

"Humor her," Luke said, his voice as tight as his back muscles.

"Who in the Nether Worlds are *you*?" Konig asked.

Luke responded by cocking the gun.

Konig lifted his hands in a gesture of surrender. He only had eyes for Marion, as though Lucas were no more than a window between them. "You and I met at the after-party for the last election for Alpha. We were at the werewolf sanctuary. You wore a white dress."

That told Marion nothing. Memories wouldn't work. "Physical things. Things I could prove right now."

"You've got to be kidding."

"I'm not," Marion said.

He laughed again, with even less genuine amusement than earlier. "You've got a scar on your ribs where you were accidentally shot with an enchanted arrow while visiting my home at Autumn Court. I tossed Saoirse into the dungeon over it, but you insisted that I have her shoot at you again so you could learn to dodge." His smile made Marion's heart skip a beat. "Does that prove I'm not a changeling?"

She lifted her shirt, tilting her side toward the light. There it was—a faint, glistening line of white. A scar. The rest of the memory was meaningless, but the scar was not. "What was I doing in the Autumn Court? Isn't that where sidhe live?"

"You only agreed to date me if I trained you how to fight against the unseelie, and the Autumn Court's training grounds are the best in the Middle Worlds," Konig said.

A date in exchange for some kind of martial training. It did sound like the kind of thing Marion might do.

And Konig knew about her scar.

She stepped hesitantly around Luke.

"Marion..." Luke said warningly.

Konig lowered his hands as she approached, letting them hang by his side. The way he smiled warmed the chill violet shards of his eyes. "You've been out of touch for weeks. I was so worried—we started posting ads online in the hopes someone would spot you, but you vanished as soon as we got a tip. Are you okay?"

"I've lost my memory," Marion said. "I can't remember anything that happened before two days ago."

"You've forgotten me?"

"Everything."

His eyes flicked up to look at Luke over Marion's shoulder. "Who's *that*?"

"Dr. Lucas Flynn." She rubbed her shoulders.

She was colder than she'd been before Konig showed up, as though the overwhelming power of the sidhe was shutting down her system's defenses against the bitter ocean air. "Luke. He's been helping me."

"A doctor," Konig echoed skeptically. Luke was still holding the gun, but not aiming it. Probably because Marion had gotten in the way.

"I can explain more, but not here," Marion said. "Can you magic us, perhaps, to the island...?"

She hadn't finished the sentence before Konig waved.

They appeared on a rocky beach Marion didn't recognize, without an instant of blurring or a spark of magic.

"Of course," Konig said.

She turned quickly, searching for Luke. He wasn't there. "The doctor," she said. "Bring him with us."

"Who is he?" Konig asked, a hint of anger tipping the words with razor-sharp danger.

"I was found in Ransom Falls, California," Marion said. "He works in the emergency department of Mercy Hospital. He's been helping me."

"Helping you, or hiding you? Did he abduct you?"

Her cheeks warmed. "Dr. Flynn has saved me from assassination attempts. Get him off of the boat. Now."

Konig waved again.

Luke appeared a few feet away. Relief flashed

across his features when he saw Marion, though it was quickly replaced by annoyance. He still hadn't holstered his gun.

"I'm okay," Marion said quickly.

"You can't blame me for wanting to protect my princess." Konig wrapped his arm around her shoulders with utter, possessive confidence. "If you've been...helping her...then I'm sure you've noticed how priceless she is. And with the summit at the United Nations approaching—her disappearance at this time had us all thinking the worst."

Marion's heart skipped a beat. "I'm involved with the summit? The one that they're talking about on the news?"

"Gods above," he said. "You've really forgotten everything, haven't you?"

"That's what I told you," she said.

"Have you even forgotten this?" Konig asked. He kissed her. The brush of his lips against Marion's was like rolling ice over her skin. Her blood pulsed in time with distant drumbeats. Konig certainly seemed familiar with the way she liked to be kissed—even though Marion, until that moment, wouldn't have known that she liked the stroke of his thumb along her jawline, or how confidently he claimed her tongue with his.

It was an intimate kiss, deep enough that Marion felt no doubt that she'd been much more intimate with Konig before.

She stepped back, fingertips lifting to her mouth. Somehow, her skin wasn't frosty-cold, even though it had felt like such a pleasant chill in the moment.

"Even that," she said faintly.

Now Konig looked worried. "I should get you to my parents. They'll be able to fix this."

"Who are your parents?" Marion asked.

"The king and queen of the Autumn Court," he said, taking her arm. "We're not far from the ley lines. I'll pull you through."

"Wait." She turned to see that Luke had finally holstered his gun. He wasn't watching them, though. He'd wandered down the beach and was staring at the ocean. Giving them privacy. Lost in thought.

"I have to talk to my friend before I go anywhere," Marion said. "In private."

Konig's eyes narrowed. "Alone?"

"He won't hurt me."

"I can phase away momentarily, but I'll return in five minutes to take you with me." He clasped her hands in his, pulling her against him. "I've already lost you once, princess. I'm not going to let you out of my grasp again."

His second kiss was a little more urgent, but no less thrilling. He tasted of peaches ripening in the late summer sun and magic with roots entrenched deep within the Earth. Konig was as much a piece of the world as the trees, the grass, the sky.

Her boyfriend, a sidhe prince of the Autumn Court.

Marion obviously had a *lot* of remembering to do.

There was no sign of other sirens or naiads when Marion joined Luke by the ocean's edge—only solemn, thoughtful silence from the doctor, and a breeze that bit at her salt-crusted flesh to send shivers into her marrow. "I should go with Konig," Marion said. "If anyone can restore my memory, it will be the sidhe."

Luke sighed, like he'd been waiting for her to say that. "Fine."

Marion had known him for all of two days. It shouldn't have mattered to her if he disapproved. "He is my boyfriend."

"Yeah, that's what he claims. He's appeared out of nowhere, he's unseelie sidhe, we don't know anything about where he comes from—"

"Whereas I know so much about you? You're just some surgeon from a hospital in the middle of nowhere," Marion said.

"Just some surgeon. Yeah." He raked a hand through his hair. "We're on Vancouver Island now, so close to your home."

"Should I take this danger back to my family when I have an alternative?" She rested a hand on his shoulder. "Konig knows things about me that he would have to be very close to know."

"There's no way to be sure he's right about how you got that scar," Luke said.

She hadn't been thinking about the scar so

much as how he'd known exactly what kind of touch would stir her body. "I believe him. I do."

"I don't want to see you hurt."

"Thank you." Her hand slid from shoulder to elbow, and she relaxed into a genuine smile, beaming at him with the relief that she wanted to allow herself to feel. "We're going to be okay."

The corners of his lips lifted momentarily. Marion wondered if having a strong physical reaction to a man's smile—a man who wasn't her supposed boyfriend—was criminal enough to make her worthy of assassination.

It was just that she felt so much closer to Luke than she had any right to be. There was so much more to the doctor than she could see on the surface. A man as depthless as the ocean, a doctor and skilled sharpshooter who easily defended her from assassin threats.

What if Konig wasn't the only man in her life that she'd forgotten?

"Have you ever been to a garden before?" Marion asked abruptly. "A garden with very big trees, filled by blue light, and without a visible sky?"

"What?"

"As I told you, I remembered something the last time I cast magic. I remembered a garden with a boy, a black boy, whose skin was almost your color, and—and I think there might be other similarities too." Like Luke's jawline. Marion could easily imagine the boy having grown up to look very much like Luke. "I think it would be the right

age difference. I was perhaps four years old. You're
—ten years older than me? Nine? He was a young
teenager, so..."

"Marion, when you were four, I was an adult.
My fiancée had already left me. I'm not the boy
from your memories."

"You *can't* be more than ten years older than
me," Marion said.

Luke gave her that lopsided smile. "I'm not the
guy you remember. I promise."

"You've never been in that garden, then."

"Not *that* garden," Luke said.

"You're not telling me something important."

"I'm not telling you a lot of things. Believe it or
not, Marion, I don't have to tell you *anything*."

His tone was identical to when he'd been
telling her that he wasn't going to buy her clothes,
and it triggered the same feelings of shame. "I
thought that we were getting to be friends."

"Marion..." He brushed his knuckles down her
shoulder, tracing along the hem of her sleeve. "If I
thought that I was locked up anywhere in your
missing memories, I'd tell you."

Marion believed that. She also believed that
the idea of leaving without him was unbearable.
"You'll come protect me in the Autumn Court,
won't you?"

"I thought you trusted this guy, this ErlKonig,"
Luke said.

"I *want* to. But he appeared fifteen minutes ago,
whereas you've been with me for two days."
Marion weighed the words she wanted to say. "I'd

be afraid to go without you."

He sighed again. "I'll stick around. You're still my patient, for the time being."

She would have hugged him if it wouldn't have been weird.

Marion settled for saying, "Thank you."

The Autumn Court was unlike anywhere Luke had been in his current lifetime: a place so magical that when Prince ErlKonig yanked him into the Middle Worlds, Luke's brain shut down completely.

Before his senses failed him, Luke got an impression of a road. Of trees glimmering like gemstones in the midday sun. Of a beach, an ocean, and clouds.

They were only impressions. Luke's eyes were open and receiving information, but he was experiencing a short between eyeballs and brain. Instead, he was sustaining assault on his every sense. He smelled rotting leaves and moist dirt and pumpkins split open in bitter sunlight, while his flesh crawled with the sensation of spiders. He heard music played in sharps and flats, with a rhythm akin to a rapid reel.

Luke pressed the heels of his palms to his temples and tried to shove away the sensations. The world swirled around him.

"I don't think I can do this," Luke gasped.

There was a hand on his sleeve. He looked

down to see Marion's slender fingers gripping the leather. If she moved her hand up six inches to his jaw, or down a few more inches to his hand, their skin would make contact. And gods only knew what would happen after that.

"Can you see, Doctor?" Her voice danced in and out of his ears.

Luke tracked up her hand, her arm, her slender throat patterned with blue veins, her heart-shaped face. That pair of Husky-bright eyes was the only real thing he could focus on, so he did. "I can only see you."

"We should go back."

"No." That was Konig. "I'll fix this." Another hand appeared, and this one was neither slender nor friendly. It was heavily boned. A fighter's hand with skin that shone like brass.

Luke jerked back. "Don't touch me."

"Let me touch you, or I'll kick you back to Earth alone," Konig said.

"Please," Marion said. He wasn't sure if she was pleading with Luke to stay or go.

He wasn't going to leave her with Konig. He'd promised. Dammit, why had Luke promised Marion anything? "Fine," Luke said.

He gripped the unseelie prince's fist. His senses snapped into place.

No longer were the road and beach mere impressions. He was standing on rocks that shimmered in shades of gold and copper. Cold, colorless water sloshed over his feet. Dying trees etched jagged outlines against a crystalline sky.

The turrets of a castle stood on the horizon, far beyond a pumpkin patch with thorny vines as thick around as Luke's waist.

Myrkheimr. Home of the royal family of the Autumn Court.

He'd heard of Myrkheimr before. It was supposed to be one of the more sizable properties in the Middle Worlds, second to Niflheimr in the Winter Court. He'd never imagined it could be quite so vast, though. Its towers brushed the clouds and the walls climbed the hills beyond.

Marion was watching him with concern etching her brow. "Doctor?"

Luke shook his head to clear the lingering cobwebs of confusion. "I'm fine. I can see now."

"The Middle Worlds are challenging for mere mortals," Konig said in an irritatingly lofty tone. It was still hard for Luke to look at him directly. Even when everything else made sense, the prince distorted the world the same way the bottom of a beer glass distorted an alcoholic's view of a bar. "I've placed a filter over your brain that will allow you to see the commonly accepted reality of the Autumn Court. What you perceive now isn't truth, but it's as close as your mortal senses will ever be able to accept."

And what a perception it was. Ravens wheeled through the chilly sky and gave mournful shrieks as black as their feathers. Leaves twirled and whirled in gentle spirals on winds Luke didn't feel.

Marion provided strange contrast to the hot colors of the Middle Worlds. Her eyes glowed faintly. Her hair shimmered with a pale halo. And her skin remained cool in tone, more blues than peaches.

If Luke only looked at her from the corner of his eyes, he almost thought he could see wings.

"My parents will be relieved to see you, princess," Konig said. He pulled Marion along the beach and plunged into the depths of the forest as though he'd instantly forgotten Luke.

Or like he wanted Luke to feel forgotten.

Luke followed more slowly, careful to keep Marion within sight.

Most of her assassins were sidhe, and this world was filled with them. He heard their voices among the trees. They soared with the ravens above and crawled with the worms chewing through the soil below. His feet slipped on the rocky beach and people laughed in response, as though mocking him.

There were foxes along the trail, flitting in and out of the bushes. They watched him with brassy eyes the same shade as Konig's magic.

Thorny vines reached for him. Luke elbowed them away.

"Are you coming?" Marion threw a glance at him over her shoulder, a pink flush on her cheekbones and delight in her eyes. She liked the Autumn Court. He wondered if memory was stirring now that she was with *him*. Her boyfriend.

"Coming," Luke said. Though he wasn't sure why. A prince of the Autumn Court would be as capable of protecting Marion from assassins as

Luke.

The path to Myrkheimr looked like it should have been miles long, but they reached the castle within moments. All it took was a momentary distortion of forest, as though it were folded in half, and then they were at the gate.

The castle grounds were guarded only by a low fence winding between the trees. But there were archers in the high branches, concealed by the gold foil of the leaves, and Luke caught glimpses of arrows leveled at them when Konig approached.

"It's me," the prince called. "Is Dad home?"

An archer leaped nimbly from the branches, landing on the path. She had white hair twisted into twin braids and leather pants the same color as fox fur.

"The king and queen are home," she said. "They've been waiting for you." A smile danced in her eyes. "All of you."

TEN

For Marion, entering the halls of Myrkheimr felt like coming home, and not because the surroundings were familiar. Everything was immaculately clean. Better still, the entryway was being actively cleaned by servants with dusters, rags, and wands. Magic sparkled over the wood floors. Marion could smell soap, and when she traced her fingertips along the edge of a table, she felt not even a speck of dust.

It was amazing that Myrkheimr could look so clean when the rest of the Autumn Court was distinctly worn. The stone pillars ringing the entryway were cracked, and the flowerbeds were shriveling from the first bites of winter. Nothing looked old, exactly. Just weathered.

But it was all clean. Immaculate, in fact. And *rich*. Every chair and crumbling brick had a distinctly artisanal, handmade touch to it. Marion could even see the tooling marks on the portrait frame hanging above the fireplace.

"You really don't remember," Konig said when he noticed how Marion stared. Gods, but he was a beautiful man. Since entering the Autumn Court, his skin had taken on a metallic sheen more like copper than mortal flesh. His jacket hung open around his linen shirt, which was thin enough that the hard lines of his muscles glimmered through the material.

And his *eyes*.

The surreal violet color was the least shocking part about his gaze. If it hadn't been obvious before, it was now incredibly obvious that Konig knew Marion well.

He loved her.

"Have I spent much time here?" she asked tentatively, walking along the ring of chairs at the center of the foyer. She touched the backs of the chairs, hoping for some kind of tactile sensation that would stir memory.

"Many days." Konig's gemlike eyes smoldered. "Many more nights."

The dizzying realization that she was surrounded by a court that knew her—a court that she should have known—made Marion want to reach out to Luke for comfort.

The doctor didn't seem awed by the surroundings. The fact that he kept his hands off of his sidearm must have meant he was trying to look as non-threatening as possible, but Luke moved like he was ready to fight. He didn't turn his back toward any of the unseelie sidhe who flitted around the periphery of the foyer, and he stuck close to Marion.

"Then I'll show you to the throne room, I suppose," Konig said. His fingers laced with hers, shooting exhilarating warmth through her veins.

The grand staircase was draped in cobwebs and more shriveled golden vines, leading to a hallway as open as the foyer itself. Some of the window frames were filled with stained glass that fragmented the light like prisms; others were open to the crisp air, giving it all an open feel that appealed to Marion. It was as though she'd be able to jump out and fly away.

Marion could tell that they were drawing near to the queen. As Konig led her closer to the end of the hallway, the air grew thick, but chilly. It made the marrow within her bones vibrate unpleasantly.

That was sidhe magic. She'd felt it frequently enough when the assassins were coming for her that she could identify it now.

The end of the hall was capped by a pair of towering double doors. Detailed scenes were carved into the four panels, each one showing a different woman who wore a crown or diadem.

On the first, there was a woman seated on a throne with a scaled tail like those of the sirens who had attacked Marion and Luke.

The panel to the right of that one was decorated with a pregnant woman with butterfly wings.

On the third panel, the one below the first quadrant, was a woman with twin pigtails decorated with pearls.

The fourth was a woman with claw-like fingernails and sharp eyes.

All those carvings were so detailed that Marion imagined that they must have been modeled after real people. "The queens of each sidhe court," Konig said helpfully.

"So one of these is your mother?"

"This one." He tapped the woman with the pigtails and pearls. Once he pointed it out, Marion couldn't help but notice the similarity to their features. She had the same lean bone structure in her face and intelligent eyes. "She's the Onyx Queen. You call her Violet."

Marion called the queen of the Autumn Court by her first name. How close was she to Konig, in order to address his mother so informally?

Only one way to find out.

"Go ahead," Konig said, gesturing toward the door.

Marion reached for the handle as she stepped forward. She hesitated with her fingers hovering an inch above the metal. "Interesting."

"What?" asked the prince.

She tipped her head to the side as she studied the door. The carvings weren't its only unique feature. Once Marion opened her mind, she could tell that the door didn't exist in merely one plane of existence. There was the physical thing that she was a hairsbreadth from touching, but there were layers under layers.

It was a magical door that tunneled straight through reality.

The spells didn't speak to her in a language she knew. It was like trying to understand the clicking of bats that flitted through the night. Clearly the work of another species. But power recognized power. The magic of the sidhe resonated with her on some level.

Instead of opening the door to the throne room, she lifted her fist and knocked. Her knuckles connected with more than wood.

The throne room on the other side became exposed. Marion saw the thrones clearly—not with her blurry, nearsighted eyes, but with a sense that superseded the physical.

She saw *everything*.

The spells under her feet, which would have appeared like a mosaic of tile to a mundane like Luke.

The illusions woven into the windows, making it appear as though the throne room overlooked the beach even though there was nothing beyond the walls.

She even saw the fibers of life that wrapped through the thrones themselves. The thrones looked like they'd been carved, but Marion understood that they had been grown from the same matter as the hair and fingernails of the royalty who sat upon it.

The king and queen waited at the epicenter of the magical hurricane.

SM Reine

"Marion," the king said, getting to his feet.

She blinked rapidly, struggling to retract her vision from the depths of the magic so that she could perceive a man. The king had the same muscular build as Konig. The same lofty stature. The same lazy way of standing, as though they were too cool to bother standing upright.

The queen lounged in her seat beside him. Her hair was wrapped into two thick braids that hung over her shoulders and puddled on the floor. There was no way to tell where hair ended and the tangle of vines began. She wore the same oversized pearls that she did on the door, along with blossoms dotting her hair that were almost the same creamy shade as her flesh.

A tiara was set into the mass of her hair. A delicate chain held a crescent suspended between her eyebrows, which matched the pendulums in her ears and the chains draped around her throat to nestle in her cleavage.

"I can't begin to say how relieved we are to see you, dear girl," the queen said warmly. She had no pupils, no irises. Her eyes were blank, eerie white.

Marion remembered that she was in the presence of royalty, and she was probably supposed to show some kind of respect. She fell into a clumsy curtsy. It must have looked moronic since she was wearing scrubs. "Your Majesties."

The king chuckled. "I never thought I'd see the day that you bowed before me. Heather was right. You've forgotten everything."

She wasn't supposed to bow to him? She

straightened awkwardly. "I'm sorry, Your Highness."

"Please," he said, "call me Rage."

"Rage?" What kind of name was Rage?

She half-expected to be punished for echoing his name with such disbelief, but the king only laughed. "That's more like it." He looked over her shoulder. "Who is this?"

"Dr. Lucas Flynn," Luke said, stepping forward. "I'm a doctor from Ransom Falls, California. I was there when Marion was found, and I was escorting her home to Vancouver Island."

"Home?" Rage's brow furrowed. "Why would you have gone there first, of all places?"

"Because she doesn't know," the queen said softly.

Marion glanced between them, unable to keep herself from frowning. She didn't understand. "What don't I know?"

"Anything, it seems," Violet said. Her blank eyes could have been focused on anything, but Marion felt like the queen was staring at her.

"What's at my house?" Marion pressed.

"Nothing, right now," Rage said. "You're due at the summit. Your live-in assistant will be waiting for you there."

"And my parents?"

"No. Here, let's make this easier." Rage stepped down from the dais, and his throne seemed to sigh, as though it were saddened by his distance. "You don't seem to remember much, so we've got a lot of ground to cover. Why don't we start by figuring out what you *do* know?"

Marion opened her mouth to respond. She wanted to tell them about the garden and the curly-haired boy, but instinct stopped her.

That wasn't something that she should tell *anyone.*

"I know that my name is Marion. I'm a mage. A half-angel, half-witch girl. And..." She shrugged. "I like things to be clean, I like designer clothes, and everyone seems to want me dead."

Luke made an odd noise behind her. She knew him well enough now to tell when he was trying to smother a laugh.

Violet stood from her throne, smoothing her dress around her thighs. She wore multi-layered ruffles, much like the carving. "This is surely the work of people trying to keep you from the UN summit. It should be easier to bring your memories back than to try to fill you in on everything that you've 'missed.' Why don't we see if we can take care of that for you?"

Marion's heart stopped beating. "Yes," she said. "Yes *please.*"

Violet led them out of the throne room and down a hallway to another wing of the castle. The king didn't come, though Marion could feel the weight of his eyes following her all the way out the door.

Marion had a great view of the surrounding forest as they weaved through Myrkheimr. They were only bordered by trees on one side. A steep precipice carved through the earth on the other side of the hall, and waterfalls foamed off the side, spilling into a lake the color of the cold sky. There was a village at the bottom.

"That's where most of our guards live." Konig seemed reluctant to let her go. He had his arm wrapped around her shoulder, and his grip only tightened as they moved down the hall. "The rest of the Autumn Court lives on the fringes of our world. We like our space."

"It doesn't look real," Marion said.

"The courts were designed by the Summer Queen, Titania," Violet said. "She's a dramatic soul." They spiraled down a staircase and into a hall set along the side of the cliff.

"What can you tell me about...me?" Marion asked, looking thoughtfully at her boyfriend's mother. "Do we know each other well?"

"I know you about as much as you'd expect any woman to know her son's girlfriend. I can tell you that your name is Marion Garin. Sometimes you go by Marion Kavanagh."

The name struck against Marion's skull as though it were crashing into her, a meteor entering the atmosphere to crater exactly where she stood.

Kavanagh.

She clutched her skull, heels of her palms digging into her temples.

"Kavanagh," she said aloud. "Kavanagh. *Kavanagh.*"

"Marion?" A hand touched her elbow. It was Luke. She wanted to let herself fall into him, praying that he would be waiting at the bottom of the deep hole that name had corkscrewed into her brain.

"Kavanagh," Marion whispered one more time.

"Two different last names," Luke said, hovering nearby, as though prepared to catch her. "Why?"

"I'm not sure, to be honest." Violet ran her fingers through the strands of pearls in her hair, which chimed unnaturally. "Marion's never been forthcoming about her past, even though we've brought her into our court as readily as though she were family."

Mysteries layered underneath mysteries.

Marion stood between Luke and Konig. The way that both of them stared at her was too much.

"I'm fine," she murmured, though she wasn't certain who she was reassuring.

"Here we are. The library." Violet stopped in front of another door, this one unremarkable aside from the fact that it should have opened into the cliff.

"Doctor, you can't come in here." Konig waved down the hall, vaguely indicating the direction of his servants. They had followed the sidhe royalty into the rear of the castle so silently that Marion hadn't noticed them. "Our people will take you to a room where you can rest after your difficult journey from Ransom Falls."

"Luke can't come into the library? Why?" Marion asked. Her urge to grab Luke was stronger than ever.

"The information held within is exclusive to the sidhe," Violet said.

Konig added, "And you, princess."

"Luke can hear anything I can," she said.

"Your loyalty's nice, but you don't understand what you were like...*before*," Konig said. "You don't know what you went through to earn the right to access what's beyond those doors."

What did Marion want more: to keep Luke by her side, or to find her memories?

"I'll go," Luke said, sparing her from the decision.

Marion gave him a weak smile. "Don't go far."

He didn't smile back.

Marion watched one of Konig's servants guide Luke away, frustration uncoiling within the pits of her gut. If she'd had her way, she would have been tethered to Luke, keeping him permanently within arm's reach. Like a toddler who needed her teddy bear. Now he was leaving and she wanted to throw a tantrum much like a toddler's, too.

She swallowed down her hurts and clutched Konig's hand harder.

Even so, when Luke walked away, she couldn't help but watch his retreating back and feel like she'd never see him again.

The room that the servant took Luke to was nice enough, aesthetically speaking. It was exactly the kind of thing he'd have expected to find in one of the faerie courts, with all its froufrou furniture, ridiculous rugs, and stained glass windows. Magic shimmered on every surface, so obvious that even he could see it.

The woman who had escorted him there hung by the door. "You'll let me know if you need anything?" She was a petite waif of a woman, and Luke believed her to be one of the gentry—the highest caste of sidhe. The gentry could pass for human, as Konig did. There was nothing inhuman about her willowy form, goldenrod hair, or peachy skin.

"I'm fine, thanks," Luke said, giving the servant a long, thoughtful look. There was something strangely flat about the purple of her irises. They didn't have the depth to them that Konig's did. She might have been gentry, but either she was weak gentry, or wearing a glamour.

Why? What physical attribute would she be trying to hide?

She stared back at Luke as though she expected him to say something.

"I'd like privacy," he said after an awkward moment.

"Of course you would." She bowed and backed out of the room, shutting the door behind her.

Luke was left alone in a room with proportions so overblown that they felt ready for a giant. The bed was like four kings put together. He could have climbed into the wardrobe with a half-dozen others for a party, too. It was possible that the sidhe did expect to entertain large guests. There were demons of those grand proportions.

None of that was interesting to him, though. He couldn't stop thinking about the magic that he had seen on the door to Myrkheimr's throne room —and the door to the library he hadn't been allowed to enter.

Luke hadn't put much thought into the magic circle he'd seen at Ollie Machado's house. At the time, he'd thought the spellwork had the faint hallmarks of unseelie magic, but he didn't know enough to be certain. There was a lot of overlap between human and sidhe magic.

Now he felt much more certain. The designs on Myrkheimr's doors were too similar to the teleportation spell to be coincidental.

He just didn't know what it meant. But he knew how to figure it out.

Luke pulled a cell phone out of one pocket and a battery out of the other. It was no secret that the Office of Preternatural Affairs tracked cell phone networks in conjunction with the National Security Agency, which was why Luke owned a phone, but never turned it on.

This particular cell phone was ancient technology. A pre-Genesis artifact. The battery and antenna were slathered in magic. No spell could prevent the NSA from surveilling the cell networks, but it could let Luke contact people without touching a cell network in the first place.

He popped the battery into place and pressed the power button.

The phone only got to ring twice before someone picked up on the other end. "Hey," said a woman. Her voice crackled with interdimensional interference, but Luke still heard the utter shock in her tone.

"Hi, Brianna," Luke said. "Long time."

Brianna Dimaria was the one person that Luke trusted with his identity—the one phone number he had kept of all those he'd known before becoming a doctor at Mercy Hospital.

Once upon a time, Brianna had been the high priestess of a prestigious coven, trained by the best of the best. Now she lived in Las Vegas and worked as a private investigator. She was so often contracted by the government that she might as well have been an employee.

Government contacts or not, Brianna was deeply loyal to Luke. She had enchanted the phone as a gift to be sure he could get help whenever he needed. Until that day, Luke had been convinced he'd never need that help.

Never say never, he thought.

"You answered the phone awfully fast," Luke said.

She gave a shaky laugh. "Well, *yeah*." Those two words were filled with a thousand unasked questions.

"I'd like you to contact a friend of mine," Luke said. "Her name is Nurse Charity Ballard and she works at Mercy Hospital in Ransom Falls, California." It was the first time that he'd told Brianna anything so personal about his new life. He pushed on before he could think about the sensitive information he was exposing. "Ask

Charity to go to Oliver Machado's house. I need Ollie's laptop, his spellbook if she can find it, and anything else remotely occultish that she can find."

"Okay. And where will you meet her to get those things?" Brianna could barely make that question sound innocent. She must have been dying to hunt Charity down, and Luke by association.

He wasn't going to make it easy for Brianna to seek him out. "I'll find Charity myself."

"Anything else?"

Luke gazed up at the stained-glass windows and the leafy shadows fluttering past. What could he do with the help of a witch like Brianna Dimaria? Probably a lot of things. Nothing that would be worth it. "Just don't tell anyone you heard from me. I'm not coming back."

"I wish you would." Brianna's voice went soft. "You know Rylie's sick with worry about you. Rylie and Abel both. I'm worried too."

"Call Charity for me. Please. And for the love of the stupid new gods, keep your oath."

"Of course I will. Who do you think I am? I haven't changed at all. You, on the other hand—"

"Thanks for your help," Luke interrupted.

Brianna hung up first.

The library of the Autumn Court had far fewer

books than Marion had expected. The room was composed of magical windows like those in the throne room, so there simply wasn't room for the floor-to-ceiling shelves she'd hoped to see.

A few pedestals held ancient-looking texts within glass cases. There were also freestanding shelves with other books that looked worthy of display at museums. Otherwise, the space was occupied primarily by comfortable furniture, which would give the people who sat within the library excellent views of the gardens.

Marion wandered along the pedestals, skimming the titles. None were in English or French. She couldn't read them. "What will you do to bring my memory back?"

"Are you aware that most sidhe were human before Genesis?" Violet asked.

"That's what I've been told."

"Like many others, I was a human—a witch— so I should be able to dig up a sounding spell to delve into your mind. I'll see if there's an enchantment to remove. Wait here. I'll call you once I'm ready."

Violet moved into the library's mezzanine, leaving Konig and Marion at the bottom. "Alone at last," Konig murmured, using his grip on her hand to pull her against his chest.

She gazed up at his brilliant violet eyes. "Not exactly *alone*."

"I trust my guards, and you do too."

She didn't have any choice but to trust what he said. Hopefully she wouldn't need to lean on blind trust for long if the Onyx Queen was about to bring her memories back. Marion buried her face in his chest, letting the overwhelming sensation of sidhe fade away. "Where was Luke taken?"

"The south wing. He's safe." Konig rubbed Marion along the furrow of her spine. "Want to tell me why you're wearing scrubs?"

"It was the only thing I had in the hospital. I was wearing pajamas when they found me in the forest, so this was my only option."

"Strange. I wonder when you were taken. When you were on your way to the summit?"

"I don't know. *Should* I have been going to the summit?"

"You disappeared a couple of weeks ago, so... no." He shook his head. "You were taking care of business without me, so I didn't know what you were up to. I thought you might have been visiting with the werewolf Alpha. You're friends."

Friends with Rylie Gresham. The woman whose autobiography Marion owned.

"I never would have expected to find you in California," Konig said.

"How did you find me in Ransom Falls?"

"I asked my father to place ads for you on the mortal internet. We made a tip line. Someone called it in."

If someone had reported Marion's location, then it must have been one of the hospital staff— the only people she had encountered while in Ransom Falls. "When was the last time I spoke to you? Before I lost my memories, I mean."

A smile crossed Konig's features, which instantly made her think dirty, intimate things. "You were visiting me here. It was barely three weeks ago."

Marion's gaze tracked down his broad chest to his muscled legs and the hand gripping hers. It was a very large hand. "I wish I could remember everything we've done together."

"Very soon, you will." Konig kissed her gently, thumb tracing along the line of her jaw. It didn't feel as intimate this time. It was more like he was positioning his hand to break her neck.

The paranoia was surely because of her missing memories. Even so, she couldn't help but pull away to glance at the second level of the library, where Violet had vanished. There was no sign of the queen.

"I take it we're serious," Marion said. "That we've been together a long time."

"A couple of years," Konig said. "And yes. It's serious."

She wasn't sure if the thrill in her chest was excitement or fear.

There was nothing intimidating about Konig, even if he had been carrying a sword in Port Angeles and tried to carry her away in a fog. She certainly wasn't afraid he would hurt her. Marion worried about what he expected of her—what sort of things they might have done, if she'd remembered him.

Marion was no more ready to dive into their relationship than she was prepared for the summit.

She pulled away, and he released her readily, though she remained trapped within the heat of his purple-eyed gaze.

"You look weird in those clothes. Not bad, but... strange," Konig said. "But you could make a paper bag sexy, I think."

Marion couldn't help but giggle. "I can see why I'd date you."

"There are many reasons." He arched an eyebrow.

Konig followed her as she walked along the shelves, trailing her finger over the bumpy spines of the books. They reassured her in a manner not too dissimilar to having Luke's presence, but they were as exciting as Konig's touch. These were books available to only a select sect of unseelie sidhe—and to Marion.

Rare knowledge was the very best kind of knowledge.

"What else do you know about me?" Marion asked as she strolled around the library. "My family?"

"Your family doesn't live at your home. You were emancipated and have lived alone since you were fifteen." Konig tapped his chin. "Hmm. What else? I know that you were raised by a single mother before you chose to move out on your own. I haven't met her. You don't talk about her much."

She stopped walking. "My parents are divorced?"

"Your father's dead. He's been dead for years.

Since before Genesis."

All those fleeting fantasies she'd had of being greeted by a large family back home—a large, adoring, rich family—were quickly withering. "So the angel blood I have...is it from my mother or father?" Marion asked.

"Your father. I can't believe you don't know—I never would have expected to have to explain this to you. Damn." Konig took one of Marion's hands in both of his. "Your father's the whole reason that you're needed at the summit, princess. He used to be the Voice of God, too. Just like you."

ELEVEN

Marion didn't realize that she needed to sit until she was suddenly in one of the library's plush chairs. *The Voice of God.* "What does that mean?" she asked once she remembered how to speak.

Konig kneeled in front of her, gazing intently into her eyes. "It means that you're the sole point of contact between the gods and the mortal races."

"That's not possible. The gods are dead."

"Who told you that? The doctor?" he asked. She nodded. "It's true that the average person hasn't seen the gods since Genesis. But you're not an average person. You're the Voice."

Of all the potential roles Marion had mulled since waking up in Ransom Falls—student, model, action heroine, whatever—she never would have considered "envoy to gods" as a possibility. But it did have a certain ring of familiarity to it. A very faint one. "That's why everyone's trying to kill me before the summit. The gods told me something they don't want to spread around. Right? What did they tell me?"

"Only you would know."

She could imagine why that kind of information might get her killed. If the gods had plans, and if those plans didn't coincide with what other leaders had in mind for their factions...

Gods. Marion was probably about to piss a lot of people off.

That only broadened the pool of suspects for who might have hired assassins. Not narrowed it.

"If we're as serious as you say, then I'm sure I've told you *something* about my speech," Marion said with a note of desperation. The idea that she was due to give a speech in two days with no memory of what she was expected to say was too horrible to contemplate.

Konig's eyes crinkled at the corners when he smiled. "No, you're more loyal to the gods than to me. Your independence is part of what I find so attractive about you. As a prince, I've no shortage of women hurling themselves at my feet. I like that I have to seek you out."

The prince closed the gap to claim her lips. Marion kissed him without feeling it.

Violet appeared at the top of the stairs. Konig pulled away from her quickly, though the queen didn't remark on what she'd caught them doing.

The Onyx Queen descended in a spill of skirts that trailed down the steps behind her. She set a wooden box with a gold lock on the table beside Marion, her white eyes unfocused and blank. "This holds an artifact that should help us sound into your mind, if you're ready."

Marion licked her lips. She still tasted Konig. "Of course I'm ready."

Violet passed a hand over the lock. It clicked. The lid opened easily, revealing a tarot card that glowed within a bed of black velvet.

"Card number twenty. Judgment." Violet lifted it out with both hands as though it were heavy. "I took this card from a former friend. It's for dredging truths out of one's past. I'll repurpose it for our cause." She offered it to Marion. "Take the card."

Marion's fingers tingled warmly at the contact with the waxy card stock.

The art on the Judgment card showed an angel in the sky. He had severe features and wings like a hawk's. He held a trumpet in one hand. Naked mortals were prostrate on the ground below, arms stretched toward him, as though begging silently. The detailed art was beautiful—and unsettling.

The angel looked familiar.

"Study the card and take deep breaths, dear girl." The queen touched her forefingers to either of Marion's temples. Power flowed through them.

The illusion of the tidy library warped. The books vanished, replaced by graying tree branches oozing orange strings of amber. Marion stood in a dead field peppered by gravestones. The sky was ash, the soil brittle.

The true Autumn Court.

Strangest of all was that this dying land wasn't weak, nor was it defeated. The power of the court was in death. The cold, the gray, the aged. All of that magic wound Violet and Marion tightly in chains of ivy, binding hearts and minds. Marion could hear music. She smelled rotting leaves.

Fear climbed down her throat.

They're going to see. Don't let them in.

"You're okay," Konig murmured from behind Marion, lips warm against the back of her neck. When he spoke, she saw the alluring illusion of the Middle Worlds again: the library, the comfortable chairs, the paintings hung in expensive frames.

She tried to take deep breaths, like the queen had told her to, even as magic probed her skull. Marion could feel it squirming like dried-out worms between the lobes of her brain.

That was pain. Real pain.

"Stop," she whispered as her vision blurred and whited out. "*Stop.*"

"Deep breaths," Violet said again.

As the probe delved deeper, Marion could see the memories that it was touching.

She saw a nightclub illuminated only by pillars of cold blue flame. The dance floor was filled with preternaturals. In her memories, she glimpsed human-like faces and easily assigned species to them: succubus, seelie sidhe, lamia, shifter.

The probe kept digging.

Marion sat in the grass behind a cottage,

overlooking a tepid lake. She played with a brown-skinned toddler whose crazy curls stuck out from his head in every direction. A feminine voice said, "I can't let you do that, Marion. You have no idea how much devastation it would cause." The speaker was obviously trying to sound calm for the sake of the toddler.

And Marion had responded, "I'd like to see you try to stop me."

Violet kept going, and senseless images flashed around Marion.

A tall woman with brown hair, very much like her own, nestling Marion in her lap.

Another woman with redder hair and a harsh face.

A pair of twin swords.

That boy that Marion had seen in the garden.

And then the garden itself, with towering trees, and dim blue light, and—

"No!" Marion *shoved*.

The Queen of the Autumn Court stumbled away from Marion. The gold-locked case tumbled to the floor between them hard enough that the wood cracked.

Marion tossed the Judgment card away, too. It was burning white hot. "No." She shook her head, struggling to swallow around the lump in her throat.

The vision of the library had returned. Everything looked so solid, so *real*—especially Konig beside her, and his mother glaring from against the windows.

Marion had pushed Violet away magically.

"I'm sorry," Marion said, standing quickly. "Are you okay?"

Violet lifted a hand to prevent Marion from approaching. "Yes, I'm fine. There are defenses layered in your mind, and they attacked when I tried to push through. I shouldn't be surprised. The Voice would never leave her treasures unguarded."

"You aren't hurt?" Konig asked.

His mother shook her head.

Marion sat down again, slower than before. She couldn't stop shaking. "Did you find anything?"

"Very little." Violet gestured to her guards. Two of them moved to collect the gold-locked case and the Judgment card on the floor. "The walls you've built are thick and numerous. I'm not sure they're all yours, though. Whoever took your memories away must have erected many of them."

Marion didn't want to describe whom she had remembered. It felt too private. "I didn't see anything." She pressed a hand to her aching temple. "Is there nothing else you can do to return my memories?"

"Not alone, I don't think. I'll have to confer with the other courts," Violet said. "Do you have any other leads I could suggest? Any information about your attackers?"

"Not many. All I know is that most of my assassins..." She trailed off, realizing what she had been about to say. *Most of my assassins are sidhe.*

She might as well have directly accused her boyfriend and his family of trying to murder her. "There's a listing on the darknet. An advertisement for a bounty on my head. Could you track the original poster?"

Violet beckoned to one of her servants, whispered in his ear, sent him away again. "We'll see what we can do. We don't have many technologically skilled people in the Autumn Court, but the Hardwicks are unseelie—they're the ones who originally designed the darknet. If any information exists, we'll be able to get it from them."

"Will it take long?" Marion asked, wringing her hands.

"It might. The Winter Court's still in anarchy, after all," Violet said.

"There hasn't been a queen of the unseelie court in five years," Konig explained, rubbing Marion's back in circles. "A lot of the unseelie sidhe have stuck around to try to bring things to order, including the Hardwicks, but..."

"They'll never get it in line," Violet said. "I wish the Hardwicks would give up that stupid chase and join us here. The rest of them can burn for all I care. Put that away." The last order was directed toward her guards, who took the Judgment card back upstairs.

"What can I do to help for now? About my memories, I mean?" Marion asked.

"Do your best to remember on your own," Violet said. "Seek familiar places. My son can help you with that."

"Happily," Konig said. His knuckles traced a line down Marion's cheek from the corner of her eye to the corner of her lip. "I think I might know what would get the cogs of your mind turning, princess."

Despite the kingdom being suspended between summer and winter, the foothills behind Myrkheimr were lush, and that was where many members of the court were hanging out.

Sidhe. Marion was surrounded by sidhe.

Any of them could have been assassins.

Everyone bowed deeply to Konig when he passed. Smiles faded whenever they looked at Marion, but they seemed to have nothing but affection for the prince himself. Marion wasn't nearly as popular as her boyfriend.

Konig opened a gate set into a stone wall. "This way, princess."

"Why do you keep calling me that?"

His eyebrows lifted. "You're my princess."

"Am I really? Literally?" Marion didn't hate the idea, but a royal title sort of implied having lands to control, too, among other resources. Or else it might have meant that she was engaged to marry Konig.

"You're not literally my princess." He took her hand, lifting her knuckles to his lips. "Not yet."

The brush of his skin against hers sent chills cascading down her spine.

A path climbed the foothills on the other side of the gate, carving through the center of a pumpkin patch overlooking an archery range. Several sidhe were practicing their skills. It was weird seeing so many people wearing modern clothes, like jeans and t-shirts, but using old-style ranged weapons.

"Here we go," Konig said. "Your favorite place in the castle."

"I'm supposed to recognize this?" Marion asked.

The weight of disappointment dragged his shoulders down. "You're the one who would only date me if I gave you access to the range."

"I'll try it out." She tried to force herself to sound more positive than she felt for his sake. "I'll see if I can trigger something."

They entered a shed at the end of the range. There was an assortment of weapons inside: not just bows, but some other oddities, like glaives and clubs.

Marion didn't know the first thing about using any of them. Aside from the naiad with the coral swords, the only weapon she'd seen used was Luke's firearm. "How about a gun?" At least she knew where the trigger was on one of those.

"Firearms aren't reliable in the Middle Worlds. Our magic mucks with the mechanical parts." Konig led her to a wall hung with bows. "This is what you prefer to use."

Marion picked up a bow and warmed the stave in her hands. Once she held the bow, she knew what else she needed to do. She selected a string on instinct. The more she thought about it, the less things made sense to her; it seemed better to let her fingers find the best length of cord, and better still to loop it on one end of the bow with eyes closed.

Yes. The motions were very familiar. These were things she had once done.

"Archer," she whispered to herself.

Marion was an archer.

Joy radiated from the core of her heart to the tingling tips of her fingers, wrapped around the stave.

"Let's shoot," she said.

Konig laughed as he offered her a quiver. "Most women can't even bend one of our bows. I think you're just pretending to have lost your memory."

"I'm a very convincing actress, aren't I?"

He bent to brush his lips over her shoulder. "Very."

The bow was still far from the most familiar thing about this setting.

Hesitantly, Marion looped the fingers of her free hand through Konig's. Yes. That was very familiar. Yet it didn't stir memories the way that touching Luke Flynn did, and she was disappointed by how little she felt in the gesture.

She banished those thoughts.

The archery range was occupied by several other sidhe, including the braided guard who had met them outside the gates of Myrkheimr. "I'm Heather," she said, shaking Marion's hand. "Heather Cobweb."

Marion couldn't help but giggle. "Cobweb?"

"She's a transfer from the Summer Court," Konig said, as though it explained everything.

Heather picked up on Marion's confusion. "The Summer Court is big on traditional faerie names. Everyone chooses something Shakespearean, mythological, or a name that sounds convincingly archaic. The king and queen call themselves Oberon and Titania, and Cobweb was one of Titania's attendants in a play."

"So it isn't your real name?" Marion asked.

"I like it better than the name I was given as a human," Heather said. "That's quite the bow you're holding. Do you even know what to do with that?"

"Not a clue," Marion said with a laugh.

"I taught her personally," Konig said. "She'll be fine."

Marion peered down the range. Heather had landed a tight cluster of arrows in the bull's-eye, which had a human figure hung over a dense wall of hay.

"May I?" Marion asked.

Heather stepped aside. "By all means. I can't wait to see this."

Konig wrapped his arms around Marion to position her for the shot. The heat of his body was much more distracting than helpful, and she fell easily into the stance. Arm straight out, lifted high, aiming down her wrist.

"Don't shoot if you don't think you can do it," Heather said.

"She's fine," Konig said again.

Marion *was* fine.

She nocked an arrow and drew the fletchings smoothly to her cheek, letting all the air from her lungs. She relaxed into it.

The world narrowed to the pinpoint of the bull's-eye.

Marion released.

She didn't watch where the arrow landed. She took a second arrow from the quiver and shot it in smooth, practiced motions, following with a third just as quickly.

Her body was filled with the white light of magic.

Knowledge.

She was nourished by this—the taste of something she had been taught. Success in a skill made her muscles warm and her skin buzz. Her heart was filled with song.

It took several moments for her to realize that she heard nothing because the range was utterly silent, not because she had gone deaf.

Marion lowered the bow and looked around. Heather was staring. Konig looked smug. And everyone else had stopped shooting to watch.

"Was that okay?" she asked.

"Yes," Heather said. "It was okay."

Marion finally checked the target. All three of her white-shafted arrows were clustered at the center, even tighter than Heather's.

"I said she was fine." Konig yanked her against his chest, a hand plundering her curls, a possessive gleam in his eyes. "Aren't you?"

He kissed her with as much confidence. Giddy with victory, she bowed herself against him.

Archer.

Marion knew something new about herself. Many new things.

She also knew that she enjoyed the way that the guards were cheering—whether at her skilled shooting or the prince's kiss, she neither knew nor cared. She'd impressed them. They were accepting her presence.

Even so, kissing Konig, though a pleasant distraction, was still not nearly as much fun as shooting. "I want more arrows," Marion said as soon as they broke apart.

"You can have all the arrows you want." Konig gestured to a servant to bring her another quiver.

Marion spent an hour shooting, pleased to find that her muscles responded positively to the stimulus. It felt like she was finally, truly waking up since being found in the forest outside of Ransom Falls.

She only stopped when she realized someone was watching her who wasn't a sidhe.

Luke stood at the edge of the range, thumbs hooked in his pockets, watching her with a faint, lopsided grin.

"Did you see that?" Marion set the bow down and leaped to Luke. "I hit the bull's-eye every time!"

"I saw," he said with a laugh that was wearier than hers. He took a step back when Marion tried to jump on him. His withdrawal was a splash of cold water on her enthusiasm.

She hung her head. "Sorry. I got excited."

"No, that's great," Luke said. "Looks like you're settling in great."

"And you're not?"

He only shrugged, which was explanation enough. He was a human, mundane, and no matter how extraordinary Marion found him, he didn't belong in the surreal Middle Worlds.

"You're leaving, aren't you?" Marion asked.

"Seems you've picked up mind-reading skills along with archery."

Marion had known it was coming ever since he'd agreed to take her home. It wasn't like Luke had said he was going to stick around forever. She still struggled to hide her disappointment, swallowing it down and stashing it in a dark corner of her heart. "I'm sure that Konig will be happy to take you back if you're ready."

"I am," Luke said.

On impulse, Marion embraced him tightly. She pressed her cheek against the shoulder of his jacket to keep their skin from touching, but she dug her fingers into his back and clung to him, and she was satisfied when he held her back almost as tightly.

"I want a phone number from you," Marion said without releasing him. "I'm going to call you once things are sorted out. I'm rich and famous so

I'm going to throw you the biggest thank-you party for taking care of me."

"Ah, Marion," he sighed.

"You would hate a party, wouldn't you?"

"It's nice of you to offer."

"Maybe just dinner then," she said. "You and me, nobody else. But a *nice* dinner. None of that horrible clam chowder."

"Sure," Luke said.

She suspected he was only trying to appease her.

The cold presence of Prince Konig appeared at Marion's back. "I couldn't help but overhear that you want to go home. Ready to leave, Dr. Flynn?"

"More than ready," Luke said, releasing Marion.

"I'll take you to the nearest ley line juncture," Konig said.

Marion itched to grab Luke, or Konig—either or both. "And leave me alone?"

"Heather will stay with you," Konig said. "I'll only be a minute. Come on, Doctor." He strode up the path.

Luke didn't take a step after Konig yet, though. He was still watching Marion.

She managed to smile. She also waved.

Luke followed the prince up the hill, and, within moments, he was gone.

Guards were waiting to receive Luke at the back door of Myrkheimr, radiating with danger. They weren't armed, but that was the thing about sidhe. They didn't *need* to carry weapons in order to kill. Their magic was most potent of all the gaean species.

The glow of warmth in Konig's violet eyes had faded as soon as he'd left Marion at the range. Now he glared at Luke with open mistrust. "Make sure the doctor gets home safely," the prince said to his guards. "All the way home, far from the ley lines."

"Yeah, you never know when I might suddenly acquire the sidhe power of being able to jump ley lines," Luke said. "You'd better blindfold me and spin me in a circle three times before pushing me through, too."

"You think you're funny, don't you?"

Luke knew better than to poke at him. But there was a pretty significant difference between "knowing better" and "being capable of resisting."

"You'll have to ask Marion what she thinks of me," Luke said.

Konig went very, very still, as though he'd turned into one of the numerous portraits hanging in the halls of Myrkheimr.

"It's strange," he said. "I feel like I should recognize you. It's as though we've met before."

"I've got one of those faces. And you were in my hospital hunting down Marion. But it's probably a 'one of those faces' kind of thing."

"Hunting her down. You say that like we're

among her assassins."

Luke just looked at him. He wanted to ask, *Are you?*

Konig plucked at Luke's collar, arranging it over his shoulder. "How do I know *you're* not responsible for Marion's loss of memory? Seems weird that someone she just met—a total stranger —would go to such lengths to protect her. Weirder still that you'd go into the Middle Worlds with her."

"You've met Marion before, right?" Luke asked. "She's convincing."

"Men tend to find her incredibly charming." He bit the words out.

Luke had to laugh at the obvious jealousy. He wasn't interested in fighting over Marion or anyone else—not that Konig was likely to believe Luke if he tried to say that. "Trust me, I just want to get back to life," Luke said. "You don't have to get me away from the ley lines. I'd settle for being escorted back to my pickup. Hopefully I won't ever have to bother you again."

"Hopefully?" Konig stepped forward until his chest almost bumped Luke's.

The prince was much taller than the doctor; he had to tilt his head down to glare at Luke. But Konig wasn't as tall as Luke's brother. Luke had grown up fighting men well over six feet tall, and he wasn't intimidated by the idea of fighting another one.

Even a sidhe prince.

Especially if it turned out that Oliver

Machado's magic had, in fact, come from the Autumn Court.

"If I see you again," Konig said in a low voice, "I'll make sure that it happens when there are no witnesses. I won't let you hurt Marion." He stepped back and raised his voice. "Take him away."

The guards didn't need to manhandle Luke. He dutifully followed them toward a gazebo positioned near the edge of the property, where shimmering light indicated access to the ley lines.

One thing was obvious to Luke: Konig was not a nice person. And Luke didn't want to leave him with Marion.

"Damn," he muttered.

The urge to fight off the guards and return to Marion was disturbingly strong.

Even if the Myrkheimr was filled with assassins—of which Luke had thus far seen no sign—she would be fine without him for a short time. The Autumn Court clearly wanted Marion alive for the time being.

But if Luke found out that Konig wasn't what he seemed...well, Luke had sworn an oath when he'd become a doctor. *Do no harm* and all that.

He wasn't going to leave Marion to the wolves.

Despite worrying about Konig's men trying to ditch him in some remote wilderness, the sidhe only took Luke to his pickup in Port Angeles before vanishing.

His truck still smelled like Marion.

Twelve hours back to Ransom Falls. Twelve hours before he could talk to Charity Ballard.

Luke didn't linger.

He made a quick sweep of the hotel room to pick up his bag and a few toiletries. The autobiography that Marion had been reading was still on the coffee table. Luke reluctantly tossed it into his bag, too.

Once all signs of their all-too-brief residence of the hotel were gone, he paid the check and returned to his pickup.

It was raining. A veritable downpour.

Yet someone was standing beside his pickup, outside without shelter.

Luke stopped at the end of the parking lot. He hadn't been spotted yet because the woman was staring anxiously in the wrong direction. The yellow hair cut in sloppy, asymmetrical lines didn't ring any bells for Luke, nor did her petite figure. She didn't look like an assassin, though.

The sound of his footsteps made her turn. Once he saw her face, he realized that he had seen her before. It was the servant who had escorted Luke to his room in Myrkheimr.

"What are you doing here?" He rested a hand on his gun.

She lifted her hands toward him, palms forward, showing that she was unarmed. "I followed the Raven Knights to talk to you."

"The what?"

"ErlKonig's guards," she said.

Their name explained the feathery black armor. Luke didn't release the butt of his gun. "You went a long way for a chat."

"We couldn't speak at the Autumn Court without being overheard," she said. "I was there when Marion lost her memory. I know what happened. And I know that the Autumn Court is trying to kill her."

TWELVE

"Open your eyes, princess."

Marion let her hands fall away from her eyes.

She gasped.

Konig had fetched Marion from the range with promise of a surprise so good that she wouldn't mind having Heather Cobweb's archery lessons interrupted. Now that Marion saw where he had taken her, she had to agree. The surprise was more than worth it.

He had taken her to a bedroom furnished with many bookshelves, like the used bookstore in Oregon multiplied a hundredfold. That alone would have been enough to make her swoon. But it got better than that. The bedroom had a walk-in closet with its doors open to expose a wealth of couture: both modern clothes, similar to the outfit she'd picked out in Port Angeles, and more formal dresses that would have made her match the queen.

"Is this...?" Marion couldn't bring herself to finish.

"It's your room." Konig's hands skimmed over her shoulders. He stood behind her, radiating simultaneous cold and heat. "My parents acquiesced when we demanded that you have space within the castle, as part of your delegate position, but they wouldn't allow your rooms to be attached to mine. We had to settle for...this."

All of the clothes and books were *hers*.

"Delegate," Marion echoed. "Delegate to what faction?"

"None. As the Voice of God, you move freely among all factions. If you imagine reality as a giant multifaceted chessboard, you're a queen without a single pawn, rook, knight...or king, for the moment." He gazed closely at her face. "Are you wearing your contacts?"

"Contacts? No. I don't have contacts."

"You have spare contacts and glasses in your closet...along with a full wardrobe."

Marion's vision wasn't quite bad enough that she ran for the contact lens case, but it was a relief to hear it. The forests of the Autumn Court were too beautiful for her to suffer them being blurry. Plus, she could stop squinting at things, which must have made her look stupid.

"You should change into something else while you're putting in your eyes," Konig said. "A jewel such as yourself shouldn't be wearing such..." He plucked at the shoulder of the scrubs. "I don't have words for this."

"You have no idea how happy I am to hear you say that," Marion said. She slid into the closet, suppressing a squeal as she ran her hands over all the clothes. Many of the dresses were indeed fit for a princess. Marion gravitated toward a filmy dress with decorative gems spilling over both shoulders. The cloth would wrap around her torso to form a bodice, then drape over her hips in filmy ribbons. It was semi-transparent, sexy but modest, classy but revealing.

"You also have access to any of my stylists you might want," Konig said, hanging outside the closet.

She shot a delighted smile at him over her shoulder. "You have stylists?"

"I couldn't make official appearances without them. There'd be an uproar at the sidhe prince showing up wearing sweatpants and t-shirts."

She giggled as she pulled the bejeweled dress off of its hanger. "I'd love to see the reactions to that."

"I know you would. As I said—you're a tempest. My little force of chaos."

"I'm not sure I'll need help of a stylist today." Marion measured the dress against herself by holding it to her chest. It appeared to be a bit too large. She hadn't been eating much lately.

Konig watched her twirl with heat in his eyes. "You may want to have your hair and makeup done before dinner with the court."

Her smile slipped off of her lips. "The court? The *entire* court?"

"It won't be the first time," Konig said.

But the first time she remembered.

She tried to shake off the apprehension. "I can do my own styling for the night. How formal?"

"Formal," he said. "There will be dancing and wine. Most likely an orgy, too."

Marion laughed at his joke.

But then she realized he wasn't joking.

She stuttered. "An orgy?"

"The sidhe do much of our magic through sex," Konig said. "You've seen it before."

Marion felt queasy. "Oh. Do I...?"

"Minors aren't allowed to participate, and you haven't attended one without me since you became an adult. So no. As far as I know, you haven't joined in."

But she had seen orgies while a minor. That wasn't a comfortable line of thinking. "You've known me so long that I have to ask. Have you ever heard me talk about Seth Wilder before?"

"You've never mentioned him to me. I'd remember that. I prefer to keep men away from you, princess—far away." He said that with the faintest smile, like it should have pleased her.

That intense look did give her chills. It stirred places deep within her body, within her heart.

Marion liked Konig getting possessive of her on some level.

"Who's Seth Wilder?" he asked.

"I don't know. I woke up with his name on my

mind, so I think he could help me with my memory problem."

"I've never heard of him," Konig said. "Probably for the best. I'd hate to have to murder a man for getting too close to you when we've almost reached the summit." Marion couldn't tell if he was joking when he said that.

"I'll get dressed for the dinner orgy, then," she said. He didn't immediately move, and she ventured, "Alone."

"I've seen you naked before," Konig said with a low chuckle. "But I understand. I'll be waiting outside...*princess*."

Konig left. Marion ensured the door was shut firmly before stripping. She tossed the scrubs that Charity Ballard had given her into the trash.

If Marion had any doubts about her sexual proclivities with Konig, then searching her drawers for underwear banished them: she had lingerie. A lot of it. Some of it leather. Marion could only imagine what she might do with Konig while wearing that lingerie. Hopefully that was something that she *only* did with Konig, not the entire Autumn Court.

She seemed to have a preference for comfortable underwear when dressed normally, though. More like boy shorts and t-shirt bras.

Marion picked a comfortable pair of underwear and a strapless bra, as they were the only things that would work under a semi-transparent dress. She matched the gown with a pair of heeled shoes that stretched her legs into long, shapely lines.

She missed the scrubs a little bit. Or maybe she missed the person the scrubs reminded her of.

"Traitor," she muttered.

Marion pinned half her hair atop her head and left the other half dangling around her shoulders. The filmy dress made her look more ethereal, as though the low-cut back were making room for wings. She would also be a little too colorless to blend in among the jewel-like sidhe.

She figured out how to put the contact lenses in and only poked herself in the eyeball twice. Then she selected lipstick in matte red, a bold splash of color that offset her eyes and dark eyebrows.

Marion looked every inch the Voice of God.

Konig was waiting in her bedroom when she emerged from the closet. His eyes heated with lust when he looked Marion over. He didn't have to say a word for her to know he approved of her semi-transparent dress.

Even so, she craved the verbal validation. "What do you think?"

"Perfect," he said. "This is my princess. Not the scraggly thing that I found on a boat."

The back of her neck prickled. Oliver Machado had called her a "thing" too.

He stepped behind her so that they were reflected in the mirror together, her lips dark against her flesh, his long fingers resting on her shoulders. "What do you think you were doing at the archery range this afternoon?" Konig asked in a tone of silken danger.

Her smile faded. With the way he'd been standing against her back, she'd expected words of affection. "I don't understand."

"The way you were flirting with that doctor before he left," Konig said. "You know how bad that makes me look in front of my people?"

Marion dropped her hair and turned to face him. "It's not like that. Luke's a friend." An incredibly good-looking friend who had made it clear that his interest in her ended as soon as she'd been delivered to the Autumn Court.

"You were hitting on him," Konig said. Darkness simmered under the surface of his eyes. "Did you screw him?"

"My gods, of course not," Marion said. "He helped me. He *saved* me."

"Damn it, Marion." Konig gripped her wrists, his fingers shackling her so tightly that it ached. "Don't you have any idea how scared I was when you went missing right before the *summit*? And then to see you come back like this—with some other man—"

"But I *did* come back."

"Damn it all." He embraced her tightly, pinning her against his chest, nose buried in her hair. "What would I do without you, princess?"

"I'm not going anywhere again. I promise you that."

"It's terrifying to think of all that time you spent alone with that doctor. When he left..." Konig shook his head. "I shouldn't tell you."

Her heart froze within her chest. "What? What happened?"

"I shouldn't have said anything."

"Please, Konig." Marion licked her lips, and added, "My prince." It felt strange to say that. She didn't seem like someone who would go swooning over princes, even ones as gorgeously well formed as ErlKonig of the Autumn Court.

"Dr. Flynn asked if there was a reward for returning you." When she opened her mouth to speak, he pushed on, silencing her. "He was in it for the money. I didn't want to say anything, but... he had ulterior motives."

The confession hurt as though Konig had plunged a blade between two of her ribs.

"There's more," Konig said. "When he shot at me in Port Angeles, he was using iron bullets. Iron's the only thing that kills the sidhe. It's illegal to possess iron bullets. Where in all the Middle Worlds could a doctor get something like that?"

Now she felt really queasy. "I see. Did you give the reward to him?"

"I wanted him gone," Konig said. "And I know, as you said, that you're grateful. Yes. I gave him a reward. I gave him every ounce of gratitude that the Autumn Court has for his service, and, hopefully, he won't come back for more."

Marion's eyes were burning and her throat was thick. "Good. Thank you."

He dipped his head toward hers, brushing their lips against each other. "Anything for you, my princess." His breath was colder than the first touch of winter.

Night fell over the Autumn Court with gossamer shadow. Marion lingered in her bedroom while Konig went to the courtyard ahead of her, and she could hear music playing from her bedroom—the silken wail of stringed instruments, the primal throbbing of drums, even the faint shifting of bodies like trees in the wind. The unseelie sidhe were gathering for dinner, and she was expected to arrive as a guest of honor.

Heather Cobweb waited in the hallway, wearing a formal guard uniform with billowy pants and a snug leather bodice. Her hair was in thin braids hanging down either side of her face. A bow was slung across her back.

"You look wonderful, Heather. How do I look?" Marion asked, spreading her arms so that her body would be outlined by the shimmering fabric.

"Excellent," Heather said. It sounded more like an automatic response than a studied one, as though she wouldn't have dared to answer in any other way.

She escorted Marion to the courtyard. They emerged at the top of a grand staircase. When Marion took the top step and looked over the party, a hush fell over the crowd. They turned judging eyes upon her in a thousand different gem colors.

Konig was amongst them. His coppery skin glimmered as he strode through the crowd to meet her at the bottom of the stairs.

"You look perfect," he said, brushing his lips over her knuckles. There was no sign of the anger he'd shared with her in private. Now Konig was all smooth, sunny charm again.

He escorted her to the far end of the courtyard, where a table had been raised above all others. Two of the chairs were sprawling affairs of gold, brass, and vines. The king and queen waited there. They smiled to see Marion.

This was where she belonged. She should have been happy.

Konig was seated beside his mother, and Marion to the left of him. That put her just as high as royalty—higher than the rest of the court. The sidhe sitting at all the other tables in the hall didn't look thrilled.

"Do you guys have dinner like this very often?" Marion whispered.

He laughed at her incredulity. "On most nights."

Her jaw dropped. The food that servants were bringing out on platters was the stuff of legend. Entire pigs, stews and fine cheese, sliced fruit drenched in molasses and honey.

And they did that on "most" nights.

"How do you get anything done?" Marion asked.

"We're sidhe," Konig said. "This *is* what we do."

A servant offered to fill Marion's goblet with

wine. She put her hand over the glass. "No thank you."

"No wine? For my princess? I don't think so." He gestured, indicating that the servant should fill it, which she did. The wine was an aromatic red that filled Marion's nose with a pleasantly spicy scent. "Try it. It's your favorite."

Marion lifted the glass by the fragile neck. "I don't think I want to drink." But she did inhale the scent deeply, and that was nearly enough to render her drunk on the spot.

"A toast," Konig murmured. "To celebrate my princess coming back to me."

She couldn't refuse him that. Not when she'd already put him through so much. And she didn't want to incite another angry outburst like the one in her bedroom.

They clinked their goblets together, and Marion sipped while Konig watched.

The wine was somehow even stronger than she expected. It was fantastic. She wasn't sure she'd describe it as a "favorite" though. Her mind drifted back to the Long Island Iced Teas at the Salty Barnacle, and the drippy clam chowder.

The orchestra played through dinner as everyone ate. Marion watched more than she talked. Konig was engaging his father in a lively conversation about a band called Black Death, so it freed her to allow her attention to wander.

Most of the sidhe didn't eat with utensils. They used their fingers. It didn't look like a barbaric thing, though; it was more sensual, as though they wanted to feel the food with their fingertips before consuming it. They often didn't feed themselves, either. They were feeding each other, leaning across the tables so that the breasts of the female sidhe swung beneath them and plastering their bodies against those of their companions.

At one of the nearer tables, a masked woman was straddling the lap of a female companion, sliding grapes into her mouth one at a time. She noticed Marion watching and smiled shamelessly.

Marion smiled back, somewhat more hesitantly.

"I could have them brought to you," Konig said. "The women you're watching. We could invite them to our room later." His breath smelled of wine. His cool hands guided Marion's goblet back to her mouth, encouraging her to take another sip.

Her head buzzed with warmth. "I thought you liked to keep me to yourself."

"With men," he said.

Marion took a longer drink of the wine. The burn was enough to make her start coughing. "No, thank you."

"You might change your mind. Once dinner finishes, the next phase of the night will begin."

Marion knew that he meant the aforementioned orgy because this feast was obviously foreplay. The way that the sidhe licked one another's fingers was so blatantly sexual that she was uncomfortable watching it.

She'd have been lying if she said she wasn't enjoying herself, though. She didn't want to join the sidhe in their sexual play, but it was just so *colorful*. There were so many different colors of hair and skin and eyes, so many bodies in different shapes and sizes, and they created fireworks of magic where they contacted. Minds opened as legs and lips spread, allowing Marion to peer into the briefest glimpses of their thoughts.

Marion drifted through their fantasies of food, sex, and music, like trailing her fingers through drapery while passing a window.

Half of her wine was gone. Had she drunk all of that?

Violet leaned around Konig to speak to Marion. "How did things go exploring the castle grounds earlier today?"

"It went well," Marion said, swirling the remaining wine in her goblet. The crimson fluid clung to the sides of the crystal. "I got into archery again. I have the muscle memory for it."

"She's as good as ever," Konig said. "She puts many of my guards to shame."

Violet's eyes creased at the corners when she smiled, much the same way that Konig's did. "What of your actual memories?"

"Little progress," Marion said. None since Luke had left her.

"Too bad," Violet said. "I haven't been able to reach the Hardwicks over the listing on the darknet, either. I've sent one of my girls into the Winter Court to see if we can find them like that. Hopefully—"

Dismayed shouts from the crowd cut her off.

Marion followed the gazes of the crowd up to the sky. The velvety black was interrupted by a shocking lance of white.

"A ley line is open," Konig said, shooting to his feet. "Mother—"

"Wait." Violet grabbed his arm. "I recognize them."

Much to Marion's surprise, she did too. She had seen them on the news at the Salty Barnacle.

Three people descended from the ley line. They were statuesque figures framed by wings that looked like they should have been on glossy, oversized hawks. Each wing was twice as tall as the bearer, which made for impressive wingspans. Not faerie wings, but feathered wings.

Angels.

The trio descended, dragging wisps of the ley lines behind them. They landed lightly on the carpet of dried leaves and their wings vanished, leaving only hints of glitter and a few downy feathers at their feet. They didn't have the flaming swords that Marion had seen on the news, but they were every inch as intimidating without them.

Rage suited his name for the first time. He shivered with carefully withheld fury that showed in the weft and warp of reality haloed around him. "Raven Knights," he said softly, dangerously.

Motion stirred around the edges of the courtyard as the royal guard rallied. Heather was positioned on the second level, her bow aimed at the angels. A few feet down, there was another guard, and then another beyond that. At a quick count, Marion saw at least a dozen deadly sidhe guards waiting for a sign from Rage.

The angels must have realized they were surrounded, but they looked terribly calm.

Marion drank in the sight of them—the first of her species she'd seen in person. Where sidhe were things of the Earth and elements, angels were alien, alabaster perfection. They might have passed as any mundane person on the street of Ransom Falls if not for the sculpted lines of their faces.

"What do you want?" Rage asked. Marion caught the edge of his thoughts. He knew these angels, and he was furious to see them.

"We caught rumors on the wind and wanted to see if they were true," said the central angel. "Is this how you welcome us to your court?"

Violet gathered her ruffled skirts and descended into the crowd. "Welcome to Myrkheimr." She kissed each angel on the cheek. When the sidhe queen got that close to the angels, the Autumn Court warped around her. The trees died, regrew, lost their leaves. The sky turned black. Marion swayed on her feet, pressing a hand to her temple.

When she blinked, everything was back to normal.

"We came as quickly as we could when we heard." That came from a tiny angel with Japanese features and a flat Californian accent. She must have been a good foot shorter than Marion. She seemed weirdly short for an angel.

"That's Suzume, a friend of the sidhe. It's a good sign that she's here," Konig whispered into Marion's ear. He pointed to the auburn-haired angel at the center. "Leliel, the leader from the Ethereal Levant." And then he pointed to the third. "Jibril, a messenger. Sort of a delegate, like you."

"Join us for dinner?" Violet asked, sweeping a hand toward the table.

In a flurry of motion, servants brought three more chairs up.

The music resumed, followed by an audible sigh of relief from the court.

Suzume settled into the chair that had been placed in front of Marion. The angel was dressed in a fashion that was almost masculine, with slacks, loafers, and minimal makeup.

"I knew the rumors weren't true," Suzume said. "There's no way someone like *you* would go missing, Marion. You're way too obnoxious for that." She lifted her goblet. "Hey! I don't have wine!" A servant materialized to serve her. She swigged the entire thing in a moment, then lifted the goblet for a refill. "Who kidnapped you? Get chatting. I want all the juicy gossip."

Konig wrapped an arm around her shoulders, pulling her against his body. "You can see with your own eyes that our girl hasn't gone anywhere."

Leliel settled beside Suzume. "We've also heard tales of repeated attacks on your life." Her pale eyes glimmered with unidentifiable emotion. "If you're experiencing trouble, you should be protected in the Ethereal Levant. It's what her father would have wanted."

Marion's heart skipped a beat. "You knew my father?"

Leliel turned her cool eyes on Marion. "Unfortunately."

"You're wasting your time if you came here to retrieve Marion," Violet said. "We're protecting her until her memory returns."

The angels all turned to stare at Marion simultaneously. Her cheeks lit with flame.

Until her memory returns.

She hadn't planned on telling the angels that it was gone in the first place.

Suzume laughed and took a big drink of wine. "No memory. Funny! Someone casting a memory spell on Marion Kavanagh, of all people."

"Not a memory spell," Violet corrected. "I didn't see anything like that in her head and would have easily dismantled it if I had. No—whatever has happened is more severe than that. She's been practically lobotomized. Look at her. She's a shell of her former self." Violet's wave toward Marion was painfully dismissive.

"No memory," Leliel murmured, turning a piercing look on Marion. Invisible fingers probed her mind. She didn't realize what was happening until it was over.

Leliel had invited herself to crawl inside Marion's skull and search for the memories.

"*Excuse* me!" Marion said.

"Actually, we've come here for another reason," Leliel said with a smile. In an instant, her tone went from remote to charming. "Yes, we hoped to find you here, daughter of Metaraon. We need someone to act as the speaker of the ethereal delegation at the summit, and we thought you'd serve that role well."

Suzume set her goblet down a little too hard. "We do?"

"Our plea would be taken better from someone with as much prestige as Metaraon's daughter," Leliel said.

"Strange timing to make that offer, don't you think?" Jibril asked, picking at a bowl of figs with distaste. He was disgusted by the lack of utensils and general hygiene at the sidhe dinner. "We've just learned that Ms. Garin is in the midst of some trouble."

"All the better to offer our help, in exchange for her to help us."

Konig leaned his chin on a fist. Excitement sparked in his eyes. "I like the sound of this. Go on."

"The speaker for the ethereal delegation will sit down with the speakers for the other factions at the United Nations," Leliel said. "If you joined us, then it would place you at the head of negotiations. You're a fierce negotiator."

"I am?" Marion asked, and then she coughed. "I mean, *yes*, I am."

Leliel smiled pleasantly, as though she'd missed Marion's faltering. "I'm currently planning to act as speaker, but I'm not very popular among the other factions. You would be able to get what we want. The angels have been unfairly confined to the Ethereal Levant—a region on Earth, not even an entire plane. We would be happier and safer in the Winter Court."

Marion frowned. "Why are you unsafe in the Levant?"

"We're constantly under infernal assault," Suzume said with a snort. "Spoiled demons have all the Nether Worlds and *still* can't leave us alone."

"We spend so much time defending our walls against them that we don't have time to focus on the other crises our race faces, such as repopulation," Leliel said. "We would be safe in the Winter Court. We could thrive."

"And what do I get if I act as your speaker?" Marion asked.

"Attention. Prestige. We'll also assign bodyguards to protect you from attack," Leliel said. That wasn't much of a promise, since the bounty said she needed to be dead by the summit. It was less than two days away. They wouldn't have to commit resources to her for long.

Then again, how difficult could it be to stand up for the angels' cause at a couple of meetings?

Leliel twisted a delicate silver bracelet off her wrist. "This cuff has been enchanted for honesty. Each faction's speaker has one like it. It's a powerful thing, this artifact. It doesn't merely prevent lying—it compels truth."

"There's a difference?" Marion asked.

"You should know," Konig said. "You made them."

Excitement thrilled through Marion as she looked at the bracelet with new eyes, trying to see the spells woven into the metal. "That's my work?"

Leliel offered the bracelet to Marion. "Be our speaker. Help us get a home."

Gods, but Marion wanted to take it.

"I'm the speaker for the Autumn Court, you know," Konig said. "You made me one of those cuffs in gold."

"That must look good against your skin," Marion said.

"Of course it does." He trailed his fingers atop her knuckles. "Imagine. Two factions in alliance."

"Maybe something would get done for once," Violet said with a chiming laugh. She stood and reached for her husband. "I want to dance. Dance with me, Rage."

He rose from his seat, looking at Violet in a way that reminded Marion very much of Konig looking at her. Like she was the only thing in the world.

The leather trousers encasing Rage's hips creaked as Violet guided him to the center of the courtyard. The tables were being pushed aside to clear room for dancing...as well as other things.

The orgy had begun while Marion was talking with the angels. The sidhe were stripping to allow their magic to emanate from their flesh in radiating lines of sensuality. They were kissing, bowing against fainting couches, allowing their legs and fingers to tangle together.

She had no interest in joining, but part of her brain watched with detached interest. Analyzing the way that they interacted. The collision of bodies sparked into magic that had cables reaching far beyond the Middle Worlds. Their minds were brilliant fireworks among the seamy night.

Soft fingers touched Marion's jaw. "What are you thinking?" Konig asked.

She forced herself to focus on him, but it didn't help all that much. He was as much a nexus for magic as the rest of the court who were sliding into sexual satisfaction. The sight of his coppery skin and symmetrical features tugged at some deep place within Marion.

"Nothing important." She finished her goblet of wine. She thought that she had drunk it down to the dregs, but her goblet was brimming, and she drank it all down. Spicy warmth settled into her marrow.

"We need the Winter Court." It was Leliel speaking now. Her bright eyes were intense on Marion's, and it was very much like looking into a mirror though their bodies were superficially dissimilar. "The angels need a refuge."

Marion's mouth moved, alcohol slurring her words. "I understand. I'll help."

And Konig said, "Of course you will. Dance with me, princess."

He took her hand, whirling her away from the table.

Marion didn't feel it when she stepped down from the raised dais onto the floor. Sidhe writhed, dancing with their graceful arms raised, heads thrown back in ecstasy. They touched each other. Kissed each other.

And she joined them. She touched and kissed Konig, her boyfriend, her prince.

The invading angels watched. They judged her.

Marion absorbed this knowledge with pride. They wanted her to be their speaker—a representative of all other angels, though she was only half-blood, as much gaean as ethereal.

It didn't matter if they judged her as long as they acknowledged her power.

THIRTEEN

It was late afternoon in Ransom Falls, and Nurse Charity Ballard was looking for an excuse to avoid working on an avalanche of paperwork, as usual. Charity brightened when a priest approached her station. Talking to an exorcist was the perfect diversion from bureaucracy. "What's the verdict, Father?"

"That patient isn't dealing with demonic possession." Witold Rolfe flipped his necktie over his shoulder before bending over the forms that she handed him. "I can't tell you more than that. My best guess is that you should order more Retrolycathol, though."

"Thank you, Father. I've already made the order, but the OPA says they're running low on supplies. I don't know if or when we'll get another shipment."

He signed off on the waiver. "Then my second-best guess is that you should get in touch with the sanctuary and tell them they'll have another shifter in six moons." The Office of Preternatural Affairs pin on his lapel caught the light, glinting in her eyes almost mockingly.

"I guess so." Charity wasn't looking forward to the additional paperwork required to refer patients to the sanctuary. She already had far too much.

Father Rolfe handed the completed waiver to her and checked his watch. "Hmm. Not really enough time for me to get down to Lake Wildwood at this point."

"More patients to evaluate for demonic possession?"

"More than I've ever seen in one year this week alone," Father Rolfe said.

Charity clutched the waiver. "That must be a bad sign."

"Agents of chaos aren't great at keeping regular schedules. I bet after this, I'll see no demonic possessions for a month." He leaned an elbow on the counter in front of the nurse's station, tracing the fake marble lines printed across the plywood. "Are you off shift soon?"

She blinked, surprised. "No, I'm pulling double shifts right now. We're understaffed." That was unlikely to change any time soon, since both Luke and Oliver had vanished. "Why? Do you need help with something?"

Father Rolfe chuckled. "Not exactly. I thought

you might be able to show me somewhere good to get dinner in a terrible little town like this one."

Oh. He's hitting on me.

Charity surveyed Father Rolfe with fresh eyes. He was one of the younger priests who worked for the OPA, ordained as part of their program to expand the reach of exorcists nationwide. At another time, she might have found the brush of dark-blond hair over his round face appealing, especially since she found chubby guys sexy. But Charity liked Ransom Falls even more, so his insults were deeply unattractive in a way that his cleft chin was not.

In any case, Charity would never date a man who worked for the Office of Preternatural Affairs.

She wasn't going anywhere as long as she was dragging Ollie Machado's spellbook around with her, either.

Charity eyed the duffel bag under her desk. It was the result of ransacking Ollie Machado's house—every occult item she'd been able to find in his house, including a spellbook. She hadn't even known the guy was a witch.

Now she was carrying stuff stolen from a coworker's house around, too paranoid to let it out of her sight until Luke retrieved it.

Father Rolfe leaned forward, as if to see what had Charity's attention. She nudged the duffel bag under the desk with her toe. "I won't be able to take you out, Father. I have too much work."

"Raincheck," he said.

Not a chance. "We'll see. Drive safely."

"G'night, Nurse Ballard." He donned his trilby and headed down the hall, glancing one more time at the nurses station. Specifically, at the bottom of it, on the other side of which was the duffel bag. It was like he could feel the magic in there.

Father Rolfe, like many exorcists who worked for the OPA, was probably a magic user. Charity wasn't. All the stuff she'd grabbed from Ollie's house felt like paperweights to her. Creepy paperweights, though. Like made of animal bones and stuff.

Charity stifled a yawn. It was only six o'clock at night, but she'd been working since three in the morning, and she wasn't going home until nine. She needed coffee, and there was already a pot waiting in the break room. She took her glasses off, stuffed them into the collar of her scrubs, and poured a big cup for herself.

By the time she returned to the nurses station, someone else was standing there.

Oliver Machado was on the other side of the counter.

Her heart skittered in her chest. "Ollie." Charity swallowed hard. "Hey! Where have you been?"

"Around." There were bags under his eyes even though he wasn't the one who'd been working double shifts to make up for the disappearances of his coworkers.

"You missed two of your scheduled shifts. I've been worried about you." When she walked up to the counter, she casually kicked the duffel bag further under her chair. It didn't budge. There was nowhere left to go.

"I had an issue with Luke," Oliver said. "I don't suppose you've heard from him lately?"

She nearly choked on her coffee. "Nope. I haven't." It wasn't a lie. She'd only heard from that friend of his, Brianna.

"Hmm." Oliver was looking at her a little too hard. Charity occupied herself by scooping some papers together, stuffing them onto her clipboard. He must have been able to hear her heart, it was pounding so hard.

She'd stolen his stuff. He was going to know. And Ollie had always weirded her out. It was nice having a big, intimidating guy like him around for the difficult patients, or the preternatural ones, but she tried to avoid being alone with him at the best of times.

Alone with him while hiding a bag of his stolen belongings was *not* the best of times.

"Grab your coat, Charity," Oliver said. "We're going for a drive."

She laughed nervously, sliding the thick-framed glasses up the bridge of her nose again. "I can't go anywhere. I'm dealing with far too much at the hospital right now."

He leaned on the counter. The posture was casual, but his tone was not. "You won't be able to deal with one gods-damned thing at the hospital if you're dead. I said we're going for a drive."

"Oh my gods," she said.

He did know.

"Come on," Oliver said, and his tone left no room for refusal.

Her whole body shook as she retrieved her jacket from the break room. She thought momentarily about running, but he was right behind her—holding the duffel bag.

He shoved it into her arms. "Let's go, Charity. We're going to see Dr. Flynn."

There were multiple advantages to running across the informant in Port Angeles. The first, of course, was the information possessed by the servant who identified herself as Nori. The second was her ability to leap through ley lines, dragging Luke and his pickup to Ransom Falls without breaking a sweat. A twelve-hour drive was reduced to the twelve minutes it took to traverse the space between the ley line juncture to Mercy Hospital.

He parked outside the back of the hospital. He kept an eye on the surrounding trees as the sun drooped toward the horizon, watching for the telltale distortion of a sidhe's presence.

"Marion isn't popular among the court," explained Nori, sitting beside Luke on the pickup's rear bumper. "Nobody trusts her, and it's not just because she's an angel. She's disrespectful to the king and queen and everyone else she meets."

Luke had a hard time imagining sweet Marion, who had walked Elena Eiderman into death, being that kind of polarizing figure. "But she's dating the prince."

"Her unpopularity appeals to ErlKonig. You know how rebellious teenagers are, and a prince is no different. With a teenager in line for the throne, you end up with a boy who wants to rebel against the entirety of his people. It pleases him to defy us."

"How would you know that?" Luke asked. "Are you close to Konig?"

"Close, as in physical proximity. He doesn't pay much attention to his servants." Nori wrung the hem of her shirt in both hands. "Marion does. She pays attention to everyone. She noticed me listening in on private conversations."

"Did she punish you for eavesdropping?" That sort of behavior didn't suit the Marion that Luke knew, but the Marion that Luke knew was also a woman who had only existed for a couple of days.

"The opposite. She recognized what I was, and she wanted me to report everything I heard to her."

Luke studied her. "What are you? A spy?"

"Among other things." She pulled a plastic case out of her back pocket. He didn't understand what it was until she screwed the top off and he saw the clear fluid inside. Then she tipped her head back, removed purple contacts, and dropped them into the case. When she blinked at him again with watery eyes, he realized that her eyes were a pale, shocking shade of blue.

"You're an angel," he said. "An angel acting as a servant in the Autumn Court."

"I'm Gray. I was fathered by Azazel before he got murdered in the New Eden Massacre. I never knew him, but I took a pilgrimage to the Ethereal Levant once I turned thirteen, and the angels accepted me."

"They decided to use you to spy on the sidhe."

"No, no. I'm just a delegate. The king and queen know what I am. We only keep it secret so that it doesn't freak out the rest of the court. But Marion—she saw me, and she instantly knew that I was like her." Nori smiled weakly. "In fact, we're first cousins. When Marion asked me to report to her on the court's secret meetings...it was an easy decision."

"So you *are* a spy," Luke said. "Just a spy for Marion."

"It casts me in a bad light," Nori admitted.

"You could say that." The sidhe were old-fashioned in their punitive ways. The Middle Worlds existed outside the mortal justice system. He'd heard that pissing off sidhe royalty could get favored limbs chopped off—or worse. Nori was talking treason.

Luke searched Nori's pixie-like features for any sign of relation to Marion and found none. They were cousins only because all pureblooded, first generation angels had been born from Eve. Marion and Nori's superficial similarities began and ended with the fact they were blue-eyed females.

"Anyway, Marion wanted to know what the king and queen have been doing, so I told her that they're planning war. I've cleaned the insides of their private quarters. I've seen their maps, their coded letters. They're rallying an army."

That didn't sound like the court that Luke had visited any more than this coercive Marion sounded like the woman he knew. Myrkheimr hadn't looked like a castle preparing for war.

"I knew I had to tell Marion about the maps once I saw them." Nori only seemed to be getting more nervous as the conversation continued. She kept glancing over her shoulder, up at the clouds, out at the trees that lined either side of the road. "I asked her to meet with me at Original Sin so we could discuss it, but our meeting somehow leaked and assassins set a trap. A werewolf and a demon."

Now Nori had his attention. "They're the ones who took her memory?"

She shook her head. "Marion dispatched them and told me to run. I shouldn't have run—but I did. Before I got out of earshot, I heard her talking to someone other than the assassins. She said, '*Mon dieu. Qu'est-ce que toi, tu fais ici?*'" If the blue eyes hadn't convinced Luke of Nori's angel blood, the smooth transition between languages would have. Angels were masters of language. "Essentially, it means 'My God, what are you doing here?' The tone is sort of rude or incredulous."

Whoever had jumped in on the assassins trying to trap Marion was someone that she'd known. Someone she was, presumably, very familiar with.

Someone like Konig?

"Interesting," Luke said.

"When I ran, Marion was holding down the werewolf assassin. He might have seen her attacker. He could have more information." Nori took a crumpled piece of paper from her pocket. "I drew the assassins in case you'd like to be able to find them."

Luke smoothed the paper out on his thigh. Nori's inherited ethereal talents clearly didn't include drawing. But the assassins had a few distinguishing features, even in the horrible illustrations. For one, the werewolf had a twisted nose and unusually squinty eyes. The other assassin was clearly a megaira, a demon who fed off of mortal aggression.

How many werewolves would be working with something as rare as a megaira?

"Why didn't you take this to Marion?" Luke asked, tucking the drawing into his jacket.

"I hadn't seen her since running from Original Sin, and she's not all there anymore. She looks different now."

"Different how?"

"It's her attitude. She's more casual with Konig than she was before. Their relationship has always been tumultuous—they all but shake the castle down when they argue. When I saw them at the archery range today, it was the sweetest they've ever been with each other, at least where I can see. And I see a lot."

Luke was feeling worse and worse about leaving Marion behind with Konig.

"I didn't know what Marion would do with that information now. She's clearly a few pages short of a novel," Nori said. "But you—I'm sure you could make use of it."

"Why me?"

"Because you're *you*," she said. "Your power is incredible."

"I'm not following," Luke said.

She started to respond, but he lifted a hand to cut her off.

There was movement at the back door from the hospital.

Charity Ballard emerged with a duffel bag slung over her shoulder. It must have been the evidence that Luke had requested from Oliver Machado's home. Luke hopped off of the pickup to meet her.

Then Oliver Machado himself emerged from behind Charity, and Luke froze.

"Shit," he said, drawing his gun.

Ollie pushed Charity into a sedan. He glanced around furtively before getting in the driver's seat, and then pulled away.

"Nori—get in the pickup," Luke said. "Now."

Oliver was in a low-slung sedan, the kind that might have had hydraulic suspension and disco lights on the inside, and Luke was in a lifted pickup. Chasing the nurse through the forest should have given Luke a major advantage. Luke kept waiting for Oliver to high center so he could come up on his ass and save Charity, but Oliver seemed to have preternatural driving skills in addition to sidhe magic.

Nori had gone colorless, gripping the dashboard with both hands. Tearing around the forest off-road tossed her around the cab. "Who are we chasing?"

"Oliver Machado," Luke said. "Name ring a bell?" Nori shook her head mutely. It looked like she might get carsick. "I caught him using unseelie magic."

"He's not sidhe," Nori said.

"No. Gaean." Luke wrenched the wheel ninety degrees, launching them over a bump. They caught air. Slammed into the soil. "Does the court have affiliations with any covens on Earth?"

"I don't know, I've only been embedded in the court to facilitate inter-faction communications, and—good *gods* can you *please* slow down?"

Not until he got Charity.

It was Luke's fault that she was in that other car, getting tossed around like Nori was. Except that Oliver was a hell of a lot likelier to hurt his passenger, and he'd do it deliberately.

Brake lights flashed on the rear of the sedan. Luke slammed his foot on his brakes. The pickup bucked.

Bumpers kissed—just enough to shove Ollie's car a couple inches.

They came to a stop in the deep forest on the

edge of a grassy clearing. It was unremarkable. Worse than that, it was remote. Somewhere they wouldn't have to deal with witnesses.

Oliver emerged with his arm hooked around Charity's throat, dragging her kicking legs through the driver's side door. The pickup's headlights cast bright circles on them from the hips down.

Luke jumped out. He aimed his gun at Oliver, just over the edge of the headlights—right about where his heart would have been. "Let her go!"

Oliver pressed a gun to Charity's temple. Poor Charity Ballard was shaking more than a Chihuahua abandoned in a hurricane. "Throw the duffel bag at him, Charity," Oliver said. She tossed the bag to Luke's feet. Strong arm, good aim. "Go ahead, doc. Look inside."

Luke's gun didn't waver. "What do you think you're doing, man? Why'd you bring us out here?"

"The circle," Oliver said. "Look at the circle." He jerked his head back, toward the other end of the clearing.

For the first time, Luke looked beyond the nurses.

Between sunset and the blanket of gray clouds, the clearing was dark enough that the grass was a murky gray blob beyond Oliver's feet. Luke could only see within narrow half-circles of lights on either side of Ollie's shadow.

There was a circle burned into the grass, sort of like a crop circle. Rain and time had faded it.

Luke still recognized a circle of power.

"This is where I found her—that angel kid,"

Oliver said. "Do you recognize the marks?"

Luke didn't. They weren't like the runes he'd seen at Myrkheimr or in Ollie's spell pages. "Get away from Charity right now. Slow movements. Don't make me shoot."

"Come on, doc," Ollie said. "Don't be like this. Just...do what you've gotta do. You *know* you have to."

He legitimately had no idea what Ollie was talking about.

Maybe the nurse didn't know who Luke was after all.

That was a problem. It meant that Luke couldn't give the crazy bastard what he wanted, and Charity looked like she was about to faint from the nerves. If she dropped, Luke couldn't trust that Ollie's trigger finger wouldn't twitch.

"I'm going to count to five," Luke said. "One. Two—"

Ollie screamed. Blood sprayed.

The movements happened so fast that Luke thought, at first, that Ollie had shot Charity. But there was too much blood for that—fountains of dark arterial blood. The scent of it was overpowering, and it sprayed so wide that it splashed on his shoes.

Luke jerked back, eyes widening, nostrils flaring.

The blood wasn't Charity's.

Oliver collapsed, and Charity rode him down, fingers gripping his shirt and knees on either side of his hips. He fired his gun into the air. He didn't hit her.

Only then did Luke realize that Charity was ripping his throat open.

He was numb, motionless, as she sank her teeth into the meat of his neck and snapped her head back, ripping the esophagus free. Another spray of blood. Another scream. This one gurgled in the shredded remnants of Ollie's throat.

Charity didn't seem to appreciate the sound. She smashed her hand into his face, collapsing his cheekbones. And then she smashed again, wrenched the bottom of his skull off. His shrieks grew louder.

She bit down on the meat of his tongue and scraped it out of his jaw with her teeth.

His eyes rolled under all the blood. His chest hitched.

Luke could only stare as she picked the shreds of tongue muscle free, swallowing them down with greedy slurps. He knew he should have been shooting at someone—something. But he was transfixed by the blood. The screaming.

Charity dug her fingernails into Oliver's neck and with a single, swift motion, decapitated him. She lifted his severed skull above her head. A few vertebrae from his spine dangled, framed by strings of tendon. She dribbled the remaining blood into her mouth.

It dwindled to drops. She tossed his head aside.

Charity straightened from his body, licking her hands clean.

Luke wondered if it was finally time to shoot

her.

"Sorry," Charity said. It seemed as if bathing in Oliver's blood had relaxed her more than a chair massage, like the kind that local therapists occasionally donated to hospital employees. She swiped her wrist over her face, smeared the blood away from her eyes, and heaved a sigh. "I got tired of having the gun to my head."

Luke stared, unable to speak.

Nori covered her mouth with both hands and screamed.

Charity Ballard's second shocking maneuver of the night was to strip naked where she stood, right there in the middle of the clearing, about two feet away from the remains of Oliver Machado. She was muscular under her scrubs. Luke had never noticed that before. He'd always thought of her as mousy, hiding behind those big glasses and thick hair.

Turned out the mouse was actually a lion.

"Revenant." She toweled the blood off of her bare body. "I'm a revenant."

"That's a kind of vampire, isn't it?" Luke asked. Of all the gaean species, he had the least exposure to vampires and their various subspecies.

"Closely related, like a cousin." She rubbed the towel under her breasts, jiggling them with the motion.

Luke politely didn't look. "I can't believe a revenant got through hospital background checks," he said to the cloudy sky.

"I don't drink blood. Self-control like a monk at a strip show." Charity propped one leg up on the tailgate of Luke's pickup and wiped blood off of her inner thigh. "And the OPA doesn't know I exist, since I never registered for benefits, so..."

"There was nothing to show up on a background check."

"I graduated from nursing school before Genesis. When I came back like this, I didn't want to have to change careers, so I've just abstained. It sucks, but you do what you gotta do." Everything about Charity was different now that she'd guzzled Oliver's blood. Her voice was deeper and more silken, her skin glowing, her hair smoother. "You know what that's like, the blood abstinence thing."

Luke couldn't help but glance at her. She hadn't gotten the blood off of her thighs so much as smeared it around. "Excuse me?"

She tossed the wrecked towel into the back of his pickup. "I've seen how you stare when we're doing transfusions, so I thought you were like me." She lifted her hands defensively. "Not judging. I stare too."

He gave a hollow laugh. "It's not because I'm a vampire. I just don't like blood."

"It seems like you're not alone." She waved at Nori, who was curled into a shivering ball near the front of the pickup. "Sorry!"

Luke pulled a spare set of his clothes out of the

pickup and handed them to Charity without looking. "I never should have called in that tip," she said. "I'm sorry. I'm so sorry. I thought I was protecting you."

"What tip?" Luke asked, keeping his eyes fixed on the sky.

"About your patient," Charity said. "Marion? I saw an ad in the white pages with her picture. People were looking for her, and I thought..." She trailed off. "Anyway, Ollie showed the ad to me. I didn't think about it much. I just called."

That explained how the assassins—and Konig—had known to look for Marion in Ransom Falls. It had been Oliver and Charity. At least Charity looked like she felt bad about it, and Oliver had already gotten what was coming to him.

"You can turn around. I'm done dressing. But I'll need a shower to get this out." Charity plucked at her sticky hair and giggled nervously. "I can't believe I did that."

"I can't believe you did either." It was hard to pretend to be upset over it, though. Luke only felt a strange hollowness—the sensation of the universe shifting again, though in a less pleasant way than when he touched Marion. "I didn't get any answers before you killed him."

Charity toed the duffel bag. "There are all the answers you requested, assuming that the Brianna who called me really is your friend."

"She is." He kneeled and unzipped the bag.

The nurse had scooped a lot from Ollie's house before eating his tongue like a mussel. The bag was stuffed with his laptop, trinkets from an altar, and a bong, which she must have mistaken for an occult item. She'd even grabbed the burned remnants of the pages left from the teleportation.

And, of course, the spellbook.

Luke carefully extracted it. He was surprised to see that the cover was heavy wood bound in leather. The inside was more typical of post-Genesis witches: cheap paper with notes printed by an inkjet. The cover was a hand-me-down from some kind of multigenerational coven. The rest was hacked together from the darknet.

He cradled the heavy text in the crook of his arm as he wandered over to the circle of power. He sidestepped Oliver Machado's remains. Not out of respect, but because he didn't want to track blood around the clearing.

"You're not scared of me," Charity said from behind him.

He glanced back at her. "Huh?"

She pulled her hair back with a rubber band. Once the bloody strands were hidden, and with her body concealed by Luke's baggy clothing, she looked like herself again. Just a nurse on her day off. "You just saw me slaughter a guy, but you're not acting scared of me at all."

"I always handle the preternaturals at the hospital." Luke shrugged. "Werewolves could do to me what you did to him."

Charity smiled shyly and jammed the thick-framed glasses onto her face. "Werewolves are a lot more common than revenants."

"I've worked with you for years."

"So did Ollie."

"Are you trying to convince me to be afraid of you, Charity?"

Insecurity seeped into her eyes, edging out the calm confidence that had suffused her upon Ollie's death. "I just don't understand it."

"Don't bother trying." Luke had almost married a werewolf who had murdered a half-dozen people while suffering from silver poisoning. A revenant was nothing after that.

Flipping through the pages of the spellbook, he searched for any hints that Oliver might have designed the circle of power in the clearing. Its markings were bizarre, so they must have been crafted by an insanely powerful witch. Someone with access to arcane magic, or someone who had invented them from scratch.

If Oliver had made the circle, then there might have been notes on the ritual that had taken away Marion's memory, too.

A couple of photographs fell out of the middle pages. They were actual physical pictures, taken on film. It was common for witches to use physical media instead of digital. Mechanical means of taking pictures would often succeed when everything else failed because of magic.

The pictures were blurry, but Luke could make out the images. Two of them showed the circle of power from different angles, when it had been freshly burned into the grass.

The other photos were of Marion. "Jesus,"

Luke muttered, lingering over the pictures.

Ollie had found her standing in the middle of the circle, head hanging, eyes shut. She looked like she'd been asleep standing up. He'd been able to take pictures from multiple angles without Marion moving an inch.

He ran his thumb along the edge of one of the pictures, studying Marion's restful face. She didn't look distressed in the wake of her memory wipe. Her cheeks were flushed with color, her hair bouncy as though it had been freshly curled.

The nurse had written notes on the backs of the photos—dates, times, the GPS coordinates.

And also a name.

Seth Wilder.

"Hey Nori," Luke called. "Come over here." The half-angel gave Charity a wide berth when she obeyed. He showed her the photos of the fresh circle. "Are these marks sidhe magic?"

Nori shook her head. "Those aren't, but this is." She pointed at the page of the book he was opened to. "Can I look?"

"Be my guest." He stuck the pictures of Marion inside his jacket. They felt too intimate to share with anyone.

She flipped through the book. "Yes. All of this spellwork is sidhe in origin."

"But not the circle," Luke said.

She shook her head again and kept skimming the pages. "Now this one here... This is the work of the Autumn Court. It's privileged information that they keep in the library."

"You've been in the library?"

"I'm a servant as much as a delegate. Someone has to wipe the fingerprints off those stupid glass cases. Anyway, they don't share that stuff with outsiders, so how did a gaean get it from the Autumn Court?"

"I've got guesses," Luke said grimly. The kind of guesses that were going to send him back to the Middle Worlds to save Marion's ass from a murderous boyfriend.

Charity hung back, as though hesitant to get too close to Nori. "What are we going to do? How can I help you?"

"You can help by getting out of Ransom Falls." Luke scuffed the outer edge of the circle, ensuring it was broken. "Something's happened here. I don't know what. But it's not safe—not for you or anyone else. Especially since you've got Ollie's blood all over you, and your DNA is all over him."

"I could take her to the Autumn Court," Nori said in a tiny voice. "Not the castle, obviously, but the village is populous enough, and they get enough tourists... Nobody would notice her. She'd be safe."

It was a generous offer. Even more generous since Charity's murder had thrown Nori into shock and a good half-hour of sobbing. Luke hadn't expected Nori to be useful for hours to come— maybe days—but she obviously had more in common with Marion than he'd expected.

"I don't want to go to the Autumn Court," Charity said. "My glamour wouldn't work there."

Nori looked startled. "You have a glamour?"

"Must be a good one," Luke said.

Charity's smile was tremulous. "I don't think either of you have seen a revenant before."

"Either way, both of you need to hide. Here." Luke gave Charity keys to his pickup. "Drive as far as you can, figure out where you guys are going to hide on the road. I'll get my truck from you later."

"How will you get around?" Nori asked.

Luke lifted one shoulder in a shrug. "My legs aren't broken. You ladies should get going. I'll be in touch soon."

Charity clutched his keys in both hands. "Thank you, Doctor." The way she said that reminded him too much of Marion.

Luke took a few weapons out of his pickup: knives, guns, one wooden stake just in case. He stashed them around his body. Then there was nothing to do but watch Charity and Nori leave. The headlights soon disappeared into the trees. Luke hoped Charity was a good driver. He was terribly fond of that pickup.

Alone, he turned to survey the circle, Ollie's mutilated remains, and the sidhe magic in the spellbook. The same magic that Luke had seen in the Autumn Court.

Oliver had brought the assassins to Ransom Falls in an attempt to kill Marion, and he was working with the Autumn Court.

But the Autumn Court weren't the ones who had decimated her memory.

Luke had been around the block once or twice

—or three times—but of all the magic he'd seen, werewolves he'd slaughtered, demons he'd hunted, he'd never seen anything like the markings on that circle of power. And neither had Nori, which was even more telling.

It was something new. Something scary.

Something *big*.

Luke flipped the collar of his jacket up, pulled it tight around his body, and covered as much of his skin as possible. He glanced around the clearing. Stretched out his senses, opened his mind, searched the region for anyone who might be watching him.

There wasn't a single pulse for almost a mile. Charity was fast getting out of dodge.

That meant no witnesses.

Luke snapped his fingers.

In a whirlwind of brimstone, he slipped out of the dimension and vanished.

FOURTEEN

Marion was running, laughing, dancing. Her vision was narrowed to the man who pulled her through the open halls of Myrkheimr, their fingers hooked together like links on a chain. She had to slip through dangling vines like a veil in order to follow Konig.

The music from the dinner party chased them through the halls. It somehow grew louder as they raced away, as though they were plunging into an ocean of sound, absorbed in the beat.

Konig's fingers slipped from hers as he darted around the corner.

"Konig?" When Marion turned that same corner, hands seized her from the darkness, wrenching her behind a statue.

He pressed her against the wall. "Speaker for the ethereal delegation," he murmured, kissing a line along her jaw to the soft skin behind her ear. The play of his tongue nearly buckled her knees. "And I for the Autumn Court. Together, we'll own the summit."

She let her head fall back with a sigh as he kissed her, stroking along her ribs, her arms, the curve of her spine. The layered veils of the dress gave him access to her skin in all kinds of odd places.

"Are you two having fun?"

Leliel's cool voice made Marion look over Konig's shoulder.

The angel waited on the other side of the statue. Golden lantern light haloed her auburn hair and highlighted her shapely shoulders. Her sway-hipped posture reminded Marion of a longbow's curves.

Konig lifted his head from Marion's throat, pushing her hair back from her face in mounds. "As a matter of fact, we are having fun." He kissed Marion again, briefly, as though unperturbed by their audience. "We're not open for sharing. Find other sidhe to entertain you."

"I came to talk, not to..." Leliel arched an eyebrow. "Cast magic. Marion, can we speak?"

"No," Konig said.

Marion peeled herself away from Konig, checking her dress to make sure that it covered everything it should have. "I'll be only a minute."

His eyes burned with hunger. "Less than a minute."

She struggled not to smile or blush when she

faced Leliel again. She failed. The whole idea of making out with someone she barely knew was far more thrilling than it should have been, but there was a time and place for that. Talking to the angel who led the Ethereal Levant required at least a fraction of professionalism.

Marion glanced back at Konig. He was watching her walk away, and her cheeks burned even hotter.

Less than a minute.

It was strange to walk beside a woman even taller than she was. Marion hung back a step or two so that she could watch Leliel's graceful motions, which were those of a long-legged heron. "You seem to be adjusting well without your memories," Leliel said. "Few people would settle into the sidhe courts so easily, but you're not the average person, are you?"

"You'd probably know better than I do."

"I think not. You don't like me, and you've always avoided me," Leliel said. "You're so much more amiable since you lost your memory, so perhaps we should see this as a healing opportunity. You can join your people, as you deserve."

"My people," Marion echoed. "I'm as much witch as angel. Gaeans are also my people."

"Metaraon conspired to kill God and dragged us all into war. Even before Genesis, most of our kind were killed as a result. Our numbers are few. Very few. Like it or not, you're one of ours, and we'll all suffer if we don't find a way to stand together." Leliel wrapped her arms around her own ribcage, touching her back with long, delicate fingers. Her spine was tattooed in a color that was only slightly darker than the skin. "Look at me."

Marion peered closely at the intricate lacework of lines. She reached out to touch them, and as her fingers inched closer, the ink began to glow. "Those are magical runes, aren't they?"

Leliel shifted, drawing away. "My wings were severed in battle. Another consequence of your father's actions."

"I saw you fly into the court."

"Magic." She tapped the edge of the tattoo, then unraveled her arms. "We've a college in the Ethereal Levant intended to teach the art of mage craft. Few of us can perform such magic. Fewer of us remember how to do it. This was tattooed by our one and only competent paladin."

"It's amazing," Marion said honestly.

"His skill is nothing compared to yours." Leliel's smile rendered her breathtakingly beautiful. "It's always seemed a shame to me that you alone can perform magecraft with mastery akin to those of angels from the past. The days of the garden of Eden."

The garden of Eden.

The garden...

The memory of the curly-haired boy flashed through her mind. Marion blinked it away. "I don't have mastery of magic right now."

"But you normally do. I want you to agree to be our speaker, and then I want you to come to the

Ethereal Levant to join your people. You can teach us magecraft."

"Why should I do that?" Marion asked. "What do I get out of it?"

"Can I show you something, mind-to-mind?" Leliel's long, delicate fingers rested on Marion's temples.

She drew back. "You didn't ask last time you got in my head."

"And I apologize for that."

Leliel waited, hands outstretched.

Marion nodded. "Go ahead."

The other angel's fingertips brushed Marion's skin again. Their minds opened, unfolding like blossoms in springtime.

If Marion's mind was a vase empty of memory, then Leliel was water poured from a pitcher. She filled Marion.

Images bubbled between them.

Marion stood in a cavern dampened by clinging fog. She was surrounded by large spherical stones, most of them tall enough that the tops were level with her chest. They glowed with inner light.

Leliel stood beside her, hand resting on one of those spheres. "This is where we came from." Movements thumped from within the rock as if responding to the angel's touch.

They weren't stones. They were eggs.

Marion turned to look around. Though many of the nests were cloaked by large-fronded ferns, she still counted dozens of the biggest spheres. She estimated that there must have been hundreds. The dim recesses of the cave vanished into fog, so for all she knew, there could have been thousands.

Thousands of angels.

"This was Araboth," Leliel said, "where our holy father, Adam, spent his final centuries. He cohabited with the remnants of Eve's nests. Both Adam and the eggs were attended by Metaraon— your angel predecessor."

Before Marion had a chance to absorb that information, the setting shifted. Eggs vanished along with the foggy cavern.

They stood on a grassy hill in a shimmering city of light.

"New Eden," Leliel said. The skyscrapers ringing the knoll seemed to have been grown from white bone. They resembled trees, in a way.

Marion stepped back to gawk at the buildings, which scraped a cloudless blue sky. Winged bodies swooped from one structure to another, hawks in a forest. All angels. Almost as many of them as there had been eggs in Araboth. "My gods."

Her heel caught on something hard. She stumbled. Marion caught herself on a tombstone thrusting from the grass.

"We first began dying in the wars against Lilith's forces," Leliel said as Marion traced the name on the tombstone. She couldn't quite read it. The dreamlike state she shared with Leliel was missing information. "We hadn't known we could be killed until then. We honored every soul we lost, and attempted to regroup, regrow, restore our species though Eve was gone. But then there was the massacre."

Marion blinked.

The buildings caught flame.

New Eden was burning—the beautiful skyscrapers, the towering forests. The blue sky was clogged with choking smoke.

People were screaming.

Marion scrambled to her feet, ran to the edge of the grassy hill. She looked down on the white cobblestone streets of New Eden to find winged, decapitated bodies filling the streets. Blood raced between the stones and flooded the channels with a crimson tide.

A dark force walked among the dead. It was a faceless being, shadow taking human shape, and it carried swords.

As Marion watched, it murdered every single angel it crossed paths with.

It was coming toward the hill. Toward Marion and Leliel.

"What is that?" Marion asked.

"The Godslayer," Leliel said. "First she killed Adam, and then she came for the rest of us. She's the reason your father is dead, too. When she was done in New Eden, barely two dozen of our lives remained, where once there had been thousands. It wasn't long before Genesis followed."

Leliel clapped her hands. The shadowy Godslayer disappeared, and New Eden was silent for a moment.

Then a wall of black appeared.

It swept through the trees, chewing up branches, ripping the forest out by the roots. Wind shrieked with the pain of a million extinguished souls. It rushed toward the hill so quickly that Marion didn't have time to turn and run.

One moment, she stood among the burned remnants of New Eden.

The next moment, there was nothing.

Marion shocked back to consciousness in the Autumn Court. She had fallen to her knees in the hallway, gasping for breath.

When she looked up at Leliel, her vision was blurred by tears.

It was one thing for Luke to describe what the Genesis void must have been like—massive, merciless, and all-consuming. But to see it, *feel* it, and have no escape from the inevitability... That was another thing entirely. Marion was shaking.

Leliel helped her stand again. "That's what's become of the angels," she said gently, brushing the hair out of Marion's eyes. "So few of us remain, and you ask why you should help us. What's in it for you. Do you understand now?"

Marion struggled to catch her breath.

She understood.

"I'll do it. I'll help you," Marion said. "Starting by acting as speaker for the angels."

Leliel's eyes sparkled. Marion loved how she felt when the angel smiled upon her, as though the sun were shining on her from the brightest planes of Earth. "This is yours, then. I return it to you with pride."

She handed the enchanted silver cuff to Marion, who gripped it tightly in both hands. It hummed with magic. Marion's magic. Touching it stirred feelings much like the ones she'd experienced when stringing the bow at the archery range. The silver bracelet was something that she knew in an intimate fashion that was impossible to forget.

Yet she still couldn't change the magic. Whatever connection she should have felt to the spells was simply absent. The omission was within Marion's skull, somewhere in the hole where the missing memories should have rested. Nothing remained but lingering wisps of Leliel's vision.

"Thank you," she said, clasping the cuff around her wrist.

"No, thank *you*," Leliel said. "You can come to the EL with me tonight. We have a lot to discuss to prepare you for the summit."

"Well..." She *was* very curious to see the Ethereal Levant, and her curiosity was a powerful force. The only force more powerful at the moment was her longing to return to Konig. She needed him now more than ever, after feeling the merciless terror of the Genesis void. "Can we meet tomorrow morning, before the summit?"

Some of Leliel's glow faded. "Very well. I've already discussed everything with Violet, and our writers are collaborating to prepare your keynote speech—in case we can't bring your memory back before then. They'll deliver it to you as soon as they're done."

"The writers are working on it right now?" she asked. "I thought everyone was at the party."

"Not all sidhe are overwhelmed by their baser urges." Leliel glanced over Marion's shoulder and lowered her voice. "Though most of them are."

Marion turned to see Konig waiting at the end of the hall, long hair shadowing one side of his face, expectation in the lines of his body. He'd followed them at a respectful distance, but his expectations were clear.

"We'll talk tomorrow and transport you to the UN. The summit begins tomorrow evening," Leliel said. "Enjoy your night."

When Konig said that he wanted to show Marion something as wondrous as the bedroom with its walk-in closet, she was skeptical. After wearing hand-me-down scrubs for so long, she doubted that anything better than her closet existed, whether in the Middle Worlds or anywhere else.

But then he took her to the gardens.

"Behold," Konig said.

He was watching her closely, waiting for a reaction.

She was confident that her surprise satisfied him.

Lights on every tree branch illuminated the leaves in eerie gold and copper. The stamens on the flowers were brighter than the moon and lit the petals from within. Fireflies darted from tree to tree, darting through breaks in honey fountains that spurted from fissures in the soil.

Even as she watched, everything was growing: the pumpkins, the vines, the herbs. They were fed by that golden flow of magical honey, and everything was in constant, gentle motion.

Marion couldn't have hidden the awe the gardens struck in her even if she'd wanted to.

"I won't bother asking if you like it." Konig dragged her down the path twisting between flowerbeds. "We've discussed it before."

"The only thing I've seen that's more beautiful than the garden is your hair," Marion said.

That surprised a laugh out of Konig. "My hair, you say?"

The silver cuff on Marion's wrist had gotten warm. She lifted it to show him. "Leliel gave me the honesty thing."

"Now *that's* interesting. My enigmatic princess compelled to be utterly honest." Konig encircled her opposite wrist with his fingers, mirroring the shape of the bracelet. "What do you think of the Autumn Court?"

"It feels like home," she said.

A sly smile inched across his face. "What do you think of my parents?"

"I don't think much about Rage at all. Violet is scary. I don't think she likes me, and I don't think I like her." Marion bit the inside of her cheek to try to stop herself, but it was too late. It was out there. "I'm sorry."

"I don't like her either," he said dismissively. "What do you think of me? Aside from my hair?"

"I'm incredulous that I could be with you," Marion said. "Though I also feel like it's no surprise, as I deserve the likes of a prince." That was getting to be a little too honest for her. It was the same kind of arrogance that had embarrassed her in Port Angeles. She started trying to wiggle the bracelet off. It was tighter than she expected, as though it had shrunk to fit her.

"What do you think of that doctor, Luke?" Konig asked.

Marion wrenched the bracelet off.

"That's not nice," Marion admonished. "We've talked about him enough. I'm here with you. Isn't that enough?"

"I don't know," Konig said, his hand tight on her arm. He bowed closer to her, until she could taste his breath on her lips.

She only allowed him to kiss her briefly. Her enthusiasm for his affection had waned in the wake of Leliel's dark memories. "Why doesn't the Autumn Court let the angels regrow here, in the gardens of Myrkheimr? Or outside, in the forest. There must be somewhere safe you could put them."

Surprise touched the violet shards of Konig's eyes. "That was the first thing we attempted when the angels approached my parents for an alliance. We've just got too much magic around here. It screwed up the nest, made things grow wrong."

"Don't you think that would happen in the

Winter Court, too?"

"Not if we evacuated the survivors still in there," Konig said. "Empty everything out, and make sure the angels start their nest as far from the ley lines as possible... It'll be fine. Why do you ask?"

"Leliel showed me things," Marion said, swallowing hard. "It made me so sad. I wanted to know if we might have a Plan B if I'm not able to negotiate for the angels to win the Winter Court at the summit."

"Your compassion astounds," Konig said. "I love you, Marion Garin."

A mischievous thought seized her. "Prove it." She lifted the bracelet between them.

Konig donned it with a laugh. "All right. I love you. I have never felt about anyone the way that I feel about you. I'd die for you."

"This is delightful. Keep talking," Marion said.

"I fantasize of what an Autumn Court would be like with you on the throne beside me," Konig said. "Mage and unseelie. We would conquer the world." He pulled her tighter against him, the silver cuff burning with heat as it worked its magic. "I want to spend my life with you, and I fully intend on marrying you as soon as I can get away with it."

All the blood rushed to her head. "Oh," she whispered. Marion cleared her throat. "What do you mean, as soon as you can get away with it?"

"You only have to tell me when." Konig punctuated that with the kind of kiss that made it feel like her clothes might just melt off.

They didn't melt away, so Konig seemed interested in taking their removal into his own hands. He fisted her skirt. Lifted it to expose her calves, her knees, her thighs. His knuckles skimmed her tender flesh, and Marion almost collapsed on the spot.

"Wait, let's go to my room," she said, pushing her dress back down.

"Mine is closer," Konig said.

FIFTEEN

Marion wasn't certain how they made it to Konig's room, or even how far it was from the garden. For all she knew, their kissing had stirred sidhe magic that instantly transported them from the honey fountains to the entrance of Konig's room.

Some part of her wanted to stop and look around—to see what a prince's bedroom would look like.

It was a very small part of her.

He ripped the bracelet off and pushed it back onto Marion's wrist.

"Tell me how this feels," he said as he kissed her throat.

She couldn't help but gasp, "Good."

He pressed himself between her thighs, lifting her legs with arms hooked under the knees. She was trapped between the prince and the wall beside his bedroom door, his lips on her throat, teeth nipping the tender flesh. Her heart pounded so hard that it felt like it would punch through the bone.

Gods, he did feel good. That was the total truth.

Shouldn't this feel more than good? Shouldn't it feel...familiar?

Marion kissed him, pushing the shirt off of his shoulders to expose his chest. His heart thundered under her palm as he pulled her dress aside, exposing her breasts. Konig's lips trailed down her collarbone. Ice rolled over her flesh, followed by goosebumps.

Sidhe magic swelled between them. There was a distant orchestra playing in time to the beat of her heart, summoning ancient, primal magics that flowed through the veins of the Autumn Court.

This was how they did magic.

This was *life*.

She'd been choking with need in the garden, but now that she was facing the reality of it, in the solitude of Konig's rooms, she was suffocated by hesitation, sadness, the shadow of the Genesis void in the corners of her mind.

Konig effortlessly carried her to the bed and spilled her body across it. The prince collapsed atop Marion. His weight flattened her to the bed, and it was pleasant. More than pleasant.

She wanted him to stop.

He slipped down her body, shoving her skirts above her knees. Konig trailed kisses along the inside of her knee. "Princess," he whispered, his breath so much hotter than his skin. His finger traced up her hip, hooked in the waistband of her underwear.

The word leaped out of Marion. "Wait."

Konig didn't immediately acknowledge she'd spoken, tugging the lace down.

She pressed her knees together.

"*Wait.*"

"What?" he asked, looking up at her. His cheek rested against her thigh.

"I can't," she said.

Konig pushed up to hang over her, weight braced on knees and hands. "You...can't?"

She scooted out from underneath him. Marion splayed her fingers over her breasts to conceal them. "I'm so, so sorry. It's this bracelet making me be honest, and—I'm sorry," she said. "This all feels strange with my missing memory. I didn't want it to feel unfamiliar, but..." Marion swallowed hard. "And then after everything Leliel showed me, I'm just not in the mood."

Konig pushed back to rest on his knees. He looked as wounded as though she'd stabbed him instead of merely asking him to stop. "Seriously?"

"Yes, seriously. Slow down."

"Slow down? *Slow down?* It's not the first time we've been together, princess. This isn't *fast.*"

"I know, I believe you," Marion said. "I just need my space. I need time. And...I need memory." When nothing she said changed his expression, she apologized again. "I'm sorry."

Konig was still for a long moment, his glower tensing her muscles into knots.

He finally climbed out of bed with a sigh, plucked a robe off of the door of his armoire, and tossed it onto the bed with her. "I shouldn't be surprised."

Marion pulled the protective shell of silk around her body before slipping out of the bed. "I don't want to hurt you, Konig. I *want* to be with you." She flashed the bracelet at him, reminding the prince of the enchantment.

"You're doing a great job by accident if it's unintentional," he said harshly. "Ever since you've come back—you've been different, Marion. I don't think I like this person you're becoming. You're not *my* Marion anymore."

"Maybe I should have left with the angels tonight after all," she said, eyes stinging.

Konig gave her a long, appraising look. "Maybe you should have."

Marion's bedroom was empty when she returned to it—so empty that even the fullness of her closet and all its fine designer clothes were no comfort.

The windows stood open, curtains fluttering in a breeze that smelled of pollen and honey. She stepped through them onto the balcony. Her room was on the opposite side of the tower from Konig's, so she couldn't see his bedroom or the garden. She could only see the fringes of Myrkheimr lit by starlight, and the village half-hidden in the trees.

Marion gazed at the moonless sky and felt... empty.

She was missing something.

It wasn't a physical ache. The discomfort came from within. The feeling that she wasn't where she needed to be, and that the time wasn't right.

Marion turned to reenter her room, but its furnishings were so unfamiliar that they felt hostile. Would she have been happier if she'd agreed to go to bed with Konig? If the chemistry between them meant anything, she doubted she'd ever slept in the Autumn Court without a coppery-fleshed sidhe prince wrapped around her body.

There was a large package on her bed that hadn't been there earlier. Marion sat on the edge of the mattress and lifted the box's lid.

Inside, a longbow was nestled beside a slender quiver of arrows. The bow's strings were coiled within wax paper at the bottom. There was also a note that only said, "For my princess." Konig must have arranged for someone to leave it in her room earlier, while they were at dinner.

"Oh, Konig," she sighed to herself.

She strung the bow and hefted its weight in her hand. Why was she so comfortable nocking one of those deadly arrows when she had been totally uncomfortable kissing her own boyfriend? Marion's body wanted to shoot but it didn't want sex. That wasn't right.

Marion propped the bow and quiver beside the

bed, then stripped off her dress, unwinding the many layers of cloth from around her lean body. The dress seemed more difficult to remove than it had been to don in the first place.

For the first time, the Autumn Court felt cold. She pulled Konig's robe around herself again.

Someone knocked at her door. She answered it to find Heather Cobweb with an envelope. "From the ethereal delegates," said the archer.

Marion took it. "Thank you."

"You'll have a guard posted in the hall outside your room all night. We've been ordered to get anything you need, so just step out here if you have any requests."

"Thank you," she said again, and she shut the door firmly.

The envelope contained one page of tightly written text—her speech for the beginning of the summit, to replace the one that she had presumably forgotten.

"It's been almost fifteen years since Genesis changed our lives," she read aloud under her breath. "Where it once took Adam, Lilith, and Eve seven days to assemble nothingness into something, it took our new gods only one. The Nether, Middle, and High Worlds are a gift to us. I've been given messages about the gods' intent to help us make the best use of these gifts."

She skimmed a few more lines down.

The speechwriters had concluded her speech with, "The Winter Court deserves an appreciative population as much as the angels need a safe haven, and the gods see these problems as having a single satisfying solution. The angels must move from the Ethereal Levant to the Winter Court."

Marion lowered the paper, frowning at her pale-cheeked reflection in the mirror.

It was one thing to have the speechwriters prepare something for her, but it was another thing entirely to pretend they could guess at the will of the gods.

A gust of wind pushed Marion's window open wider with a creak. She turned to close it.

A figure stood on the balcony.

Marion thought it was Konig at first. He was tall enough, slender enough, and carrying a sword almost as tall as he was.

He entered the dim light of her bedside lamp. His skin was the dull color of dead leaves. Limp hair hung to the small of his back. His sunken eyes were fixed on her as firmly as his fingers were upon the jagged hilt of the sword.

That wasn't Konig, but an assassin. In the Autumn Court. Where she should have been protected.

Marion seized the bow from her bedside. She was quick to nock an arrow, but the assassin was quicker to dart toward her. A sidhe had the advantage in the Middle Worlds: the ability to slip from one spot to another before she could blink.

He swung the sword. She leaped back, putting the bed between them. The tip of the blade sliced smoothly through the ribbon tying her robe shut.

Marion opened her mouth to shout for the

guards.

Another flash.

The assassin seized her from behind, wrapping his hand around her mouth to smother the cry. All that came out was a muffled wail.

He was close enough to quiet her, but too close to use such a great cleaving blade with any effectiveness. And too close for Marion to use the bow. She slammed the jagged point of the arrow into her assassin's thigh instead. Cold blood gushed over her fingers.

"Shit," he hissed, blasting ice on her cheek.

She stabbed again, but he twisted out of its range. His hand shifted on her mouth. Marion sank her teeth into the pad of his thumb.

He jerked away with a shout.

Marion threw herself across the room. "Heather! Help me!"

It should have taken barely an instant for Heather to enter. She'd said that there would be guards all night barely three minutes earlier.

Nobody came.

Worse, Marion had dropped her bow by the assassin's feet, so now she only held a single, blood-slicked arrow.

She darted for the balcony. The assassin did, too.

Marion got through the doors first and leaped onto the railing, prepared to dive over the side into the forest.

A hand fisted in her hair. Jerked her back. Tossed her to the floor.

The assassin loomed over her, wrapping the magic of the Autumn Court around himself like the cloak of an executioner. He radiated greed. He was dreaming of money—a million dollars—and the thought of what he would do with Marion's body had him giddy.

He lifted his sword in both hands. Its point glistened in the light.

And then—a gunshot.

The assassin wasn't where he had been standing moments earlier, so the bullet only zipped past his shoulder.

Marion pushed up onto her elbows, searching for the shooter. Her eyes fell on a balcony a dozen feet from hers, where another man stood. The bullet had come from the barrel of a gun that had saved her life more than once before.

Luke was back, leather jacket, handguns, and all. And he looked pissed off.

He shot again.

The assassin lifted his sword in time to deflect the bullet. The ricochet shattered the window.

There was no way the guards hadn't heard that.

Luke leaped off of the other balcony and landed on hers. A choked cry caught in Marion's throat when the assassin met him with the blade, but Luke dodged under it effortlessly.

When he shot again, he didn't miss.

The assassin thudded to his knees beside Marion with a gaping hole in his chest. The sword clattered to the floor.

Blood dribbled across the stone. Marion kicked

wildly, driving herself away from the puddle so the icy amber tide wouldn't touch her.

She was caught in warm arms.

"Did he get you?" Luke asked, dragging her off of the ground.

Marion wasn't actually certain. The adrenaline throbbing through her body was so intense that she couldn't feel her body at all. There was so much blood—but all of it the color of tree sap, so none of it hers.

"I think I'm okay," she said, clinging to Luke's chest. "He came out of nowhere. How did he get at me?"

"Dunno. Let's get inside." Luke half-carried her into her room again, shutting the doors behind them. Blood crept into the bedroom near the edge of the frame and soaked the carpet.

She allowed herself to stare at Luke for only a moment. She drank in the reassuring squareness of his features and inhaled his leathery scent.

He had come back for her.

The logistics of it seemed irrelevant, just as she momentarily didn't care about Konig's accusations toward Luke. He obviously did have iron bullets. He'd just used them to exterminate an unseelie assassin. Marion had never felt so grateful before.

She was dizzy with giddy relief. "You came back."

"I couldn't help myself," Luke said. How could he manage to shoot that lopsided smile at her when he had just killed someone?

He just killed someone. Assassins are still coming

after me.

Marion peeled away from Luke and scrambled to pick up her bow. She realized her robe was hanging open, so she pulled it shut with her other hand. "How did you know—?"

"The Autumn Court sent the assassins." Luke glanced out the windows, then whipped the curtains shut. "They're trying to kill you."

All that giddy relief came to a screeching halt.

The Autumn Court?

"Just because the assassins are sidhe doesn't mean..." She swallowed hard, shook her head. "No, I don't think—"

"Oliver Machado had magic out of the Autumn Court's private library. They had to give those spells to him, so they're the ones who want you dead." Luke flung the closet open, grabbed an outfit from the drawers nearest the door.

"But *why*?" Marion asked.

"We can only guess. Let's wait to do that once we're away from the people trying to murder you." Luke tossed clothes to her. "Get dressed so we can leave."

Her door opened an inch—just long enough for Marion to see Heather on the other side.

The guard was already lifting her bow to aim.

Marion shut her door and shoved the desk in front of it. Bodies banged uselessly into the other side—not just Heather, but a half-dozen other guards from the sounds of it. They didn't sound happy.

"I should find Konig. This is a mistake. He'll

clear it up." Marion yanked the jeans on under her bathrobe and slung her bow over her shoulder.

"I think the whole court's in on it," Luke said.

But Konig had just been kissing her, trying to make love to her, showing her a beautiful garden that flowed with honey. He would never try to kill her.

"No," Marion said.

"Come on." Luke extended a hand toward her.

His bare hand.

The guards pounded their fists into the doors. Magic burned in the hallway, making Marion's skin itch all over. The handle went white with heat. They'd be through within seconds.

"Come on," Luke said again, more insistently.

Her every sense longed to take his hand, with an urgency as powerful as the one that had pushed Konig away from her that night.

Marion brushed her fingertips against his palm.

Her mind opened.

Knock knock, Marion.

The world shifted. It swirled and twisted and filled with light.

There was magic in her mind, in her soul.

They reached the balcony at the same time that Heather broke through the doors with reinforcements. Magic teemed around their fists, and when Marion tried to look directly at them, all she could see was blinding light.

"Get away from me!" Marion cried, clutching Luke's hand.

She thrust her opposite hand toward the guards.

The magic came from within—within, and without. It flowed from the pulse of her blood and from the sky above. The stars fed her. The brilliant sparks of thought roiling within Luke's mind. The books on the shelves.

She was an angel, a mage.

Even when Marion didn't understand why or how, she couldn't change who she was.

Magic punched into her would be assassins and sent them flying.

They smashed through the bedroom wall, and then the wall beyond that. The force of Marion's magic kept pushing until they were flying through open air beyond the outermost walls of Myrkheimr. Only Heather managed to push back, clinging to the hallway outside the room.

"Stop!" roared the archer, lifting her bow against the force of magic.

"Hold on to my neck," Luke said. He swept an arm under her legs, scooping her easily off the ground and stepping over the first assassin's body. Marion clung to his neck as he ordered. She was weightless in his arms.

He leaped off of the balcony.

Falling in the Middle Worlds didn't feel like it should have—as though the air thickened and gravity slowed, allowing them to float rather than tumble. The grass took their bodies gently, soft as a pillow.

Shouts followed them as they raced toward the

ley line juncture near the archery range. Lights blazed to life all throughout Myrkheimr as the entire castle became alerted to the fight—and the destruction that Marion had wrought.

Sidhe materialized in the path between Marion and Luke and that gazebo.

Marion blasted them with wind and rain and lightning that flowed from her fingertips. She flung them toward the village.

The path was clear.

"Marion!" That was Konig's voice. He was chasing them too, and he sounded desperate.

"Hold your breath," Luke said before Marion could figure out where Konig was coming from.

They plunged into the juncture.

Konig and Myrkheimr disappeared.

SIXTEEN

Marion and Luke appeared at the edge of a park on Earth, shrouded in night. The foliage was dull in comparison to the twisted gardens of the Autumn Court. Nothing about the brick buildings, the rusty swing set, or the twisting road looked familiar to Marion—or even similar to the western states where she'd woken up.

"Where are we?" she asked.

"Town in Pennsylvania." Luke unwrapped his arm from around Marion and stuffed his handgun into the back of his belt. "Somewhere the unseelie won't think to look for us, I'd hope."

Her heart plummeted with disappointment. *Konig won't be able to find me.* That should have been a good thing, if Luke was right about the Autumn Court trying to kill her. "We took their ley lines to Earth. Doesn't that mean they know exactly where we came out on this side?"

"Nah." Luke took out a cell phone. "Let's get going." He made a phone call while striding down the street. Marion followed him more slowly, watching the park behind them. It was empty. Nobody wanted to be out when it was drizzly and dark.

There was no sign of Konig.

Marion hugged her body tightly against the cold.

Luke was talking in a low voice, speaking to someone on his cell phone. "I need a car. We're in Jim Thorpe. Going to the coffee shop downtown."

Marion sped her pace so that she could hear whom he was calling. It was a female voice on the other end of the line, too quiet for her to distinguish words.

"Thanks," Luke said, and he hung up. Magic sparked over the back of the phone as he shoved it into his pocket.

"Who were you calling?"

He winced and rubbed his ribs. "Friend."

"Female friend? Former fiancée?"

"Yes, and no." He glanced both ways before crossing the street, ever the Boy Scout. "I'm in a mood for coffee."

They weren't far from a shop set into the first floor of an old apartment building. The illuminated sign said, "Open 24/7." It was warm and dry inside and, best of all, there were no sidhe in sight. Luke tucked Marion's bow in a corner by the front door, concealing her weapon behind the sofa. He tugged his jacket around his guns before going to the counter to order.

Marion tensed when she realized a barista had watched them stash the bow, but he didn't say anything. Apparently in a world filled with preternaturals, dropping in for midnight coffee while armed wasn't worthy of note.

Aside from the strange lack of reaction from the staff, the coffee shop was very much the kind of place Marion imagined she should have enjoyed: a location that was tidy, immaculate, and hip, with a chalkboard declaring the daily specials over the cash register and nary a beardless man.

She couldn't seem to settle into the sagging couch against the wall. There were only a handful of people in the coffee shop this late at night, and it felt like everyone was looking at her.

Luke sat on the opposite end of the sofa, bringing two drinks with him. "Cappuccino for you. Hope that's fine, 'cause they didn't have chocolate milk."

"It's fine," Marion said. She eyed Luke's gun, which was jutting out from his jacket.

He caught her gaze. "You okay?"

"Iron bullets are illegal," she said.

She expected—or maybe hoped—for Luke to deny it. If he denied that one thing, then Konig's other accusations would be more obviously untrue. But Luke said, "Are you surprised? You saw me casting bullets in my bathtub."

"So you're in the habit of killing preternaturals. Have you any wooden bullets for the vampires?"

"Wood would shatter in a gun, Marion."

"So you just stake them," she said.

"You seem angry at me," Luke said.

Marion certainly felt angry. She wasn't sure if it was toward Luke or Konig or the world at large, though. She'd finally found somewhere that felt like it could have been home—a court where she fit in as royalty—and they were behind the attacks on her life.

"I just have so many questions, and it feels like every answer I've gotten in the last few days turns into more questions. I don't know who I am, I don't know whom to trust..." She tried to take a drink of her cappuccino but it was too hot. She set it down hard enough that frothed milk slopped over the side. "I thought I had you figured out, and now I'm not sure."

"I work with preternaturals," Luke said. "I'm ready to defend myself against anything that could threaten my patients. But until this week, I hadn't fired my gun in over ten years. There's a difference between preparedness and murderous intent. I've only got one of them."

Marion let her face drop into her hands. "I'm sorry."

"Don't apologize." He sipped his coffee, sat back with a sigh. "Nothing to apologize for."

"Konig told me that you asked for a reward for returning me to the Autumn Court."

"He was lying," Luke said, but he looked so unsurprised by the claim that Marion couldn't help but feel a little suspicious.

"Why would he do that?"

"Jealousy. Possessiveness. And because he wanted you undefended. That's my guess. He practically drop-kicked me back to Earth after offering to do a duel at dawn over you, so I'm not shocked that he'd be manipulative in other ways."

Marion almost laughed. A duel at dawn. Luke and Konig fighting a duel over her.

She didn't laugh because that wasn't funny at all. In fact, she liked the sound of it a little bit too much.

"I don't believe Konig knows what the rest of the court is doing. He gave me the bow, he showed me things." Like the garden, and his very fine body. "No. *No.* Not Konig. He was utterly honest with me. He cares about me."

"How do you know?" Luke asked.

"I know for the same reason that you can be sure I'm being honest with you now." Marion twisted the enchanted bracelet off her wrist. "I made these for the people participating in the summit. They're mage artifacts that compel the wearer to honesty. When Konig wore it, he told me that...um." *He said he loves me and wants to marry me.*

If Marion had still been wearing the bracelet, she wouldn't have been able to keep herself from sharing that information with Luke.

But she wasn't.

"I believe that he has no ill intent for me," Marion finished, somewhat pathetically.

Luke was so interested in the bracelet that he

seemed to miss the hole in her story. "You made those for the summit? And, what, you left that one in your room?"

"It was given to me by a visiting angel. They asked me to be their speaker."

Luke's gaze dropped to the cuff again. "You said yes. Seems like a conflict of interest, Marion."

She lifted her chin, staring down her nose at him. "I'll let you know when I want your opinion on my decisions. I'm capable of making them on my own."

"Suit yourself," he said. "I don't care about politics anyway."

"You care enough to accuse the Autumn Court of trying to destroy the summit by killing the Voice of God."

"I care enough to save your life," Luke said. Her heart gave a pathetic flop in her chest. He plucked the bracelet out of her hand. It barely fit her delicately boned wrist, yet it still managed to fit over his hand. The magic expanded the metal so that it went on him just as easily. "With the evidence I've seen, I believe the Autumn Court is behind your bounty, and there's no way in hell I'm letting them hurt you. Your boyfriend threatened me, so I don't trust him. And I didn't ask for money." Luke ripped the bracelet off again. "Happy?"

Happy didn't exactly describe the feelings she was battling with.

Marion had shared dinner and wine with the people who wanted her dead. If she were this powerful creature, this Voice of God that everyone feared, shouldn't she have seen it coming?

But Konig says he wants to marry me.

She stuck the bracelet in her pocket. Marion was done with honesty for the night. "You said that you have a lot of evidence, so I take it you were busy after you returned to Earth."

"I was." He withdrew photos from inside his jacket, spreading them across the coffee table in front of her. They were pictures of Marion. She stood in a dark clearing, wearing those pajamas she'd woken up in. Her eyes were closed.

"No injuries," Marion said.

Luke frowned. "What?"

"I woke up with bruises all over. I don't see them in this picture." She pushed the photos away from herself, feeling queasy. "What's that mean?"

It looked like Luke had a few ideas, and none of them made him happy. "It means that I feel even less guilty about Oliver Machado's death, since he's the only person who saw you between these pictures and your arrival at the hospital, as far as I know."

Marion choked on her cappuccino, and not because it was hot. "He's dead?"

"He abducted Nurse Ballard."

"So you killed him."

"Nurse Ballard did," Luke said. "I would have done it, though."

She nodded. She trusted him—she did. "So you found evidence that Oliver Machado was after me because of the Autumn Court, and now he's dead. What's our next move?"

"The unseelie want to kill you because of the summit tomorrow," Luke said, "so we keep you in hiding until your speech. That's what we do." His phone rang and he answered it. "Yeah?" A pause. "Yeah, I am. Thanks." He turned the phone off and stood up. "We've got a car."

Marion stood more slowly, gathering the photos of herself off the table. She left the cappuccino. Hot chocolate really was superior. "What connections does a doctor from California have in Pennsylvania?"

"I've got friends all over," he said.

His friends were either rich or powerful, because there was a new car parked outside the coffee shop, right at the curb. It was stopped illegally in front of a fire hydrant with the keys on the hood. Luke opened the trunk and loaded Marion's bow and quiver inside.

He grimaced when he slammed it shut.

"You keep moving like that," Marion said. "What's wrong? Did you get injured fighting the assassin?"

"You might say that," Luke said. For the first time, he spread his jacket open, and Marion realized his shirt was wet. It wasn't from the rain. She touched his warm, sticky side and her fingertips came away glistening with blood. "Big sword, bad aim. I don't think he hit anything important."

"You're not important?"

"Nothing critical," Luke amended. He limped

back onto the sidewalk and opened the passenger's side door for her. "Get in."

"*You're* driving in this condition?" Marion asked.

"Do you remember how to drive?"

She wouldn't know until she got behind the wheel. "We should go to the nearest hospital."

Luke propped his elbow atop the open door. The rain misted his skin, making him shine orange in the light from the coffee shop. He almost looked sidhe himself. "I've been seen by multiple assassins and now everyone knows you're with me. I'm not going to risk bringing them to another hospital."

"But you're bleeding."

"Not the first time, not the last."

"It will be if you die!" She took the door from him. "*You* get into the passenger's seat and *I* will do the driving. I've watched you do it. It can't be harder than driving a boat."

"Marion…"

"Don't argue with me, Dr. Flynn. I'm the Voice of God, dammit."

"You can't whip that out in arguments like that," Luke said. "That's not how this works."

"Shut up and get in," she said. He rolled his eyes, but surrendered the keys to Marion. She climbed into the driver's seat and turned the engine on. "See? Easy."

"Turn on the windshield wipers," Luke said, reclining his chair to relieve pressure on the wound.

She poked a button. The radio hummed to life.

He laughed and then grimaced.

"I'm going to drive around until I find a hospital and drop you off," Marion said decisively. She kept pushing buttons and flipping levers until the wipers began whisking over the windshield. *Easy.*

"Is that what you want me to do? Go away?"

No. Never. She swallowed hard. "You need to be treated, that's all." She lifted a hand to touch his where it was pressed to his injured side.

He leaned out of her reach. "No hospitals, Voice of God. And I'm not leaving you until you're at the summit," Luke said. "Let's get to New York City. We'll talk about what to do after that."

Rain turned to snow in the mountains, thick and pillowy. The roads were salted, so they reached higher elevations before encountering slick conditions Marion wasn't sure how to navigate. They slid dangerously around a few corners before Luke spoke up. "We need somewhere to spend the night."

"Such as a hospital?" Marion suggested.

"Such as a house. Turn left up here, double back."

Luke directed Marion back down into a valley, where the snow wasn't quite as dense. There was a small farming town hidden within the trees. It wasn't too unlike Ransom Falls, sort of like its East Coast twin covered under a solid six inches of snow. The other significant difference was that it looked a lot more tired. The post office was dingier. There was an OPA benefits office tucked behind a bargain grocery store. The agricultural supply company had trash piled in its back yard.

The house he told Marion to stop at was beside something the sign called an auto shop, though it looked more like a junk yard. She parked against the curb crookedly, wincing when she bumped the front wheel into the sidewalk.

They had arrived without dying or crashing. That was a victory in Marion's book.

"There," she said, forcing a big smile. "I told you I could drive."

Luke didn't smile back. He'd gone ashen during the drive, which Marion had attributed to fear that she'd launch them straight off the side of the mountain. But now he didn't fight with her when she peeled the side of his jacket back. The bloodstain had spread across his side, dripping onto the seat underneath.

She should have gone to a hospital.

"What are we doing here?" Marion asked, slipping out of the car to carve a path through the snow to Luke's door.

"Hiding." Luke was already trying to climb out of the car on his own, but it was taking a lot longer than it should have, even if he managed not to make any pain faces. "This is an old house of mine."

"You have an old house in Pennsylvania? One that happens to be within hours of the unseelie sidhe's ley lines?"

"The ley line dumps out near New York City for probably the same reason I used to live here. It's rural, but close enough to get into town for business with a long morning's drive." He slipped and sank to his knees with a grunt. Crimson droplets spattered the snow.

Marion pulled his arm over her shoulder. She practically heard budding arguments skimming over the surface of his mind, so she snapped, "Quiet." They shuffled up the front path together. "Does anyone live here?"

"Not for over a decade, but I left a lot of belongings behind."

"Also very convenient. Were you planning to come back?"

"Not really," Luke said. "I just didn't care about the stuff I left here." He leaned against the wall. Marion ripped the yellow warning tape off of the front door and pushed it open.

Despite being a house that hadn't been inhabited in a long time, it was still in better condition than Oliver Machado's home had been. It was really was cozy on the inside. Old wood floors in good condition, some mismatched but high quality furniture, a tidy kitchen.

Best of all, the living room was filled with books.

"You didn't care about your books? You heathen," she said, pulling Luke's arm over her shoulders again.

He gave a short laugh. "Books are heavy."

She settled him atop a dusty couch as he began to tremble. The inside of the house was very cold, but not that cold—he was still losing too much blood.

Marion pressed her lips into a disapproving line. For his sake, she wouldn't talk about hospitals again. She yanked a plaid blanket off of the back of the couch and covered him with it. After one more trip to bring her bow and quiver inside, she shut the front door and locked it.

"I'm going to remember how to do healing magic now," Marion declared. "I remembered magic to care for Elena Eiderman, and I can do the same for you."

"Hopefully not the exact same," Luke said. "I'm not in a dying mood." She thought that was meant to be a joke, but he sounded so faint that she couldn't laugh.

She spread her hands in front of her and looked at them expectantly.

Come on, magic.

She'd blasted the sidhe through walls, for goodness's sake. She should have been able to summon *some* magic.

Her skin remained dull.

"I'll need to touch you to get the spells," Marion said.

This time, Luke's grimace had nothing to do with pain. "No way. We've done enough of that for a lifetime."

The immediacy of his reaction stung. "Don't be ridiculous. I'm sure I could repair you within seconds if you'd just let me take your hand."

"It doesn't hurt *that* much," Luke said.

"Why are you fighting me on this? Did I do something to make you angry?"

"I have nothing against you, but that doesn't mean I want you to touch me, either."

"I see how it is. Very well." For a man who had gone so far out of his way to rescue her, Luke was making it quite clear that he didn't actually like her all that much. Marion's throat felt thick, and she worried that she'd start crying if she talked too much, so she kept things short. "Tell me what to do."

"Bathroom," Luke said. "First aid kit. Then check the cabinet by the fridge."

Marion swallowed down her disappointment and retrieved the first aid kit. It was rather large—not surprising, considering that Luke was a doctor. She had to half-drag it to his side.

She opened it to find an array of professional tools: scalpels, bandages, painkillers.

"Oh my," Marion said.

"Cabinet by the fridge," he said again.

She opened it to find a large bottle of whiskey. "This is what you want?"

"Antiseptic." The corner of his mouth twitched. "Inside and out. Glasses are over the stove."

Marion grabbed those, too.

Luke was sitting up when she came back, trying to get his jacket off.

"Don't move," she said, swatting his arm, perhaps slightly harder than necessary. Her frustration had to go somewhere. "Let me."

She tugged it down his shoulders. She couldn't help but remember when she had pushed Konig's shirt down his shoulders earlier, though in a completely different context. It was horrible that she'd even equate the two in her mind.

Marion couldn't help but stare when she cut his shirt away, though. Dr. Lucas Flynn was, somehow, even more sculpted than a sidhe prince. How a doctor had time to provide the kind of compassionate care he'd delivered to Elena Eiderman and still carve his body into that of a god was a mystery for another day. One where he wasn't bleeding out of a wound longer than Marion's arm, slicing him open from armpit to hip.

She stared at the massive, gaping wound even harder than his impressive abdominals. "You had a calm conversation with me while hiding *that* under your jacket."

"Think I was in shock," Luke said. "The shock is fading. Unfortunately."

She tucked a couple of worn pillows behind him so that he could lean back, and then gave him a glass of whiskey. "What should we do about this?" She pointed at his wound and kept her eyes on his face. *Not* his muscles.

"First I'm going to get drunk. Then you're going to be an extra pair of hands while I stitch it up," Luke said.

"You're going to perform surgery on yourself?"

Marion was going to need at least one drink, too. She poured a glass for herself and drank it quickly. It burned all the way down and made her eyes prick with tears. "Okay, what's next?"

"Clean this needle with alcohol. Wash your hands while you're at it. Then put on the gloves at the bottom of the box."

Marion hurried to do as he told her, taking the tools to the sink. Through the kitchen window, she saw that the snow was only increasing. It was thick enough in the back yard that she could see only a few inches of the fence.

They were not going to be able to go to the hospital any time soon.

"The faucet isn't working," Marion said.

Luke muttered a curse. "Of course the water's off. There are bottles in another cabinet. Don't remember which one."

She found them hiding behind some canned green beans that looked about as appealing as roadkill. Marion set a couple of bottles aside for drinking, then took one for her hands. "I hope this melts overnight," she said, washing her hands thoroughly in the sink using old, gummy soap that was crusted to its bottle. "I don't know how I'll drive to the city in this kind of weather."

"I'll be able to drive us tomorrow," Luke said. He poured himself another drink and knocked it back. The whiskey didn't seem to bother him at all. He'd had a few more years to practice drinking than she had, though.

She brought the sterilized needle back to him,

pulling the gloves on. "What now?"

"Thread the needle for me," he said.

There was just enough room on the couch for Marion to sit between his body and the edge. While she threaded the needle, he washed away some of the blood with the cheap whiskey. He barely even groaned.

Marion struggled to do her part, and all it required was getting one stupid piece of thread through a tiny hole.

They were going to sew him shut.

She was feeling faint, and it wasn't because of that foul-tasting gasoline that was masquerading as whiskey.

Luke was watching her. "You okay?"

"Delightful," she snapped. "This is *so* much better than taking you to a hospital."

"Uh-huh. Press the sides of the skin together for me."

Marion did, and then she redirected her gaze to the bookshelves so that she wouldn't have to see the needle going in.

He was fast and neat, even when working on himself. According to the clock on the wall, the tidy stitches only took a few minutes, even though he had to span a good eighteen inches of his body. It felt like much, much longer to Marion. Her heart pounded in her temples the whole time he did it.

But then he was done.

"You can look again," Luke said, sagging back against the couch. He was even paler than when he'd started.

"There's Percocet in the first aid kit," Marion said.

"I'd rather stick to the whiskey. It's more fun. And they don't mix well." His eyes had slid shut, and it didn't look like they were likely to open any time soon.

Marion swept through the room to clean it up: the bloody remnants of his shirt, the blankets, extra gauze, the needle. She shoved everything into an empty trash bin before returning to Luke.

His jacket wasn't destroyed, but it would stain if the blood were allowed to set. She sat on the floor beside him to spot-clean it with another water bottle.

"What are you doing?" Luke asked sleepily. She thought he'd been unconscious.

"Never you mind that," Marion said. "Focus on resting."

"What if I focus on more whiskey?"

She eyeballed the bottle. The two of them had demolished half of it, but very little of that had been Marion's responsibility. "I'm not sure you should."

"I've got a hollow leg," he said.

Marion handed the bottle to him. Their hands almost touched—merely an inch apart.

It would be so easy to twitch her thumb and get that skin contact she so badly wanted. The memories she *needed*.

Luke seemed to sense the direction of her thoughts. He jerked the bottle away.

Marion set his jacket aside. "Doctor..." She

shifted onto the sofa beside him again.

He watched her blearily, mind so fogged by pain and alcohol that Marion could see the distortion of his brain signals. She hadn't gotten all that much from him before. Luke's mind was usually as guarded as the rest of his demeanor. "Marion. Marion Garin."

"Yes, that's my name," she said.

"Beautiful," Luke said, just like Elena Eiderman had.

She inched her hand toward his on the couch. "The briefest touches have given me language, memory, and magic. What do you think would happen if we touched each other longer than that?"

"We already talked about this."

"This isn't about your memories. It's about mine. What if you're the key to unlocking everything?"

"I'm not." He said it so emphatically that she couldn't help but recoil. "Whatever weird reaction strikes up whenever we touch—it's gotta be coincidence, or accident—"

"But it's *every time*. Don't you think that means something? Don't you feel something between us?"

He went tense all over.

Marion had gone too far. Brought up a facet of their relationship neither had addressed aloud.

It was too late to take it back, so she took a deep breath and plunged on. "This isn't about your memories at all, is it?" Marion asked. "It's because of this...um, this chemistry between us." Gods, she hoped she wasn't hallucinating the chemistry. She could only handle so much humiliation for one night. "We have a special connection. I felt it from the moment I saw you in the hospital."

Luke set the whiskey bottle aside. "I won't say chemistry. Connection—maybe. I feel connected with a lot of patients."

"Would you *really* follow most patients into the Middle Worlds to save them from assassins? Or are you trying to hurt me by pretending that you would?"

The look he gave her in response to that was very much like the one he'd given her in the clothes store in Port Angeles. "You know I'm not trying to hurt you."

"Then are you resisting me because of your ex-fiancée? Your ridiculous oath to remain alone?"

"I shouldn't have told you about that," Luke said. "No. My ex has got nothing to do with this."

She flung her hands into the air. "Then what is it? I'm not asking you to get married to me. I'm not even asking to go on a date. I'm asking you to help restore my memories and my magic! It's ridiculous that you won't do that because you're afraid we'll touch and—and that it will turn into something romantic."

It sounded much stupider when she said it out loud than when she had considered the idea. Now she was on a roll and she couldn't stop herself. The verbal diarrhea just kept getting worse.

"You shouldn't flatter yourself, Dr. Flynn! Don't even imagine that you're at risk of having a romantic *thing* with me. I'm the Voice of God!"

"This again," he muttered.

"I am the Voice of God," she repeated, more firmly, "and my boyfriend is a sidhe prince. I can touch you without consequence. I'm not afraid of falling in love with the likes of a mundane man like *you*."

Although once she said that hideous four-letter word, she realized that it might have been a little too close to truth.

Marion hadn't left the Autumn Court because she genuinely thought Konig wanted to hurt her.

She'd left for Luke.

Her mouth snapped shut. She slipped off the couch and sat on the floor by his jacket, where she should have been the whole time.

"I'm not drunk enough for this," Luke said, leaning against the back of the couch again.

Marion's eyes burned. "Me neither." She poured herself another glass and drank it down. It was just as awful as it had been the first time.

Gods, she hoped he was drunk enough not to have noticed what she'd said.

His tone was a lot gentler when he started talking again. "You don't know me. We only met a few days ago."

Yet Marion felt as though they were so much closer than that. She trusted him more than anyone else she had met in her brief memories. She wanted to open herself to him, and have the favor returned.

It was naïveté. Illusions of emotion cast around

the confusion of memory loss and adrenaline.

Luke had told her no.

No, she couldn't use his money.

No, she couldn't touch him.

But yes, he would save her. And he'd keep saving her as long as she needed it. Couldn't Marion be satisfied with that?

She folded her hands under her arms, squeezing them tightly to her sides. "It's absurd you won't help me when you can do it so easily. That's all I'm trying to tell you."

His hand slipped down to rest on her clothed shoulder. "I don't want to hurt you, Marion. It's just *complicated*."

She inched away from him.

"Angels can read minds," Luke said.

Leliel had proven that quite effectively. "Yes, I know."

"The more you touch me, the likelier it becomes you'll read my mind." He sighed. "Look... this is the thing: you're important. You know a lot of people. Tomorrow, you're going to go to this summit where all these other important people are waiting, and if you've gotten something out of my head—if they get something about me out of *your* head... It's just not safe."

"You're important too, aren't you?" Marion asked. "That's why you're such an enigma."

"You don't have to be important to make important enemies. We aren't touching again for my safety." After a pause, he said, more quietly, "And for yours."

Marion finally nodded. "I'm sorry."

"Don't apologize," he said. "We're just going to hole up until it's time to get you to the summit. All right? Giving that speech is the only way we're going to shake off your assassins."

He didn't say it, but Marion understood that it was also the only way that Luke would be able to get rid of her, too.

SEVENTEEN

Luke could only tell when morning came because his senses told him that the protective cloak of nighttime had been stripped away. There was no sunlight to indicate the time: the snow was too thick, the clouds too heavy, the valley too deep. It was always too deep. Morning had never touched his old home in the mountains.

It was strange waking up to that timeless twilight the way that he used to. When Luke had last awakened in such a fashion, it had been a different world, a different time.

He'd been a different man.

Sitting up was difficult, which had less to do with the stitches woven into his side and more to do with the sheer volume of whiskey that he had drunk the previous night. Even Luke, hollow-legged as he'd claimed to be, could get a hangover.

It wasn't easy, but he'd managed somehow.

He groaned, resting a hand on his stitches. The skin was hot. His human body was struggling to heal as best it could.

Luke was acutely aware of the fact that the pain was his fault. He could have avoided it. Could have been healed by other methods.

Marion could have fixed him.

But he'd made his choices, and he was going to stick with them.

He drank the last half-inch of whiskey in the bottle before forcing himself off the lumpy couch and into the kitchen.

The bedroom door was cracked open a fraction of an inch. Marion rested atop the comforter, hand on the pillow beside her face, curls arranged so neatly around her head that it looked deliberate. Luke hung by the doorway to watch her sleep, feeling the weight of the snow outside the building as it pressed in on them, confining the two of them in the tomb of Luke's old life.

Her heart pulsed steadily, shooting blood through the lacework of veins patterning her pale throat. Her brow was furrowed even though she was unconscious.

Marion was unhappy. He'd done that to her, and no amount of migraine would make him forget it.

"Damn," Luke muttered.

There was nothing to cook for breakfast. He could only crack open old canned food, so old that they still had the barcodes with the black parallel lines stamped on white. He opened the tops, drained the liquids from the fruit, dumped it in a bowl.

Not much of a breakfast, but at least it would be enough to keep them from being hungry for a little while. Long enough to plan how they'd get out of the house, get to New York, deliver Marion to the summit. Twelve hours wasn't nearly enough time.

"Good morning." Marion had sneaked up on Luke and stood by the bedroom door, hair tousled and face puffy from sleep. She wore the same jeans as the night before, but she'd replaced the shredded bathrobe with one of Luke's t-shirts. It overwhelmed her slender form.

He set the canned food on the table, a rickety little thing with barely enough room for one of them to sit by it, although there were two rickety chairs to match. "Morning."

Marion slipped into the seat across from him. Her hands were folded in her lap, posture hunched. Her usual arrogance had faded.

"Marion," he began.

"How does your injury feel this morning?" she interrupted.

"Fine," he lied. "Better."

She nodded and didn't offer to heal him again. He was grateful for that. "How will I reach the summit in time with this snow?"

That wasn't where Luke had planned to begin their conversation, but it was probably better. "There are Snowcats we could borrow. If we can just get out of the valley, we should be able to get another truck to take us the rest of the way."

Or he could touch Marion long enough to give her the magic to heal him and then burn their way out.

Much faster, but much more dangerous.

She rose from the table again without eating. "Would you like to see something I discovered last night?" She didn't wait for a response before ducking into the bedroom and returning with a box. He recognized it even before she opened it.

Marion had found an old battery-powered TV. Its screen was the size of Luke's palm.

"That doesn't still work, does it?" he asked.

She turned it on, fiddled with the antenna.

The news faded in. Luke could make out reporter January Lazar's blurry features.

"—the summit beginning tonight, the final members of the participating factions are arriving," she said. "The infernal delegation arrived in its entirety yesterday, along with Deirdre Tombs and Jolene Chang, leaders of the American Gaean Commission, representing non-sanctuary gaeans. There's no sign of the sidhe from any court as of yet."

Marion kept swiveling the antenna, trying to bring the signal into focus. "I spent an hour watching the news after going to bed. They've been talking about the summit nonstop."

"Anything interesting?"

"Everything," she said. "Unfortunately, all that I've learned isn't enough to write a new speech."

"We'll have to get you into the United Nations before we can even worry about that," Luke said. "I was awake last night, too. Doing some planning. The sidhe will be around the UN, trying to catch you before you get inside. We'll have to sneak you past them."

"That means I'll have to disguise myself without magic." Marion smiled a little. It wasn't as bright as her usual smiles had been, as though she'd lost some of her spark. "I don't suppose you have a fake mustache in here somewhere?"

Someone knocked on the front door. Marion and Luke lifted their heads simultaneously to look at each other.

Who would go to an abandoned house in a rural valley in this snow?

The potential answers weren't good.

Marion was on her feet in moments, bow lifted, arrow nocked.

Someone knocked again.

Luke stood just behind Marion with gun drawn. "I'll get it," he said softly. He stepped beside the door, back pressed to the wall, and unlocked the deadbolt.

He waited until Marion nodded her acquiescence before throwing the door open.

Luke leaped around the doorframe, lifting the gun.

But he knew the person who stood on the other side.

It was Nori. The half-angel girl who had told him about the Autumn Court's plans for war. She sucked in a breath at the sight of Luke and Marion aiming their weapons at her.

"It's okay, Marion," Luke said, lowering the gun. "She's an ally."

Then another woman stepped out from behind Nori.

It was Brianna Dimaria. The witch that had given Luke the enchanted cell phone and the car.

The witch who knew who he really was.

"Hey," Brianna said with a big smile. "Can we come in?"

When Luke had spoken to Brianna on the phone, the witch's voice had sounded identical to the last time he'd seen her. In his mind, Luke had envisioned she would look the way she had at that time, too.

More than a decade earlier, Brianna had been a petite girl with shaggy brown hair who wore long tunics, ratty jeans, and ridiculous amounts of wooden jewelry. She'd been—still was—a witch of the Wiccan persuasion with a twist of modern hippy on top.

Thirteen years had elapsed since their last investigation together. Thirteen years since Luke had realized something had changed and that he couldn't live a life with his peers anymore.

Brianna had aged from early twenties to mid-thirties. The years had worn her down and added a few lines to her face—not the kind that came from smiling, but the kind that came from frowning as she struggled to resolve mysteries.

She still had all that enchanted wooden jewelry, though. That hadn't changed. Nor had her sterling ability to corner Luke and make him feel like she'd sucked all the oxygen out of the room.

"The kid thinks Seth Wilder can bring her memories back?" Brianna had backed him into the bedroom near the closet—the only space in the house with a door that shut, aside from the bathroom.

"Keep your voice down," Luke said. "Don't say that name."

"But if Marion thinks that Seth Wilder can save her…"

"He can't." Luke shot a look over the top of her head, through the doorway, and into the living room. Nori hadn't arrived with Brianna alone. Charity Ballard had come, too. Now Nori, Charity, and Marion were talking, and there was enough power between them that it felt like the house should have exploded around them. "How did you even find us?"

He didn't bother asking how Brianna had gotten there through the snow—Nori's ethereal ability to walk between planes meant that weather presented no hindrance to travel.

"I tracked your pickup down and found those women in it. They told me what's been going on. What they know about it, anyway. And then I used the pickup to cast a tracking spell to find you."

"That's better magic than you used to be able to do," Luke said. Brianna was a good witch, but she wasn't strong. Mostly she was clever. Dangerously so. "Why bring Nori and Charity?"

"They didn't give me any choice. You've still got that way of making ladies follow you everywhere you go, you dog. Thirteen years and nothing changes. Literally nothing."

"Keep your voice down," he said again, even though Marion was distracted.

"God," Brianna whispered, gazing at Luke like she'd never seen him before. "You haven't aged a day." She reached up to touch his cheek. He knew that she was feeling for the lines that should have been on his face. For texture and pores and blemishes that didn't exist. "How is this possible? I look like I fell out of the old lady tree and hit every branch on the way down, while you look like you did when—"

"You shouldn't have come for me."

"I couldn't leave you alone if you were in trouble. We might not be partners anymore, but I still want to help." She pinched his cheek. It was a sororal gesture, almost a maternal one. That was how much his frozen age had shifted their relationship. "You'll want my help to disappear again, too."

Luke glanced again at Marion, who was talking with Nori in French in the other room. From that angle, he could only see a sliver of Marion's face concealed by her wavy brown hair. "Yeah, I'm going to have to disappear, so don't tell her who I am. She'll pass it on. And then Rylie..." He sighed. "Just don't tell her who I am."

"I'll help you, like I always did." Brianna finally backed away, giving Luke room.

Charity was exploring the kitchen. It was impossible to tell she was a revenant in this setting. She was hiding behind those big glasses again, along with a baggy sweater. She smiled when she saw Luke, and the teeth she exposed were both charmingly crooked and a little too big for her features. He smiled back.

If he was going to have to disappear again, it was nice reconnecting with the life he'd have to leave behind. He'd really liked being Dr. Lucas Flynn and working with Charity Ballard. He would miss it.

"Nori is the solution to our problems," Marion said, smoothly transitioning to English. "There's a ley line juncture just over the ocean near the United Nations building. She can pull us through there, and then magic us to the shore."

Luke remained in the doorway, shoulder leaning against the wall, arms folded. "That's only the solution to one problem—getting us to New York."

"What other problems do we have? She's expected at the summit, isn't she?" Charity asked. "They should be thrilled to see her."

"I see Nori and Brianna filled you in," Luke said.

Charity smiled bashfully. "I felt bad for calling in the tip that got the sidhe on your butt. Sorry,

Marion."

Marion inclined her head. "Thank you."

"I want to be able to help, whatever it takes," Charity said.

"Then you can help us figure out what to do about this." Brianna pulled a newspaper out of her jacket and handed it to Luke.

He unfolded the newspaper. The front page was plastered with Marion's photo—a beauty shot where she was smiling wide, showing her dimples. The headline said, "Keynote Speaker Reported Missing Hours Before Summit."

And there was a sketch of a man at the bottom with a wide nose and hard eyes.

A sketch that could conceivably be Luke, as drawn by someone who had only ever heard him described in vague terms.

"They're accusing Dr. Lucas Flynn of abducting Marion," Brianna said.

Marion edged nearer to peer at the newspaper over Luke's shoulder. "*Merde.*"

"This is worse than you realize, Marion," Nori said. "In the past, they haven't publicly shown your face in order to protect your identity—to keep you from becoming a celebrity." She tugged the newspaper from Luke's hands to skim it again. "This seems to be a full profile on you."

"*Merde,*" Marion said again, with even more feeling.

Luke felt the same.

Marion would never be able to lurk in anonymity again.

And he was getting dragged into the spotlight beside her.

The article on Marion had been written by ErlKonig. At least, it had been attributed to him. It was so lengthy that she had a hard time imagining the prince writing it personally.

All of the information must have been provided by Konig, though. There were details about her that she hadn't even known. It was an impassioned piece about their relationship, which was written more like a romance, really, what with the way he talked about "when our eyes first met" and how he "instantly knew we were destined."

Konig wrote that he was crushed about her abduction. All he wanted, with his whole heart, was to have her returned safely to him.

Marion read through the whole thing while sitting on the couch. She lowered it to her thighs and stared at the wall.

"Help bring my princess back to me." That was how the article had ended—with as much passion as he'd expressed to her in the gardens of Myrkheimr.

He only wanted her back.

She reached over to flip the battery-powered TV on again. After a moment's fiddling with the antenna, the news appeared. Marion's face was displayed on the screen beside the sketch of Luke

Flynn used in the newspaper. She couldn't get away from it. Everyone was looking for the Voice of God and her supposed abductor.

The couch creaked as Luke sat beside Marion. He turned the TV off. "Don't watch that." He took the newspaper, tossed it aside. "And don't worry about that, either."

"Everyone's looking for me."

"That's why we'll have to be careful getting you to the United Nations," he said. "If we can get you on stage, the killers will have to give up."

"How can we do that?" Marion said.

"All I know right now is that I *will* get you on that stage," Luke said. The confidence in his tone was comforting. She'd have been even more comforted if he actually had a plan.

"I could escort her," Charity said. "I want to be helpful so let me help."

"No," Luke said. "That wouldn't be subtle."

"Having a nurse escort me into the United Nations? I should say not. There's no way someone like *her* has the clearance," Marion said.

Shame tinged Charity's thoughts. The nurse looked at her feet.

"Cut it, Marion," Luke said.

She straightened her back. "Don't talk to me like that."

"Don't talk to Charity like that and I won't," Luke said. "We need to get you to the stage without killing the hundreds of people who get in your path. No offense, Charity. It's a good idea otherwise."

Marion's eyes widened. How would a nurse kill hundreds of people?

"I wouldn't need to kill *everyone*, would I?" Charity asked, pushing her glasses up her nose. "Just assassins."

"Yeah, but everyone in New York City is going to be looking for Marion. Not just the bounty hunters, but civilians hoping to get a reward for finding her," Brianna said. "There's no way we'll be able to get near the United Nations building without someone reporting her to the sidhe. And once they do, there'll be a lot more than a handful of determined assassins to contend with."

"So I can't be seen at all." Marion offered a weak smile to Luke. "As I said, I think I need a fake mustache."

He wasn't looking at her. His focus was still on the nurse, Charity Ballard.

"I've got a better idea than a mustache," he said.

Nori spirited them from the ley line in the snow-heavy clouds to a rooftop near the United Nations. Once Marion had solid concrete under her feet, she had plenty of time to study New York City: the distant streets, the fog lit by office windows, the drifting zeppelins.

Marion's first impression of New York was that it was, in its own way, as magical as the glimpses of

New Eden she had seen in Leliel's mind. She had a hard time imagining that its skyscrapers could have been built rather than grown with magic. They surrounded her like tombstones honoring the beautiful dead of Earth's past. Old buildings and new, from before Genesis and after, all shimmering with gaean life.

The United Nations building was the tallest of the skyscrapers. Its elegant white lines were identical to New Eden's once-glorious monuments. The throb of ethereal magic within its foundations whispered the story of angels laboring to spin its beauty the way a spider spun webs.

The angels' web had caught a thousand tiny bugs. Some of them spiders, and others prey. The black-clad security that skittered around the courtyard were spiders—little ones compared to the angels who'd designed the building, but spiders nonetheless. The humans milling outside the barricade hoping to see a preternatural celebrity were prey. Barely more than gnats.

If the search for Marion erupted into violence, there would be a lot of collateral damage.

"Get away from the edge," Luke said from behind Marion. "You're making me nervous."

She'd stepped up to the farthest corner of their rooftop without realizing it, compelled to approach the kindred magic of the United Nations. Marion hopped back down. "Did you see the screens?"

"They're impossible to miss," Luke said.

Massive screens had been hung from each side

of the United Nations building—big white rectangles that covered easily twenty stories each. The auditorium, where the kickoff speeches would be held, was projected on those screens. The stage was empty at the moment, but if Luke's plan were successful, the screen would soon show Marion taking the podium.

Luke was assembling a sniper rifle nearby, screwing a scope on top of it at the moment.

"You'll be staying here when I give the speech," she said. "Won't you?"

Luke peered through the scope as if to test it. "I'm going to cover your back while you enter the building. Yeah."

Marion wrapped her arms around her body, shielding herself from the ice-heavy wind. Her hair whipped in front of her face. "You said you'd stay with me until the summit. That you wouldn't leave me alone."

"You won't be," he said. They planned for Nori to guide Marion into the United Nations while Charity Ballard created a distraction. Marion would have preferred a plan that kept Luke at her side, but he didn't want to go inside.

Charity, Nori, and Brianna were chatting in the shelter of an air conditioning unit, huddled where the wind couldn't reach them. They didn't look like an intimidating team.

"Is Brianna your ex?" Marion asked.

"We dated for about a week."

Marion should have figured that Brianna wasn't Luke's ex-fiancée. She was too old, and the feelings that drifted on the surface of her mind weren't intense enough for them to have been engaged. "You said you choose to be alone. Why break your rule for a week?"

Luke lowered his eye to the scope again. Adjusted the sniper rifle. "It's easy to date someone when you're not afraid it'll get serious."

"That's cold."

"She knows how I feel," he said.

"She must still care about you to track you down like this."

"Guess so." He didn't seem like he wanted to talk about it.

Marion couldn't help but continue to push. "Would you break your oath for Charity? She wants you."

That got his attention. Luke finally looked at her. "You've been reading Charity's mind?"

"I get some feelings," Marion said. "She has a lot of them where you're concerned."

He glanced at the women huddled behind the air conditioning unit. "I didn't know that." Luke shook his head, standing from the gun. "I wouldn't date her."

"Afraid it would get serious?"

"No," he said. "I'm not."

Charity crossed the rooftop, pulling her glasses off. Her eyes looked bigger when she wasn't wearing them. "Your speech is scheduled to begin in an hour, Marion. I think it's time for me to create the diversion."

"I'm ready when you are," Luke said.

Surrounded by snow and the spires of New York, his irises truly looked a depthless shade of black.

Marion looked Charity over again. It was hard to imagine such a shrunken woman could be distracting enough to distract OPA security. "How will this work, exactly?"

"I'll give you my glamour, and then I'll go walking down there," Charity said. "That's all it will take."

Surprise washed over Marion. "You have a glamour?"

"Yep, in my glasses. All you have to do is press both thumbs to the gems set into the inner arms, then put them on. The glamour will automatically be removed from me and pass over to you. Only one of us can wear it at a time."

Marion took the glasses. She hadn't even noticed the tiny gems when she'd considered stealing them from the break room at Mercy Hospital. She had to look closely at them to notice the faintest sparks of magic, inside which glimmered a universe of complicated spellwork.

"Once you're inside the building, press your thumbs to the gems while you fold them and the glamour will end," Charity said. "It's easy."

"Once the glamour settles on Marion, we'll head downstairs and across the plaza," Nori said, jiggling her leg, twisting the hem of her shirt in both hands. Nerves had turned her into a flurry of fidgeting. "You've got to have the guards away before we cross the street, Charity."

"No problem," said the nurse.

"No problem at all," Marion echoed, gazing at the glasses without putting them on.

It was almost time to give a speech she didn't remember.

"What's wrong?" Luke asked in a low voice, quiet enough that only Marion would hear him. "Are you ready?"

All of her ire from the night before, when he'd hurt her feelings, drained away at the idea of leaving. She whispered, "I'm afraid, Doctor."

He pulled her against his side. Gave her a hug. Didn't touch her skin, but held her tight, for just a moment. "You're going to be fine, Marion," Luke said. "I promise."

I promise.

The words rang in her mind as she pressed her thumbs to the gems in the glasses. She slid them over her nose.

Magic hummed through Marion.

Nothing changed on her end of things. She could only tell that the glamour had taken her by the way that Luke stared.

Nori and Brianna, however, were staring at Charity.

The glamour fell away from the nurse.

She grew taller. Thinner. Her skin became pallid and her cheeks hollowed, while her eyes sank deep into her skull. Charity's lips peeled back to expose uneven teeth with sharp points and a black tongue too long to be contained by her jaw. It was the same shade of glossy black as her fingernails—which were more like claws, really.

Her gut was hollow under her ribs, as though she didn't have any organs.

But even though she was every inch the monster, the expression on her face was embarrassment.

She would never pass for human. She was too tall to blend into the crowd. It was worse when she moved, because her skin faded into transparence, as though she were little more than a ghost.

Now Marion could imagine how Charity could serve as a distraction.

"I'll count to thirty and head down," Charity said. Her voice was a low hiss, the whisper of wind through cadavers dangling at the gallows. "I'll keep them busy as long as possible, but...don't take your time crossing the street."

"We won't," Nori said.

She grabbed Marion and ran.

EIGHTEEN

A cyclone of snow whipped around Marion and Nori as they crossed the street, huddled together for warmth. The blizzard was thick enough to blind Marion to the world more than a block away. The city was turned to little more than ghostly shapes in the night.

They couldn't reach the barricade surrounding the United Nations. There was too much of a crowd hoping to see politicians on their way into the summit. Not a single one of them realized that the keynote speaker was among them, hidden behind thick-framed glasses and a glamour that made her look like a mousy healthcare professional.

Marion's nerves jolted when the guards glanced at her, even though they didn't react. Her face was plastered on every newspaper, every television, and more than a few billboards. But now Marion's face wasn't Marion's face.

She squinted up at the office building where Luke waited with the sniper rifle. At that distance, she couldn't even see the roof. It was unlikely that he'd be able to see her, either.

It didn't matter. He wouldn't be able to protect her once she ran inside with Nori.

"Take a few deep breaths," Nori whispered.

Had Marion looked that afraid? She forced herself to smile. "Thank you."

Apparently she wasn't very convincing. Nori squeezed her hand tightly. "Believe it or not, you're in your element. You thrive in danger and politics. That hasn't gone anywhere, even if your memories have."

"I'm sorry, do I know you?" Marion asked.

Nori's smile wavered. "You told me once that I was your only friend in the Autumn Court."

Secretary Friederling appeared on the screens hanging on each side of the United Nations building.

Cheers spread through the crowds as bodies shifted for a better view.

"Mr. President, Madame Alpha, fellow delegates, ladies and gentlemen," he began. He spoke in the same clipped tones that he'd used to write the preface for Rylie Gresham's autobiography. "Nearly fifteen years after Genesis, it's worth reflecting on how far the world has come, together, and how much more we can accomplish in the future."

"Let's try cutting through over here," Nori muttered to Marion, tugging her toward the barrier on the right.

The OPA secretary went on. "Out of the ashes of Genesis…"

People began to scream, drowning his voice out.

Charity had descended down the street.

The revenant was far enough away that Marion could only see the shape of her in the light of the street lamp. Her silhouette was extending, stretching, twisting. She was at least twelve feet tall.

The crowd buffeted against Marion, running and screaming. Only Nori's hand anchored her.

"Stay close," Nori said. "We're almost there."

The black-clad security guards ran in the opposite direction of the crowd. They were heading toward Charity, not away.

Nori and Marion were the only ones who moved perpendicular to the flow of traffic, straight across the courtyard. Nori lifted the chain. Marion ducked under it and entered a restricted area, unseen.

The courtyard was paved with white stones that had been textured so they wouldn't be slick in the snow. Marion couldn't tell where the base of the building was, given that it was made all of white stone too. For a few dizzying moments, heading into the United Nations, she felt like she was running straight up the side of the building.

A glass door appeared in the swirling snow.

Secretary Friederling's voice continued to thunder from the speakers as Marion ran for it.

"...the ideal that this body must pursue, even when we are imperfect, and so often fall short of our ideals..."

Then they reached the door. It was shut.

Nori slammed her snow boots into the glass hard enough that it shattered. She elbowed the cruelest shards out of the frame, and then they plunged inside.

There was only one path into the lobby, which was demarcated with ropes, and ended with a metal detector. The room beyond was massive. Its walls were entirely glass, shimmering with enchanted magic. A crescent-shaped desk stood at the center to block the elevators, though it was currently unstaffed.

The entire lobby was empty, in fact.

"Where is everyone?" Marion asked. Her voice had changed to sound like Charity's when the glamour had taken over. That was the most unsettling part.

"The auditorium," she said.

Marion's pulse stuttered. "How do we get there?"

"Well, the main entrance to the auditorium is that way." Nori pointed to a wide hallway to the right of the elevators. The hall was curved so that Marion couldn't see into the auditorium, but the doors must have been open. Secretary Friederling's authoritative voice resonated through the whole bottom floor of the United Nations building. He would be preparing to introduce Marion, oblivious to the fight outside.

"Let's go," Marion said.

"Wait, we have to get you backstage. You'll never make it through the audience. Let's go around the other way." Nori broke into a jog, heading to a door marked for staff only. She pushed it open. "Come on," she said to Marion over her shoulder.

There was a guard on the other side. Nori didn't see him in time, and he came up on her quickly.

"Look out!" Marion said.

Nori didn't turn quickly enough. The guard brought his baton down on Nori's skull. The instant it made contact, her eyes went blank, and she crumbled into a puddle.

Marion muffled a cry and wheeled backward.

The guard came at her swinging.

She dodged and the baton smashed into her shoulder. White hot pain bloomed over her collarbone.

A gunshot.

Glass shattered.

The guard's baton dropped out of his grip. Blood dribbled from his wrist.

Marion looked from his bleeding wrist to the neat hole in the lobby window. It was angled perfectly for the shot to have come from above. High above. As in the rooftop across the street.

Luke was protecting her, just as he'd said he would.

More guards would be coming, though.

She leaped over the man Luke had shot and plunged into the employees-only hallway.

The hallway behind it was plainer than the lobby, with cement floors and tan walls. An area never meant to be seen by visitors. Pain pulsed through her shoulder with every strike of her feet against the carpet.

Marion yanked Charity's glasses off of her face and shoved them into her pocket. The glamour dropped away, revealing her true face. Anyone who saw her would know who she was. And there could be assassins anywhere.

She turned a corner, following the sound of Secretary Friederling's voice blindly.

Leliel stood at the end of the hall. The angel was watching the speech through a window, giving Marion only a profile view of her beautiful face. The auditorium's light tinted her nose and lips and rimmed her auburn hair with gold.

Marion skidded to a halt, heart pounding and lungs heaving. "Leliel. Oh, thank the gods."

"Marion." Surprise crossed Leliel's features. "I heard you'd been abducted from Myrkheimr."

"I wasn't abducted. I ran away. The Autumn Court is trying to kill me."

"Is that so?" Leliel asked.

The sound of bodies moving at the end of the hall echoed toward Marion. There were more pounding footsteps, more people muttering. Reinforcements were heading toward Marion and Leliel. Once she heard them coming, she sensed the magic. Sidhe magic.

She stretched out her mind, feeling the specific fingerprint of the energy. Marion couldn't tell if it was unseelie or seelie yet. But she knew that it was powerful, and that it reminded her of being kissed under fountains of honey.

"Konig," she whispered. Her gut exploded with frenzied butterflies. She wanted to see her boyfriend, look into his eyes, *know* if he was complicit in her assassination.

Leliel's mild surprise shifted into alarm. "We need to get you on stage."

"I want to see Konig," she said.

"If the Autumn Court wants to hurt you, then you can't," Leliel said. "We should move. This way." She peered around the corner before striding down the hallway, the folds of her peach skirt fluttering behind her.

"Wait," Marion said. How did she know that Leliel wasn't going to hurt her, too? She thrust the enchanted silver bracelet toward the angel. "Put this on. Promise me that you're on my side, that you're going to help me."

Leliel slipped it on. "I have no intent of harming you, dear girl. Now let's go!"

Marion followed, and it felt like her heart was shredding to know she was moving away from Konig.

Leliel turned another corner, and another. Her legs were so long that Marion had to take three steps for every one that Leliel took, and Marion was hardly short. "Are you ready to give your speech?" the angel asked, twisting the silver cuff on her wrist.

"Not at all," Marion said. "I'm hoping it will magically come to me when I get on stage." She wasn't joking about the "magically" thing.

Displeasure darkened Leliel's eyes. "What of the speech we wrote for you?"

"I'm not going to use it. The Autumn Court helped write it. I can't trust their speechwriters if they want me dead," Marion said.

"Are you sure you won't use that speech?" Leliel asked. "Absolutely certain? Because I helped write it, too."

"I'll still help you as speaker," Marion said. "I just can't give the speech."

"Shame. We're almost there," Leliel said. She pushed a pair of double doors open.

There was an empty ballroom on the other side. It was even bigger than the lobby had been, with balconies overlooking the glossy wooden floor and tapestries hanging from every wall. There was also a small stage and an orchestra pit in front of it.

Marion stepped in behind Leliel, confused. She didn't hear Secretary Friederling's voice anymore. "This leads to the summit?"

"No," Leliel said.

Pain bloomed in Marion's midsection.

She looked down to find a knife embedded left of her navel, still clutched by Leliel. The enchanted honesty bracelet glowed.

"So," Leliel said, "you do bleed red. You're not

as much an angel as they say."

Marion's pulse throbbed in her skull. She gripped Leliel's wrist in both hands, trying to push her away. The angel was so strong. "What are you doing?" Marion stuttered over the question, slick fingers sliding on the angel's arm.

"I'll assume that question isn't because you're stupid, but because of the shock," Leliel said. "Obviously I'm killing you."

She yanked the knife free. It actually hurt worse being removed, probably because of the serrated edge that tore Marion's skin.

Marion touched the wound. Blood dribbled between her fingers.

"You made me speaker," she whispered. "The bracelet..."

"It doesn't work on me," Leliel said, "thanks to the same magecraft that gives me the ability to fly. Should I have mentioned that?"

The reality of the scenario caught up with Marion.

Obviously I'm killing you.

Leliel drove the knife toward Marion again. Marion flung herself away, scrambling across the floor. She slipped on her own blood. It was so slick, puddled on the floor of the ballroom.

She hurled herself into the orchestra pit. She didn't fall nearly as gracefully as she had when leaping off the balcony in Myrkheimr with Luke. Marion thudded to her knees, and the shock of pain through her belly was so intense that she couldn't get up again.

"What about everything you said before, about wanting my help to save the angels?" Marion asked. Her throat was thick with tears.

"Sure, if you'd just given my speech. But you won't. I can't trust you. Honestly, this is a far more satisfying result," Leliel said. "Especially since it's your father's fault that so many angels are dead in the first place." The angel stepped up to the edge of the orchestra pit, gazing down at Marion with unconcealed disdain. Marion's red blood slid along the cutting edge of the knife.

Leliel's magicked wings snapped wide. She leaped into the pit, knife uplifted, her face formed into a mask of determination.

Marion needed to access her magic to save her own life—without touching Luke.

If she was the Voice of God, then surely there were gods who cared about her. Deities who wouldn't want her to die.

They might not have loved her enough to protect her from memory loss, but surely they wouldn't want to replace her. Who else could speak for the gods? Who was as special as she was, the half-witch daughter of the angel who had last been the Voice of God?

Nobody.

The gods wouldn't let her get killed—not like this, not now, when she was so close to delivering their message to the summit. Whatever that message was.

Marion prayed to powers she should have been acquainted with.

Give me my power.

Leliel landed inches from Marion. The knife descended toward Marion's face.

"No!" Marion grabbed Leliel's wrist.

Magic crashed through them on contact.

Scraps of a bond lingered from where they had shared memories in the Autumn Court. Marion seized upon that. She used it to punch directly into Leliel's mind.

Leliel brimmed with thousands of years' worth of memories—so many more memories than the brief scenes in Araboth and New Eden. Her experiences predated Genesis, stretching all the way back to the days when the old gods had still been thriving.

Marion ripped her mind open to expose ancient cities and oases, long stretches of empty desert, armies clashing in midday heat. Marion searched back as far as she could go, absorbing the enormity of Leliel's experiences.

If she couldn't have memories of her own, she could have this woman's.

"Get out!" Leliel roared.

Their minds beat against each other. Marion had lost all sense of her body, the wound in her belly, the blood pouring out. She only felt magic against magic.

The harder Leliel fought to repel Marion, the deeper she sank into the angel's memory.

She saw Leliel in the Ethereal Levant, at a modern palace with a thousand hollow rooms and only a dozen living occupants.

"They won't want us in the Winter Court," Jibril said. He was sitting primly at a table, frowning at a chessboard. He was in the middle of a game against Leliel. "There's a reason that the demons were given the Nether Worlds in Genesis while we were banished to one small region on Earth."

"I don't care what the gods want for us." Leliel had slid her pawn diagonally to take one of Jibril's.

"The others at the summit will care. When Metaraon's daughter tells everyone the will of the gods, the vote will follow her words."

"We'll buy the votes," Leliel said.

Jibril moved his knight. "It won't be enough."

And in that moment, Leliel had decided that Marion needed to die. The decision had been emotionless and instantaneous.

Leliel shoved Marion out of that memory. Marion wheeled through the canyons of the angel's mind.

Genesis was in there, repeated a thousand times over. The roar of a black void consuming the world, sucking entire cities into nothingness, quenching billions of souls. That hadn't traumatized Leliel as much as having her wings cut off. That memory was drenched in crimson, too wrought with emotion for Marion to interpret it.

Marion pushed back. She dived deeper.

Leliel screamed in an endless, wordless way that resonated through the memories. Marion's magic was stronger, though. She was a mage, a bearer of old powers that Leliel couldn't reach on her best of days.

The memories became more vibrant as Marion delved deeper. Leliel was fondest of her youth, when she had lived in a garden.

A garden?

Marion lingered over those parts of Leliel's mind. It was the same place that Marion had remembered when drawing on her magic to fight the sirens: the place with moss underfoot and a canopy of trees high above.

Leliel gave the garden a name.

Eden.

Marion had lived in Eden when she was a child, and that was also where Leliel—and all angels—had been born many centuries earlier.

But the Eden that Leliel remembered was far more vibrant than the one in Marion's memories. Eden hadn't been an empty garden, but a booming metropolis filled with thousands of angels. A flourishing species at the peak of skill in art and magical science.

With the memory of Eden came memories of Marion's father.

Metaraon had been an imposing man, even for an angel. He had been taller than his brethren, brighter-eyed and darker-skinned. Marion could see so much of herself in him. She had the more delicate version of his nose, the diluted version of his deep olive flesh, the thickness of his hair. The similarities ran deeper than the surface. The imperiousness in his stance was something

SM Reine

Marion had seen in every mirror she passed. He was frightening, arrogant—powerful.

He was the real reason Leliel had decided Marion needed to die. In truth, Leliel had wanted Marion dead for years. Metaraon had been gone for a long time. There was no chance to get revenge against him now—only the last, lingering remnants of his blood on the Earth.

This death had been coming ever since Marion had been born.

Marion gazed upon Metaraon's cruel eyes, so similar to her own, and she ached for the father she would never know.

Father, she whispered into Leliel's mind.

Metaraon reached for her with one hand. *Daughter*.

Sudden, powerful fear bucked through Leliel.

"Get out of my head!"

It wasn't Leliel's scream that finally exorcised Marion from the angel's memory. It was a sudden shock of electricity in Marion's physical body.

She crashed back into her own mind. Her eyes flew open.

Marion was flat on her back in the orchestra pit. Leliel was hunched beside her, tears streaming down her cheeks, magicked wings drooping. The knife was on the floor between them.

Another shock of electricity.

It originated from the wound in Marion's belly. She gripped it with a groan. Fresh blood spurted between her fingers.

Leliel lifted her head at the sound of Marion's

cry. Her eyes fell on the knife.

The angel seized the hilt. Before she could lift it, a boot slammed into Leliel's wrist, pinning her hand to the ground. Marion's eyes tracked up the booted foot crushing Leliel's hand to a muscular leg, narrow hips, and chiseled features.

It wasn't Luke, but an unseelie prince with blue-black hair and coppery skin.

"Princess," Konig said. He clutched a fistful of sidhe magic, which pulsed in time with the healing magic that she felt in her stab wound.

Konig was healing her. He was *saving* her.

Marion passed out.

NINETEEN

"There we go, sixteen thousand." Brianna counted out the last of the hundred dollar bills and dropped them next to Luke's sniper rifle. "Gimme your pinks."

Luke wasn't listening. He was watching the screens hanging on the outside of the United Nations building, which had showed Secretary Friederling's face until twenty minutes earlier. He had introduced Marion, stepped off stage, and then...nothing.

Marion still hadn't taken the podium.

The crowd gathered outside the UN were getting restless—what few of them remained after Charity's attack. Most had fled at first, but some had returned after the revenant's arrest to watch the rest of Secretary Friederling's speech, and probably to watch Marion's too. But she wasn't there.

"Hello, pay attention," Brianna said, waving a hand in front of his face.

He jerked back. "What?"

"Sixteen thousand for your pickup," Brianna said. "I just need you to sign the title over to me, please. That way I don't have to spend as much time at the DMV. I've got way better things to do than that."

Luke didn't bother counting the money to make sure it was all there. He signed off on the paperwork for the sale of his pickup and shoved it back at Brianna. "That's too much. It might be only three years old, but it's over ninety thousand miles."

"And in pristine condition, thanks to your mechanical skills and anal retentiveness. Bet you I flip it for twenty grand." Brianna plopped onto the roof beside him. She folded the title and stuck it inside her jacket. "You're going to need the money if you want a complete do-over on your identity again. That doesn't come cheap."

He made a noncommittal sound. Luke wasn't short on money. He'd been smart. Kept a lot of it in cash. He didn't even need to access his bank accounts in order to be set for the next ten years—more than enough time to get established as a new person.

Sixteen thousand wouldn't hurt, though. And the pickup had been his baby.

His eyes wandered to the screens again.

Still no Marion.

"Something's wrong," he said.

"Yeah, you've blown your identity in a big way," Brianna said. "Your sketch is floating around. It's a bad drawing, sure, but Rylie will figure out who that drawing represents once when she talks to Marion long enough."

That was true. And Rylie was an Alpha werewolf, so if she knew to go looking for Luke, all it would take was putting her wolfish nose to the ground to seek him out.

"Pack up the sniper rifle so we can go," Brianna said, snapping her fingers impatiently. "We've still got about a million pages of paperwork to do before you can start over again. It's worse than getting a mortgage."

His eyes snapped to hers again. "Sorry. Distracted."

She glanced at the empty screen hanging on the side of the UN. Her mouth twisted in a wry smile. "I see that."

He began to disassemble the sniper rifle as Brianna took out her cell phone.

"Do you want a total reboot?" she asked, tapping out a text message to one of her contacts. "Licenses, degrees, and insurance under your new name, new bank accounts...? And I bet you'll want a glamour for a facial change since your sketch is going around. We should have asked Charity where she got hers. It's awesome."

"Sure, I'll take one of those," he said distractedly, shoving the pieces of his rifle into a duffel bag.

Why wasn't Marion on stage? Had the Autumn Court gotten to her?

He zipped up his bag. He stood.

"Where should I have all your paperwork sent?" Brianna asked. Her expression was innocent, but he knew that she wanted to know where he was going to settle down. She was too nosy to let him vanish a second time without keeping tabs on him.

The curtains on the stage moved, and a random OPA agent stepped up to the podium. He apologized. He said that the keynote speaker had been delayed.

Even on video, Luke could tell that the OPA agent was lying. The flush in his cheeks and racing pulse just under his jaw spoke volumes.

Something had happened.

Who cared if Rylie smelled Luke around? He was about to vanish again, even more completely than he had thirteen years earlier. He couldn't abandon Marion like this. Not when she needed help.

"I'll meet you at the Roasting House in an hour," Luke said. It was Brianna's favorite coffee shop in New York.

She stood too. "Don't tell me you're going in there. Rylie will smell you. You'll get caught!"

"Thanks for your help," he said. "I'll see you soon."

And he jumped off the side of the building.

Marion awakened to the sensation of pressure on her belly. She groaned and tried to push whatever was resting on top of her away.

"Hold still, I'm almost done."

Her eyes popped open. "Konig?"

The unseelie prince kneeled over her, the violet shards of his eyes warmed by concern. "Hold still, princess. You'll make it worse if you move too much."

She lifted her head to look down. Both of his hands were pressed to her stomach where Leliel had stabbed her. Not only had the wound closed, but the blood was evaporating, leaving her flesh and shirt clean. "Oh my gods. How...?"

"You have the Alpha to thank for your survival," Konig said. "I wouldn't have been capable of responding so quickly if she hadn't rallied her security to close in on your position. As soon as we saw the attacks outside, we knew you must have been close, and she immediately deployed her entire team to search for you."

Konig helped her sit up, and Marion saw a middle-aged blond woman standing behind him, conferring with the black-clad OPA agents who had chased Marion through the building. Her heart leaped with anxiety until she remembered she was allowed to be there—nay, one of the key speakers.

The blond woman wore a nude-colored skirt

suit and carried her heels in one hand, as though she'd been running. Her hair was a frazzled mess, cheeks pink. This was Rylie Gresham, Alpha of all of the North American shapeshifters, and arguably the most politically powerful preternatural alive. Marion had seen her author photo on the autobiography.

Rylie shot a dangerous warning look at Marion.

"Did I make her angry?" Marion whispered to Konig.

"You could say that," he said.

Magic jolted through the ballroom. Leliel was surrounded by another ring of guards, who had her contained with a circle of power. It didn't look necessary. The angel wasn't fighting them. She also wasn't crying anymore.

Marion stood gingerly, checking her abdomen. There was only a one-inch patch of cold on her belly where Konig's hands had been. "You healed me."

"Of course I did," Konig said. "What did you expect?"

She'd expected him—and the entire Autumn Court—to kill her.

Rylie stepped away from the guards. She picked up her pace, and by the time she reached Marion, she was practically running.

She yanked Marion into a hug so powerful that it felt like every bone might break. This woman was irrationally strong, so much stronger than a person her age and size had any right to be, as though the power of a dozen bodybuilders had been folded into her slight figure.

Rylie seemed to think that she was close to Marion. Hugging-to-death close.

Marion gave a tiny squeak. "Pain."

"Sorry, sorry." She eased up the pressure enough for Marion to breathe. "Where have you been?"

"Um...here, at the United Nations? Since about twenty minutes ago?"

"Why didn't you call me? I could have escorted you to the stage without having to deal with..." Rylie shot a look at Leliel. The angel responded with a serene, chilly-eyed glare over the shoulders of the OPA agents.

"I didn't know that calling you for help was an option," Marion said.

"I mentioned that you were friends with the sanctuary shifters," Konig pointed out.

Had he? Marion couldn't remember. Even if he had, she wasn't certain that she would have acted on the information.

"Forget about that," Rylie said, flapping her hands as though to dismiss the prince. "Where were you *before* twenty minutes ago, Marion? And don't you dare tell me something facetious like 'the street outside.' I have been worried sick about you for weeks. You go missing like this without telling anyone where you've been, without making a single phone call—"

"She was abducted," Konig said.

Rylie gave Konig an are-you-kidding look.

"Marion can speak for herself."

"I can't," Marion said softly, "because I don't remember anything since waking up in California a few days ago."

The Alpha's eyes widened. "Are you serious?"

"Deadly so," Konig said. He gave her a brief explanation of the week's events: Marion's appearance in Ransom Falls, her attempts to get home, and her brief visit to the unseelie court—along with the Onyx Queen's failed attempt to restore Marion's memory. He didn't mention the doctor. Marion knew, with nauseating certainty, that Konig was angry she'd left with Luke.

"Memory loss," Rylie finally said. "I can't believe someone got you with an attack like that." It was sort of nice to know that the werewolf Alpha had such faith in Marion. "And you still don't remember anything?"

"I don't even know what speech I'm supposed to give in, um..." Marion glanced up at the ballroom's grandfather clock. "Fifteen minutes ago." At least she hadn't been unconscious for long.

"Interesting." Rylie dropped her shoes and stuffed her feet into them. "Let's see about fixing that, shall we?"

She marched over to Leliel.

"Don't look at me," the angel said with unsettling calm. "I had nothing to do with her memory loss. Only the tragically unsuccessful attempts to kill her."

Marion's jaw dropped. "You're confessing to my

attempted assassination? Right now, in front of all of these witnesses?"

"Of course she is." Konig held Marion a little tighter. "There's literally nothing that we can do to punish her over that. She has immunity."

"*Immunity*?" Marion whirled on Rylie, looking for confirmation that this ridiculous claim couldn't be true.

Rylie sighed. "Everyone has immunity for the duration of the summit. In any case, angels can't really be detained for long unless the ethereal faction helps us hold them...or unless you do it with your magic, Marion."

The magic she still couldn't remember.

"It's a shame, isn't it Rylie?" Leliel asked. "You must be itching for a chance to detain me after all these years. So close, yet so far." Yet something was shimmering over Leliel's mind—some truth she was trying to conceal. Marion peered into Leliel's skull, trying to extract details, but Leliel stared back without revealing anything.

"You're taking the blame for this to protect somebody specifically because angels can't be punished," Marion said softly.

The angel's eyes gleamed with cruel amusement. But there was surprise skimming over her thoughts. Marion was onto the truth.

Leliel hadn't placed the bounty.

"Pray tell, daughter of Metaraon—whom would I protect?" Leliel asked.

Luke had believed it was the Autumn Court, but Marion couldn't exactly accuse Konig's parents while he stood beside her. Instead, she asked, "If you placed the bounty, then why were so many of the assassins sidhe?"

"Sidhe don't have a support system on Earth the way that most gaeans do," Leliel said. "If they want to live outside the courts, they need money. Becoming hired guns is better than getting real jobs. They're too prideful to become wage slaves."

"Heather Cobweb is an employee of the court, and she attacked me too," Marion said.

Konig cleared his throat. "She attacked the man trying to abduct you. She was trying to save your life." He smoothed his hand down her wavy hair. "Surely you don't think that my kingdom would have been out to get you, Marion."

"I don't think you'd ever hurt me," she said, clutching his hand.

And that was true. Marion didn't think Konig would try to hurt her.

Rage and Violet, on the other hand...

Marion turned to Rylie. "What do we have to do to keep Leliel in custody until we have more opportunity to investigate? She already confessed to trying to kill me."

"We can't do anything," Rylie said. "There are laws around the summit. Magical laws, which *you* established. They're firm."

"I could take care of Leliel outside those laws," Konig said threateningly, magic shimmering over his copper flesh.

"Don't burn your bridges with me, princeling," Leliel said. "Marion is still going to deliver the speech recommending the angels take the Winter Court."

Marion's eyes widened. "I am?"

"Absolutely. If you don't agree to give us the Winter Court, we will take it. We may very well carve our route into the Winter Court straight through Myrkheimr."

Konig's magic lashed hard enough to make his wind gust through the ballroom. "I'd like to see you try."

Marion winced. She definitely did *not* want to see Leliel try any such thing. "You told me yourself that there aren't many angels left. Would you really wage war against factions as big as the sidhe?"

"At least if we fight and lose, we'll be extinct faster. The alternative is watching our loved ones die out over the centuries to come." The fervor in Leliel's words was frightening. "I don't think we'll lose, though. Even two dozen angels could decimate the sidhe armies."

Marion turned to Konig, looking for some signal that it wasn't true.

She saw in his grim anger confirmation that Leliel was right.

"You're due to give your speech shortly, daughter of Metaraon, Voice of God," Leliel said. "You *will* give the speech I wrote if you want to prevent war. And I'll have won whether you're dead or alive."

Marion felt sick all over.

"We may not be able to arrest you, but we can eject you from the UN for now," Rylie said.

Leliel lifted her chin. "Hardly. I lead the ethereal delegation."

"Marion leads the ethereal delegation because you named her speaker." Rylie turned to the OPA agents. "Please show Leliel out."

Leliel didn't need to be manhandled. She glided away in the custody of security, shooting one last smirk at them over her shoulder. Marion watched the angel go, surrounded by the remaining guards and feeling numb. Despite the size of the ballroom, she felt like she was suffocating.

"You think that the Autumn Court is behind the bounty, don't you?" Konig murmured under his breath, ensuring only Marion would be able to hear him.

Guilt wriggled through her stomach. Her probes about the sidhe assassins hadn't been subtle. "It's just that Oliver Machado—the human witch who found me in Ransom Falls, who summoned assassins to kill me—was using unseelie magic. As in, magic that you guys keep locked in the library. How else could he have gotten that if someone important in the Autumn Court didn't give it to him?"

"The unseelie of the Winter Court used to have human allies among the triadists," Konig said. "That's a church of witches who worship the new gods."

"So you think the Winter Court is trying to kill me too?"

"I don't know," he said. "But what I *do* know is

that it's not me, nor is it my parents. If you had doubts, you should have asked me so that we could figure it out—you and me, *together*."

He was right. Her cheeks burned hot with shame. "I'm sorry."

Konig gathered her into his arms. "This is all my fault, princess. You'd have remained under my protection in Myrkheimr if I hadn't picked a fight with you. I've been afraid I'd lose you. It made me act like..." He shook his head. "Not like the prince you deserve."

She gazed up at the sculpted lines of his face. "I read your article about me. What you said was so sweet." And he'd said it after she had fled from Myrkheimr with Luke Flynn. "I think I don't deserve you, especially if you think this behavior is your worst."

"Then let's be undeserving together," Konig said. "Never leave me again."

"She'll have to leave for at least five minutes," Rylie said lightly as she hurried back from the doorway, through which Leliel had just vanished. She ran her fingers through her hair, tidying it up. "Unfortunately, Leliel was right about one thing. You have to give your speech, Marion. The summit is counting on your guidance. Everything will fall apart if you don't get on stage."

Marion tried not to tremble. "But I don't know what to say. I can't give Leliel what she wants."

Konig's expression was deadly serious. "Do you realize how many people would die if angels attacked the Middle Worlds?"

Until she had invaded Leliel's mind, Marion wouldn't have been able to picture it.

But she had seen into Leliel's memories. She had seen ancient armies, infernal and ethereal, battling on the planes of Earth. It had only taken one angel to fight every ten thousand demons. Even if Leliel were the last of two dozen angels, as she claimed, they could truly wreak devastation on the entire world.

They'd start with beautiful Myrkheimr, its gardens of honey, and people like Nori and Konig.

Rylie studied Marion with worry furrowing her eyebrows. "Are you ready?"

Marion took the speech Leliel and the Autumn Court had prepared out of her pocket. She skimmed the words again and swallowed hard.

Konig was right. If Marion had the opportunity to prevent war, she had to do it. What harm could there be in giving the Winter Court to the angels anyway? It was in anarchy, a world without leadership. It wasn't like the angels would be invading an established kingdom.

Marion took a step toward the door, but stopped when a thought struck her. "Wait," she said, rounding on Rylie. "The attack outside, and in the lobby—those were diversions created by friends who were trying to help me get into the UN safely. I need them to be released." As an afterthought, she added, "Please."

Shock flashed through the Alpha's eyes. "Did you just say please?"

"I told you Marion's memory is gone," Konig

said.

Rylie looked more unsettled by this than anything else that had happened that day. "I'll see to it that your friends are released." Satisfied, Marion moved to follow Konig into the hallway—toward the speech she still had no choice but to deliver. Rylie paced her. She whispered urgently to Marion. "If Elise and James don't want the angels to have the Winter Court, you better do what they say."

Marion frowned. "Who are Elise and James?"

The doors opened. Secretary Friederling stepped inside. He was shorter in person than he'd looked on the screens hanging outside the UN, and he was leaning heavily on a cane with a hawk's head and glimmering gemstone eyes. "What's the holdup? Everyone's waiting." He snapped his fingers impatiently. "*Today*, Ms. Garin."

He was speaking to Marion.

She took a deep breath and squared her shoulders.

It was time to give her speech.

The OPA agents escorted Marion backstage at the auditorium. She struggled to take each step toward the theater. Marion's body was filled with lead.

You can't give Leliel what she wants. She tried to kill you, and you're going to piss off the gods if you obey her.

But the gods probably don't even exist. You haven't seen them, have you? You've been on the brink of death a dozen times and they didn't save you.

You can save lives by giving the angels what they want.

There has to be a catch. Leliel is evil.

You can't give that speech.

Marion could hear how restless the crowd was from behind the curtains. Voices and magic hummed throughout the entire room.

Everyone was waiting for her.

"Go," urged a security guard. It looked like he was about to push her on stage. If Marion were going to humiliate herself in front of everyone, she wouldn't be pushed. She'd do it with dignity.

She walked out on stage and winced into the bright, hot lights. The intensity of them was a mercy. It meant that she couldn't see the expectant faces of all those powerful people who were wondering what a fraud was doing on stage wearing the mask of Marion Garin.

Rylie Gresham would have gotten back to her seat by now. The Alpha of all shapeshifters was waiting to see what Marion would do.

Deirdre Tombs, chair of the American Gaean Commission, would have a booth of her own. She'd be accompanied by a dozen of her toughest allies with the strongest connections to the media. Some of them were surely filming Marion.

Konig would have joined his parents and the other members of the Autumn Court, too.

Marion's face would be on televisions

everywhere, including the screens hanging on the outside of the United Nations building. She could imagine Luke standing on the rooftop to watch her fail. It was easy, since a few large monitors were positioned around the stage, and Marion could see her own desperately confused face staring back at her.

She stood stupefied before an entire room of deadly creatures—people who held the strings of the world and made nations dance as puppets. People who trusted Marion to deliver the word of the gods even though she was lucky she could tie her shoes without help.

She unfolded the speech on the podium. She gripped the microphone so tightly that her knuckles were white and her forearms trembled.

"It's been almost fifteen years since Genesis changed our lives." Her voice was hoarse, cracking, shaking. "Where it once took Adam, Lilith, and Eve seven days to assemble nothingness into something, it took our new gods only one. The Nether, Middle, and High Worlds are a gift to us. I've been given messages about the gods' intent to help us make best use of these gifts."

But I don't remember the message.

She couldn't make herself keep reading. She struggled to keep standing, to keep her calm, to keep *breathing.*

Murmurs rippled through the crowd. Motion caught the corner of her eye, and she turned to see the curtains swaying.

Luke stepped onto the stage with a faint whiff

of sulfur. Snow clung to his hair and the shoulders of his leather jacket. His eyes looked blacker in the brilliant stage lights, and his skin warmer, almost more like burnished gold than brown.

He strode toward her without even glancing at the audience.

Murmurs erupted into shouting. Marion couldn't understand what anyone was saying because the summit's attendees were yelling over one another.

All the tension in her body melted into blind gratitude.

Luke was there. He was going to save her one more time.

She rested a hand on the microphone to make sure that it wouldn't pick up her voice. "What are you doing? How did you even get inside?"

"That's not important." He ducked his head to whisper into her ear. "Knock knock, Marion." Luke's bare, chilly fingers clutched Marion's.

The doors of her mind opened.

Warm surety flooded Marion, accompanied by the buzz of magic and frothing memory. It was too much for her to pick through all at once, so she focused on the thing that mattered most: leading the summit, as was her birthright, her job, and her honor.

Marion knew what the gods wanted. She was, after all, the Voice.

She crumpled the speech written by the angels in her fist, dropped it onto the stage, and spoke from memory.

"We meet this week to discuss the fate of the Winter Court," Marion said. Luke's fingers tightened around hers. "It's been in turmoil ever since the previous leader was arrested by the Office of Preternatural Affairs. It's a travesty that none of the sidhe have stepped up to take care of this precious jewel. Even now, Niflheimr is in ruin, and the court is rocked by anarchy. The surviving unseelie within the court are frozen in battle. They have been abandoned."

The murmuring voices were quickly subsiding.

She could *feel* the eyes of the angels on her, waiting for her to give them the Winter Court.

But the message of the gods was stronger than any other influence on Marion. It was a living thing coiled in her belly, speaking through her lips. She was no more than Pythia, the oracle who spoke the words of Apollo.

"The gods want to make one thing clear: the Winter Court must not be yielded to angels or demons," Marion said. "The sanctuary of the Middle Worlds is solely intended for gaean occupation. They are prepared to enforce this with blood."

Shouting erupted anew.

Screaming.

Marion gripped Luke's hand tightly and leaned toward the microphone to finish her speech.

"As the Voice of God, I will be taking immediate custody of the Winter Court," Marion said. "Vote as you will in the days to come, but know that the summit's decisions bind only mortals. I speak to the will of the gods. Niflheimr is mine. Those who dare to defy me will know the gods' wrath." She smiled when she spoke, and she could see her cheeks dimpling on the monitors around the room.

Dread filled her even as she smiled.

She hadn't meant to say that. She hadn't had a clue what the gods' message was.

But now it was out there, and she couldn't stop the war it would incite.

The attendees descended into something resembling a riot, and security moved swiftly to remove Marion from the stage. She stepped behind the curtains with Luke and the guards, breaking her grip with the doctor's hand. The instant they no longer touched, the gods' words fled from her, draining all the confidence along with it. Marion's magic and memories slipped back into murky oblivion.

It didn't matter. The damage was done.

But she still had Luke's company.

She turned to security. "Leave us," she ordered.

They didn't question her. She was too important for that.

It wasn't until the doors shut and Marion was alone with Luke that she allowed exhaustion to replace adrenaline.

"Oh gods," she whispered, half-giddy and half-horrified. "I can't believe I did that." And then she realized exactly what had happened. "Oh no. I can't believe I did that."

"Why would the gods want *you* to have the Winter Court?" Luke asked, eyes narrowing as he studied her face. It looked like he thought he would be able to find answers if he stared at her hard enough.

"I don't know. I didn't mean to say that." The shaking started all over again. "I can't take over one of the Middle Worlds. I'm not really a princess. I'm just...gods, I don't know who I am."

He took her shoulders. Marion couldn't help but notice that Luke avoided touching her skin again. Her mind was far dimmer without his contact. "You did what you had to do, and you'll keep doing it. You should be proud of yourself." The corner of his mouth lifted in a lopsided smile. "I am."

Her cheeks got hot, and she ducked her head. "It wasn't the sidhe trying to kill me. It was Leliel. She nearly murdered me before I could get on stage, and that's why my speech was so late."

"Leliel? I'm not surprised to hear that. But I don't believe the Autumn Court is innocent. They're allied with the angels."

"Leliel confessed," Marion said. "Konig was shocked."

"Maybe Konig doesn't know what his parents are up to," Luke said. It sounded like giving that concession to the prince pained him.

It equally pained her to say, "I agree with you."

"At least you're safe now," Luke said. "Be careful, Marion. Watch out for yourself." He squeezed her shoulders gently. "I have to go."

"Go? Where?"

"Away," he said.

"For how long? When will I see you again?"

"I don't know." The way he said it was more of an answer than the words themselves. Luke didn't plan on coming back. "Good luck, Marion. You're going to do great things with the Winter Court. I can tell."

Before she could protest, Luke stooped to brush his lips over her temple. The briefest kiss was electricity through her brain.

It whited out her entire mind.

Marion was a little girl in a garden of towering trees. She was running free, bouncing off of springy green moss, splashing through the icy churn of a brook that babbled her name. She was searching for doors in a skyless world.

And Luke was there.

He had *always* been there.

Someone was shouting. "Seth!"

Marion's vision cleared. She was still standing backstage, but Luke Flynn was nowhere in sight. She brushed her fingertips over her temple where he had kissed her. The skin was hot and cold all at once. Her back hurt. Her ribs felt as though they'd been squeezed.

But somewhere, deep within, in a place that she hadn't found yet—a door had opened, and it was permanent. A door that would never shut again.

"Seth!" Rylie Gresham burst backstage, nose lifted, sniffing the air like the wolf she was capable of becoming. Her private guard was barely two steps behind her. They had golden shifter eyes and held big guns. Marion didn't even care.

The sound of that name she'd been whispering to herself for so long—*Seth*—was almost as electric within Marion's gut as the brush of Luke's lips. "What did you say?"

Rylie seized Marion's hands. "Why didn't you tell me you found Seth when we were talking in the ballroom? You know I've been looking for him for years!"

"Seth," Marion echoed. "Do you mean...Seth Wilder?"

Rylie gave a disbelieving laugh. "Of course I mean Seth Wilder. What other Seth would I care about? Why was he on stage with you?"

Luke is Seth Wilder.

All this time, Marion had been traveling with the man she needed to find.

She spun on the spot, scanning the area behind the stage for any sign of him. It was rapidly filling with people who wore werewolf sanctuary-branded t-shirts—people who belonged to Rylie's delegation.

There was no sign of Lucas Flynn.

Seth Wilder.

Whoever he was, he had already disappeared, leaving nothing for Marion but a few lingering memories and the brush of a kiss on her temple.

And he'd made it clear he was never coming back.